The
Storm
Makers

The
Storm
Makers

BY JENNIFER E. SMITH

ILLUSTRATED BY BRETT HELQUIST

LITTLE, BROWN AND COMPANY
NEW YORK   BOSTON

Copyright © 2012 by Jennifer E. Smith
Illustrations copyright © 2012 by Brett Helquist

Little, Brown and Company

Hachette Book Group
237 Park Avenue, New York, NY 10017
Visit our website at www.lb-kids.com

Little, Brown and Company is a division of Hachette Book Group, Inc.
The Little, Brown name and logo are trademarks of Hachette Book Group, Inc.

The publisher is not responsible for websites (or their content)
that are not owned by the publisher.

First Edition: April 2012

Library of Congress Cataloging-in-Publication Data

Smith, Jennifer E.
The Storm Makers / by Jennifer E. Smith ; illustrated by Brett Helquist. — 1st ed.
   p. cm.
Summary: Twelve-year-olds Ruby and Simon have been growing apart since their parents moved them to a Wisconsin farm, but weird weather events that seem tied to Simon's emotions bring a stranger into their lives who introduces them to the Makers of Storms Society, strengthening the bond between the twins.
ISBN 978-0-316-17958-4
[1. Weather—Fiction. 2. Supernatural—Fiction. 3. Magic—Fiction. 4. Brothers and sisters—Fiction. 5. Twins—Fiction. 6. Family life—Wisconsin—Fiction. 7. Farm life—Wisconsin—Fiction. 8. Wisconsin—Fiction.] I. Helquist, Brett, ill. II. Title.
PZ7.S65141Su 2012   [Fic]—dc23   2011025419

10 9 8 7 6 5 4 3 2 1

RRD-C

Printed in the United States of America

For my dad, whose obsession with Doppler radar probably led me here... Thanks for always refusing to turn off The Weather Channel!

There are some things you learn best in calm,
and some in storm.

— WILLA CATHER

one

ONLY RUBY KNEW about the stranger in the barn.

It was the dogs who had first given him away. She'd been watching from her bedroom window as they danced at the double-doored entrance, bounding in and then out again amid a small cloud of dust. They were a cowardly duo, a pair of oversized brown mutts that seemed perpetually startled by the mob of barn cats in their midst. But Ruby had begun to get up anyway, in case it turned out to be something worse—a garter snake or a rat. And when she saw them suddenly dart away, streaking back up the drive and toward the house, she pressed her face closer to the window just in time to see a man walk out of the barn.

He yawned and stretched, tilting his face toward the paling sky, then moved casually out into the open as if he were waking up in his own bedroom rather than the McDuffs' crumbling barn. He was tall, perhaps the tallest person Ruby had ever seen, with long legs that seemed to account for an unusually large percentage of his body, giving him an overall storklike impression, which wasn't helped by the length of his nose. There was something in his manner that she found unsettling, an air of confidence, like he was somehow entitled to be there.

Ruby knew she should probably yell for Mom and Dad, or at least wake Simon, who was still asleep in his room next door. But even so, she remained frozen on the edge of her bed, unable to move from the window.

As she watched, the man pulled a hat from his back pocket—a raggedy gray thing that barely held its shape—and placed it carefully on his head. He wore dark pants and a blue shirt with buttons that glinted in the sun, which seemed to Ruby an outfit better suited for

an office than for stowing away in someone's hayloft. He thumped a hand against his chest as if to give himself a kick start, then yawned once more before turning to walk purposefully up the drive.

Ruby waited for another minute, her eyes still wide, her nose still touching the glass, and then vaulted out of bed and ran down the stairs in her pajamas.

She saw Mom half turn from the griddle as she passed the kitchen, and she forced herself to slow to a somewhat normal speed. Dad looked up from the table, where he seemed to be examining the tines of a fork, turning it in circles and humming to himself.

"Breakfast in ten, okay?" Mom yelled as Ruby hurried past, but she was already out the front door. She paused for a moment and swept her eyes around in search of the stranger, but it was as if he'd simply disappeared in the acres of wheat that bordered the farmhouse. As she headed toward the barn, the scorched earth was hot against her bare feet. The sky overhead was still pink at the edges where it touched the fields that stretched in every direction, flat and endless and unchanging.

The dogs had returned and were now milling about at the entrance to the barn. Their tails fanned the air as

4

Ruby approached at a jog. "You guys are fantastic security guards," she said, giving each a pat as she stepped around them. "Really."

Inside, the barn was stiflingly hot—like everything else these days—and there was a crackling dryness to it, as if the hay might go up in flames at any moment. But other than the recent rise in temperatures, very little else had changed in the year since the McDuffs first bought the place.

Their ten acres of land could be called a farm only in the very loosest sense of the word. From the outside, someone might be fooled into thinking they knew what they were doing; they'd planted just enough crops to get by, a half-dozen acres of corn and wheat, all of which was wilting badly in the drought.

But the inside of the barn told a different story; there were no cows or pigs or sheep, just a few bales of hay in the very back, where the cats liked to curl up in the afternoons. The building's main function was to act as Dad's workshop. This was where he now spent his days, bent over a thick wooden table, struggling to give shape to the yet uninvented invention that had brought them all out here in the first place.

In their old life, in a small suburb of Chicago, Dad had been a high school science teacher, and Mom a florist. But a year ago, just after Simon and Ruby turned eleven, their parents had traded in their perfectly good jobs and their perfectly acceptable lives to pursue their own separate dreams of becoming an inventor and an artist.

So far, Mom had finished painting only a single picture of the barn, which looked about as dire as the thing itself, and Dad had amassed a stable full of wires and bolts and rattling sheets of metal, though not much else.

"Imagining the thing is half the battle," he always said when Ruby watched him work, his face screwed up in concentration as he examined this tool or that, pausing every now and then to turn the page of one of the many books that lined the uneven floor.

He knew exactly what he wanted to build. He'd come up with the idea to put a device beneath the floor of every major train station and airport and sports stadium in the country, places with steady flows of traffic, people walking back and forth all day long, running for their trains or pacing during delays or jumping up and down for their teams. And the force of all those footsteps would be harnessed by his invention, which would turn them into enough energy to power the buildings themselves.

Everyone agreed that it was a brilliant idea.

The only problem was, he hadn't quite figured out how to make the thing work yet.

Now, Ruby made her way past the bookshelves and the lights and the radio Dad listened to while working, all the way to the back of the barn, where a small pile of hay bales were stacked along the wall. As she approached, thinking that it looked altogether too neat and that perhaps she had only dreamed the man in the blue shirt, she noticed one of the kittens crouched between the bales, batting at something with her paw. When Ruby drew near, she sprang up and loped off with her tail held high, disappearing into one of the stalls and leaving behind a silver button with the faintest of etchings on its metallic surface: a tiny, perfect *O*.

⚡

By the time Ruby skidded into her seat at the breakfast table, Simon was already there, eyeing his plateful of pancakes.

"About time," he said, stabbing one with his fork. The McDuffs had a rule about waiting until everyone was at the table before eating, and Simon's appetite—Mom called it *healthy*, though Ruby would have gone with *disgusting*—usually meant he was the first to arrive. Dad slid a pancake onto Ruby's plate while Mom poured her a glass of orange juice.

"Sorry," she said. "The dogs were acting funny."

"Shocking," Simon said, raising his eyebrows. He was still in pajamas, too, and his blond hair looked more like feathers than anything else this morning, sticking out in all directions. His eyes—the same shade of blue as Ruby's—were still heavy with sleep. "What was it this time? The kittens? A mouse?"

She slipped a hand into the thin pocket of her pajama pants, where she'd tucked the silver button. Dad was reading the newspaper and Mom was buttering a piece of toast, and Ruby took the opportunity to give Simon a long look, a look intended to be meaningful, but that obviously fell somewhat short.

"What?" he asked, wiping his sleeve across his face. "Syrup? Did I get it?"

Ruby sighed and shook her head. "No, you're fine."

It wasn't long ago that they'd been able to read each other's thoughts without even trying. Or at least it had seemed that way. They'd grown up side by side, slept in the same room for most of their lives, whispered secrets in the dark, invented languages, and murmured stories. They'd come into the world together at nearly the same moment, and because of this it had always seemed they were meant to stay that way.

But if there was anything Ruby had learned in the last year, it was that things change. In summers past, she and Simon had explored their old neighborhood together. They'd raced their bikes and built a tree house; they'd invented a new flavor of Popsicle, and held a contest to see who could keep their goldfish alive the longest. They'd done all this amid sidewalks and driveways and rows of hedges. On concrete playgrounds and back porches and soccer fields.

But now the backdrop to their lives was so much starker, so much wider, and sometimes Ruby couldn't help feeling like the landscape itself was to blame for all that had changed between her and her twin brother.

How could you be the king and queen of a place with no boundaries, where the sky fell like a blade against the horizon in every direction?

Maybe they'd never really been inseparable so much as they hadn't ever had room to separate.

Ever since they'd turned twelve last month, Simon had grown moody, often stalking off into the fields or locking himself in his room for no reason at all. On rainy days, he'd taken to lying on his bed for hours at a time, mindlessly tossing a baseball up at the ceiling. Even the dogs had begun to avoid him, shying away in a mystifying display of wariness.

Now they were keeping a wide berth around Simon's seat as they circled the table, their noses twitching at the smell of the food. When he accidentally dropped a piece of pancake near his foot, both dogs hesitated, then one of them—the braver one—darted over to grab it before scurrying away again as if being chased.

"So what's on the agenda today?" Mom asked as she reached for the syrup.

Simon groaned. "Trying not to melt."

"It's like an oven out there," Ruby agreed.

"Oh, come on," Dad said in the same falsely cheerful

voice he'd begun to use for nearly everything these days. "It's not *that* bad."

"Actually, it sort of is," Mom said with a grin. "Sorry, hon. But I spent half of yesterday with my head in the freezer."

Dad shook his head mournfully. "How did I manage to get stuck with a family of such big wimps?"

"Luck, I guess," Mom said, nudging the empty bread basket in the direction of the twins. "Would one of you pop in a few more pieces of toast?"

Ruby was the first to put her finger on her nose, so Simon rose with a sigh and grabbed the basket. Rules were rules.

"I know, I know. Life is *so* tough," Mom teased him as he moved sullenly around the kitchen. "And not to add to your troubles, but you're on laundry duty later."

"Can't Ruby do it?" he asked. "I'm helping Dad this morning, and then I wanted to get in some pitching practice this afternoon."

"You've got all day," Mom said, unmoved. "And it's your turn, not Ruby's."

Simon rolled his eyes, though Ruby couldn't tell if it was meant for her or for Mom or for them both. Right now, he seemed to be upset with the toast more than anything, jamming in the first slice of bread so hard that it crumpled like an accordion.

"If Dad needs you this morning, we'll get to it later this afternoon," Mom continued, spearing a piece of pancake with her fork. "But it's got to get done, okay?"

"*Okay*," Simon said, his voice heavy with frustration as he angled the second slice into the toaster, his hand brushing up against its metal paneling. As he did, there was a sudden spark, followed by a quick popping sound, and then the lights in the kitchen went abruptly dark.

Simon dropped the bread and took a swift step backward, his mouth open. The hum of the air conditioner had gone silent, and the numbers on the microwave had disappeared. Everyone stared at Simon, who stood absolutely still.

A few beats of silence passed, and then a few more. Finally, Dad cleared his throat. "Must've been a short circuit," he said, looking vaguely pleased at the idea that something electronic might need fixing. "I'll go down and check it out."

But Mom was still looking at Simon. "You okay?" she asked, and he held up both hands like a criminal caught in the act.

"It wasn't my fault," he said quickly, and Mom let out a little laugh.

"Of course it wasn't," she said. But from where Ruby sat at the table—the dogs cowering beneath her feet, the kitchen dark and silent—she wasn't nearly as sure.

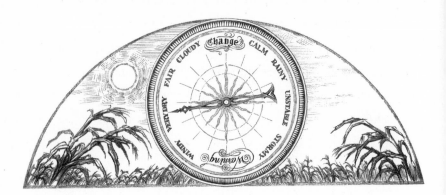

two

Ruby still hadn't had a chance to tell Simon about the button in her pocket. As soon as Dad had finished fixing the circuit breakers—letting out a triumphant whoop from the basement when the lights flickered on again—the two of them headed out to the barn together, leaving Ruby on dish duty with Mom. .

They stood side by side at the sink, looking out the window as the dogs ran circles around the scarecrow. The sun had risen higher now, making the fields look washed out and pale, and the heat quivered above them like something you could reach out and touch.

Behind them, on the little TV set that was perched atop the microwave, the morning news showed images of the tornadoes that had been ripping across the Plains States with uncommon frequency — a montage of torn shingles and uprooted road signs — before switching to a story about unusually high rainfall and heavy flooding in New England. Ruby swiveled to watch, and Mom set down a soapy dish with a sigh.

"Wish we'd get some of that rain up here," she said, looking out grimly over the cracked fields beyond the window.

On the TV, the lens of the camera was being pelted by raindrops that looked as big as quarters, and two people in slickers stood waist-deep in water. Ruby shook her head. "Not rain like *that*."

"No," Mom agreed. "But we need *some*. Otherwise..."

"Otherwise, what?" Ruby asked, feeling a faint tug of hope at the thought of their old life in the suburbs. This move was supposed to make life better, but the crops had been meant to keep them afloat until Dad had some luck with his invention or Mom got a letter back from one of the art galleries she was always writing to in Chicago.

Nobody could have foreseen such an epic drought, though, the worst in a hundred years, at least according to the old farmers at the general store in town, their leathery faces set with worried wrinkles. Their first summer on the farm had been fairly normal, and the winter no worse than the ones in Chicago, but it was only the beginning of June, and already this had been the longest summer of Ruby's life. It was the summer of heat and the summer of humidity, the summer of sweat and the summer of fans.

But mostly, it was the summer of dust.

Dust had become a fact of life. It was everywhere: in their teeth and in the creases between their toes, in their hair and in their eyes. Even after taking a shower, Ruby seemed to always find it in her bed at night, and it came through the window on the blades of the fans, determined to coat every inch of the house. To make things worse, there'd been a spate of freak wind gusts lately, rushing breezes that kicked loose the dry dirt in the fields and sent it sailing in great hazy clouds across the farm, stinging anyone who dared to venture outside.

Ruby couldn't help it. She hated the acres of land here, with hardly a tree in sight, and the vast and complete darkness that settled over the farm every night. The water in the shower was always cold and the house creaked and sang its way through the nights, and though she now had her own room, it felt big and lonely and not at all like she'd always imagined it.

When she thought of home, it didn't include a barn or a scarecrow; it was the house she'd grown up in, and she'd give just about anything to go back.

Mom turned back to the sink, fishing around in the foamy water for the sponge.

"Otherwise, what?" Ruby asked again, hoping the answer might be that they'd have to move back, pick up where they left off, pretend this year had never happened. But Mom's mouth was set in a thin line, and she gave her head a little shake. They stood there like that for a while, one washing, one drying, neither speaking.

"So," Mom said eventually, her voice a bit too bright, "any big plans for the day?"

"No," Ruby said shortly.

"You two could go for a ride," she suggested, and when she saw Ruby's face, she laughed. "It's not like it's all that much cooler in here. At least on the bike you might catch a breeze."

"I'll ask Simon," Ruby said without much hope. She was pretty sure neither of her parents had noticed the distance between her and her brother, caught up as they were in their own separate projects.

There was enough space here that it was easy to lose sight of one another.

After the dishes were put away and the table was wiped off and she'd changed out of her pajamas, Ruby headed back out to the barn. The sun burned her scalp and parched her throat, but she was used to that by now. The worst part was how the heat had started to make every day seem exactly like the one before, a never-ending chain of moments, all melted together like candle wax.

Now, as she neared the barn, she could hear a sound like drumming, punctuated by Simon's laughter. Once inside, she could see that he was jumping up and down on a flat piece of metal that was suspended above another by thick, coiled springs. Beside him, Dad was frowning so hard at the lightbulb—connected to the contraption by a cluster of wires—that Ruby was surprised it didn't light up out of sheer intimidation.

"Any luck?" she asked, letting her eyes adjust. They'd taken to calling it the TGI—the Totally Genius Invention—but so far, it had done little more than give off a few accidental sparks.

Dad seemed not to notice that she'd joined them, but Simon shook his head. "Makes a pretty good trampoline, though."

"Want to go for a bike ride?" Ruby asked.

"Maybe later," he said, but the way he said it, she knew better than to wait around. Instead, she crossed the width of the barn and unhinged one of the stall doors, then wheeled out her bike. But when she walked by Dad, he looked up sharply.

"Hold up," he said, sitting back on his heels. "We were thinking of maybe heading into town. Any interest in coming?"

"What for?"

"New tires for the truck," Simon said, wandering over to kick at the old ones, which were shiny and bald.

Ruby hesitated. The nearest town was a ten-minute drive, and though it wasn't much to get excited about—there were more antique shops than stoplights—she rarely passed up a chance to go in. Still, she wasn't exactly dying to spend the morning at an auto-repair shop.

"There'll be air-conditioning...." Dad said, wiggling his eyebrows. "And maybe even ice cream."

"Okay," Ruby said, dropping her bike. "I'm in."

While Simon ran inside to change out of his pajamas, Ruby assumed a perch beside Dad, handing over tools when he needed them.

"I'm thinking maybe this thing just needs a jump start," he said, glancing over at the truck. "What do you say we give it a shot when we get back later?"

Ruby nodded.

"Remember what I taught you about the positive and negative charges?"

"Different poles," she said, and Dad beamed.

Science had always come naturally to Ruby. Ever since she was little, Dad had shared trivia the same way other fathers told bedtime stories, quizzing her about the animal kingdom and the solar system and the way tides work. Simon had little patience for all this, much preferring baseball to anything even remotely bookish, but for Ruby, this type of knowledge settled in the corners of her mind with an ease that surprised everyone. Most kids knew jokes. Ruby knew facts.

Dad squatted beside her with the jumper cables, the colors faded beneath a thin layer of dust. He pointed to the red one.

"Positive charge," Ruby said, and before he could ask, she reached out for the black one. "Negative," she said. "This is the ground one."

"Right-o," Dad said, giving her a little pat on the shoulder.

At the entrance to the barn, Simon appeared—now dressed in shorts and a striped T-shirt—and kicked at the ground impatiently. Behind him, the wind picked up, blowing the loose dirt from the driveway in lazy circles.

Ruby noticed that Simon's face had clouded over at the sight of them. As usual, Dad was completely oblivious, but Ruby could feel Simon's eyes on her as she worked, and she understood the reason without needing to be told. Dad never asked her brother to help in any kind of real way. When there were boxes to be carried or sheet metal to be scrapped, Simon was the one he called. But if there was anything more delicate to be done, anything scientific in nature, it was always Ruby he asked, and she could feel Simon's resentment like a kind of heat as she worked.

"Hey," Dad said now, eyeing one of the coiled pipes beneath the platform. "What if we tried connecting the wires to the base itself?"

Ruby wiped her hands on her shorts. "Town," she reminded him, conscious of the fact that Simon was still waiting. "Let's try it later."

At this, Simon bolted over to the truck, hurdling a stack of books as he crossed the floor of the barn. "Shotgun," he called out triumphantly, coming to rest with a thump against the passenger-side door.

Ruby shrugged. As she climbed into the back of the truck, her legs sticky against the hot vinyl, Simon reclined his own seat so far that it nearly rested in Ruby's lap. She slammed the heel of her palm against the back of it, but he refused to move it up again, and she wondered why she was still so concerned about her brother's feelings, when he'd clearly stopped worrying about hers.

But she couldn't help it. Some lingering instinct, some fragile connection, still remained between them, like the last dying embers of a fire, and despite everything, Ruby was determined to keep it burning.

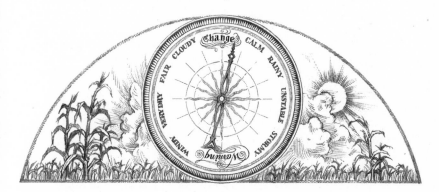

three

THE TOWN WAS as flat and brown as the land all around it, a collection of low-slung buildings that seemed to hunker down against the biting dust. The acres of fields stopped just outside the barber shop and picked up again three blocks later, where one of four antique stores signaled the abrupt end of civilization.

In the year or so that they'd lived here, Ruby had been to nearly every store in town—not exactly a difficult feat—but this was her first time at the mechanic's, which was on the outskirts, an openmouthed garage big enough for three cars, set back on a sizzling apron of black asphalt.

There was only one car occupying the space at the moment—an ancient yellow convertible—and as Dad pulled the truck into the stall beside it and they all tumbled out, a tiny woman in a gray jumpsuit appeared, a streak of grease on one cheek like war paint. The name stitched across her uniform in loopy letters read DAISY. She wiped her hands on a rag and regarded each of them in turn.

"What can I do for you all?"

Simon's face was scrunched up, and Ruby could tell just by looking at him that his definition of an auto mechanic wasn't exactly a blond woman named after a flower. He wandered over to examine the yellow convertible, peering under the open hood, and Ruby noticed Daisy's eyes following him warily.

"We need some new front tires," Dad said. "I think those are pretty much shot."

Daisy crouched beside the car and brushed a hand over the smooth rubber. "You could go skiing on these things," she agreed, then gestured toward a second building, which sat just outside the garage. "Why don't you go pick something out in the office?"

Dad hesitated as he watched Daisy straighten to lift the hood of the truck, which opened with a small cough of dust.

"It's really just the tires," he said, but Daisy didn't even look at him.

"We're full-service."

"I'm actually pretty good with mechanics myself," Dad insisted, and from where they were both now leaning against the convertible, Ruby and Simon rolled their eyes.

"Looks like you could probably use an oil change, too," Daisy said. "I'll fix you up while you pick out some new tires."

It seemed there was no point in arguing, so Dad began his retreat to the office with a shrug. When he looked back for Ruby and Simon, he saw that neither had followed him. They stood just behind Daisy, both of them on tiptoe to look into the engine.

"They can stay," she said without turning around, and when the echo of his footsteps on the concrete floor had disappeared, she pointed into the guts of the truck. "You two know how you can tell if you need oil?" She reached in and pulled out a long stick, which was black and slick. "This is called the dipstick."

Simon laughed, and Daisy half turned to them with raised eyebrows.

"He's always calling *me* a dipstick," Ruby explained, and Simon nodded sheepishly.

Daisy looked amused as she wiped the stick clean with the same rag she'd used on her hands earlier. "Now," she said, "we need to put it back in there to see how high the oil level is. Who wants to try?"

"I do," Simon said, pushing forward to grab the stick. Daisy helped him climb up onto the bumper, pointing to where it should go. He leaned over the engine, his whole body pitched forward, his tongue poking out in concentration.

"Be careful," Ruby said, the words escaping before she could think better of it.

"I'm fine," Simon muttered, then jammed the stick into the depths of the engine.

There was a flash of light as he removed his hand again, and the faintest tracing of electricity seemed to stretch between him and the engine, so quick and bright that even as she watched it happen, Ruby couldn't be sure it was happening at all.

For the second time that day, a sharp cracking sound rent the air around them. Even before the noise had faded, Daisy had Simon around the waist and was yanking him back off the hood.

A thin curl of smoke drifted up from the engine, and the three of them simply stood there, watching in stunned silence.

After a moment, Daisy turned to Simon with wide eyes. "Are you okay?"

He nodded, glancing down at his hand as if looking for an explanation, some sign of why this had happened. But it was only a hand, grubby and sweaty and lined with dirt.

"Was that..." Ruby began, but she couldn't seem to get the question out. "I mean, that looked like..."

Lightning, she wanted to say. *It looked like lightning.*

But Simon's face was twisted in confusion, and Ruby left the sentence unfinished. Daisy stepped back up to the engine, her face unchanging as she peered inside. The smoke had tapered off, but the smell of it still hung over the garage like a fog, and for a long time, they were all quiet.

Finally, Simon cleared his throat. "Sorry."

Daisy shifted her gaze from the engine, regarding him in the way that someone might study a painting, her eyes narrowed with focus. Outside the wind picked up, and they could hear the door to the office creak open and then bounce shut again.

"Has this happened before?" Daisy asked, and Simon looked down at the oil-stained floor.

"No," he said finally, but Ruby shook her head.

"Sort of," she said, looking at him hard. "This morning? With the toaster?"

Daisy nodded; her face was impossible to read, but her eyes never left Simon, who shifted uncomfortably from one foot to the other.

When Dad appeared at the entrance to the garage, they all seemed to tense up, and Ruby braced herself for Daisy to tell him what had occurred.

"Is something burning?" he asked as he handed over a slip of paper, the name of the tires he wanted scrawled across the page.

Daisy glanced once more at Simon, who seemed to be holding his breath. "You've got a faulty battery," she said after a moment. "You're lucky we caught it."

"What?" Dad cried, flying over to the truck. "There's no way. I just checked it."

"It's completely dead," Daisy said patiently. "Why don't you guys come back in an hour or so? I'll get you fixed up with a new one, and put the tires on."

Dad sighed. There was really no choice. This was their only vehicle, and their only way of getting home.

"We need the battery later anyway," Ruby reminded him. "To jump-start the TGI."

"Fine," Dad agreed, leaning to examine the engine once more with a doleful look. "An hour?"

Daisy nodded, her eyes on Simon. "Try to stay out of trouble till then, okay?" she said, and though it was meant to sound casual, there was something strained in her tone.

To pass the time, they wandered over to the hardware store, where Dad filled a paper bag with bolts and screws and the twins filled their own bags with gumdrops and sour balls. As she replaced the lid on one of the old-fashioned candy jars, Ruby caught the briefest flash of gray out of the corner of her eye. She whirled around, her heart racing, her mind filled with the one possibility that had been trailing her like a ghost all morning.

There, on the highest shelf, resting above the rows of hammers and duct tape, the bath mats and the kitchen knives, was a gray hat.

It wasn't even the same one; it was stiff and new, with a price tag hanging from the brim. But for a moment, Ruby had been absolutely sure of it: that he was there again, right over her shoulder—the man from the barn.

She let out a shaky breath and saw that her knuckles had gone white around the bag of candy. As she turned to make her way up to the counter, where Dad was waiting, her eyes swept the aisles. *It was nothing,* she told herself.

But even as she worked to settle her busy mind, to tell herself that nothing was lurking at her back, her foot caught her other leg. She tripped, pitching forward so that the bag went flying out of her hands, candy scattering across the wooden floor like marbles. When she spun around, Simon had a hand clapped over his mouth.

"Sorry," he said. "I didn't mean for it to spill."

Ruby glared at him until he dropped to his knees and began scooping up the skittering sour balls with both hands. It was just one of Simon's many annoying habits, this trick of his: He loved to walk behind her, and then, with the slightest tap of his foot at just the right moment, send her stumbling over herself.

"One foot in front of the other," Mom would always say, and Ruby would give Simon a withering look as he skipped ahead in triumph. Now was no different. As he handed her the ruined bag of candy, she could see the amusement scrawled across his face. But she noticed that his eyes were also glassy, his face paler than usual.

"You feeling okay?" she asked, and his expression darkened.

"I'm fine," he muttered, then wandered away again.

By the time they got back to the garage, Daisy was just finishing up the last tire. Once they were ready to go, she watched them all clamber back into the truck before knocking on the door, her fist making the whole thing clang.

"Thanks again," Dad said, starting the engine. "We'll let you know if anything else comes up."

"I hope you do," Daisy said, but she wasn't looking at him at all; she was looking at Simon. "Good luck with it."

By the time they arrived back home, Ruby had decided she'd had enough of engines and wires and electronics for the day, so when Dad asked if she still wanted to help out with the invention, she shook her head.

"Can we do it later?" she asked. "I still want to go for a bike ride."

"You sure?" he said, squinting out over the fields, which looked wavery in the heat. "It's almost noon. Hottest time of the day."

"I can help," Simon offered, appearing at Dad's elbow.

"Great," he said. "You and I can clear out that wrecked metal, and then we'll try the jump start when Ruby's back later."

Simon's face fell, and Ruby pretended not to notice. "Sure you don't want to come?" she asked, but he was already walking off toward the shed with Dad, trotting to keep up with his long stride, and so Ruby slipped into the barn alone.

Once she'd wheeled her bike outside she mounted quickly, then glided down the driveway, the tires grumbling over the rocks and dirt. She swung left down the road for no particular reason; every direction was much the same as any other, all square fields with roads running between them like the stitching on a quilt, and there was little to mark off her journey: a neighbor's barn or a chipping silo, a sagging fence or a field of listless cows. The newly planted corn was uniformly brown where it should be green, and the wheat was stiff and parched. The world looked like something too long forgotten.

She wasn't sure how long she rode, farther than usual perhaps, though the air was heavy with heat and her shirt was stuck to her back. The road held straight for so long that Ruby began to wonder if she could follow it all the way south to Chicago. But it wasn't until she saw the windmills that she realized just how far she must have gone.

They stretched tall against the blue sky, looming white poles with slow-moving rotors that spun like giant insects in the air. She counted seven in all, staggered across the skyline with no apparent pattern, an eerie grouping of modern machines amid the pastures and cornfields. She was so busy looking up that she didn't notice the old hay wagon parked just below the nearest one until she was just a few feet away.

There, sitting with his back to her, his legs dangling off the edge, was the man in the blue shirt. His hat was perched atop his head at a skewed angle, and he was leaning back on one hand, while the other twisted a piece of hay lazily in the air.

Somehow, the most surprising thing about seeing him there was just how very *unsurprising* it was, as if Ruby had been drawn not by the powerful windmills or the arrow-straight road, but by the man himself.

She gripped the handlebars of her bike as she tried to make sense of the situation, worked to formulate some kind of plan, to come to a decision about whether to speak up or run away. But before she could decide, the man cleared his throat.

"Nice weather we're having," he said without turning around. He swung his legs up onto the bed of the wagon and then swiveled to face her incuriously, like he'd been expecting her any minute, like it was only a matter of time. But before Ruby could disagree, before she could say anything at all, he removed his hat and twirled it in his hands, glancing once at the sky, and then, just like that, it started to rain.

four

THE FIRST TIME Ruby ever watched *The Wizard of Oz*, Mom had smiled and leaned in close during the part with the ruby slippers.

"Just like you," she'd whispered, kissing the top of her head.

Even then, Ruby suspected it was her duty to wish for a pair herself, as all little girls undoubtedly should. But it wasn't the sparkly shoes that had fascinated her.

She soon got into the habit of skipping the beginning,

fast-forwarding right through the munchkins and the good witch, the banding together of friends along the way. Her favorite part was the end, the march through the field of poppies only to find that the wizard was nothing more than an old man with white hair.

Simon was always as disappointed as Dorothy by this revelation, that a wizard could turn out to be just a normal person.

But Ruby saw it differently: Normal people, it seemed, could be wizards.

And she couldn't help feeling a bit like Dorothy now, the endless crops stretched out all around her, the rain falling fast as if the man on the wagon had conjured it himself. She closed her eyes and let it stream over her, the water impossibly cool, loosening the layers of dust and dirt and sweat that had clung to her for what seemed like forever.

When she looked up again, the sky behind the hay wagon had turned flat and gray, and she saw that the man's hair was nearly the same color. His face was deeply tanned and lined with creases, but in a way that made it difficult to tell just how old he was. As she watched, he turned his hat upside down, peering into it as the brim grew soggy and the hollow part began to fill.

"It's been a while, huh?" he asked, but Ruby couldn't find the words to answer. She wiped the water from her eyes and stared up at him, unsure whether to stay or go, unsure whether he was crazy in a harmless way or a dangerous one. It occurred to her that he might be homeless, but even in the rain she could see the expensive silver buttons on his shirt, which matched the one in her pocket. Perhaps he was a thief, though if that were the case, he couldn't be a very smart one. All the McDuffs had to steal was a pile of scrap metal in the barn and a roomful of blank canvases upstairs.

She propped her bike on its kickstand, then took a step forward. The man smiled graciously, like a host happy to see that his guest had finally decided to join the party. There was something about his features that made him seem almost a caricature of himself, his nose a bit too long, his eyes large and owlish. Ruby stared up at him as she tried to collect her words, to put together some kind of question, but after a moment, he nodded as if she'd already asked it.

"I'm here to help your brother."

Ruby wasn't sure what she'd been expecting, but it certainly wasn't that. She took a small step backward. "He doesn't need any help."

The man tipped his face up to the falling rain. "Not yet," he said. "But the winds are starting to change."

His smile was infuriating, utterly cryptic and completely untroubled even in this strangest of situations. And at that very moment, the winds *did* change, the rain coming down at an angle, blowing the wheat sideways. It stung Ruby's face, and she wiped at the end of her nose, where the water had collected into a single drop. Above them, the windmills continued to churn, the water falling in sheets from the blades. She narrowed her eyes, suddenly angry.

"It's not right, you know," she said. "Staying on someone else's property."

"I'm only visiting," he said, as if it were the most obvious thing in the world.

"Well, don't."

He grinned. "Or what?"

"Or else I'll tell," she said, though this sounded silly even to her. "I'll tell my parents. Or call the police."

"You would have done that already."

Ruby blinked, feeling the color rise in her cheeks. A flash of lightning whitened the sky, and in that brief moment of illumination, she saw a look of worry cross his face. The thunder that followed reached them with a scraping sound, like the sky itself was being hollowed out by the storm. They watched a second fork of lightning touch down in a nearby field, a blue-tinted scribble in the surrounding grayness.

The man reached into his pocket and glanced down at what looked like a watch. His eyes narrowed. "You better get back now," he said, but Ruby straightened, holding her ground in the mud. He slid off the wagon in one fluid motion, and once he was unfolded, she could see just how tall he really was. "Go on."

"No," she said, so softly it was nearly lost in the weather.

He gave his hat a little shake, but it was too soaked through to wear now, a flimsy, dead-looking thing. "Simon needs you."

Ruby stared at him. "How do you know his name?" she asked, but he was already walking away from her, pushing back the damp stalks of wheat until he seemed to disappear altogether into their midst.

By the time she turned into the long drive leading up to the farm, Ruby was shaking all over, and her fingers were numb on the handlebars of her bike. The storm had only grown stronger, and the wind blew with such force that, every so often, she had to stop and plant her feet on the ground for fear of tipping over.

As she neared the barn, she could see Dad pulling open the heavy doors, his legs braced against the gravel drive. When he saw her, his whole body slackened.

"There you are," he said, jogging to meet her. Ruby had been expecting him to look thrilled about the unexpected arrival of the rain, but his face was grim. He threw an arm up over his eyes to keep out the cutting rain. "I was about to drive out to look for you."

"Sorry," Ruby said, swinging herself off her bike. "That came up fast."

"I'll meet you inside," Dad said, grabbing the handlebars. He began to wheel the bike toward the open barn, then paused and turned back. "Your brother's not feeling well. Mom's upstairs with him."

Ruby froze, her stomach suddenly tight. What had the

man said about Simon? That he'd come to help him? The wind ripped the leaves from the corn and set them loose like confetti, and the sky was an angry purple now, the light almost completely snuffed out, though it was only mid-afternoon. She hurried toward the house.

Inside, the downstairs was quiet, and Ruby stood in the hallway, water dripping from her hair. The rain beat at the screen door, and she could hear the dogs moving restlessly in the kitchen. She was still there, standing in a small puddle on the wooden floor, when Dad came in, unzipping his jacket.

"What're you doing?" he asked, frowning. "You're gonna freeze."

"What's wrong with Simon?"

Dad shook his head. "I think he's got a fever. He was feeling hot out in the barn, and came in to grab a drink. Your mom said his hands were like ice, so she put him right to bed."

"But he's okay?"

"I'm sure he'll be fine," he said. "You better go grab some dry clothes or you'll catch something, too."

Ruby nodded and began to climb the stairs slowly. At the top, she peeked into Simon's room, where Mom was sitting on the edge of his bed. Ruby watched them for a moment—the way Mom fussed with his blankets, the way Simon's eyelids fluttered in sleep—and she didn't realize she was holding her breath until Mom looked over, put a finger to her lips, and then tiptoed out of the room.

"You're soaked," she said, closing the door behind her and then leaning to kiss the top of Ruby's head. "Go get changed, and I'll make us a warm drink."

"Is he okay?"

Mom nodded, pressing her lips into a straight line. "This fever came out of nowhere, though."

Later, as the three of them drank cups of tea in the kitchen, watching the weather report through the static on the television set, Dad said the same thing about the storm.

"It came out of nowhere," he muttered, glancing out the window, where the rain was still thrashing against the house.

"It's a good thing," Mom said. "We need it. Badly."

But Dad looked unconvinced. "How could nobody have seen it coming?"

Ruby stared off in the direction of the barn, her thoughts drifting to her conversation with the strange man. She thought of the way he'd smiled up into the rain, and then the look of concern that had passed over his face at the first sign of lightning. *I'm here to help your brother,* he'd said. But what could that mean?

She took another sip from her mug, shivering as the old husk of a farmhouse trembled beneath another fit of thunder.

All afternoon they took turns checking on Simon, who tossed and turned in his bed, his sheets in a sweaty knot at his feet, his forehead damp. Outside, the clouds broke across the sky like the yolk of an egg, green running into yellow, and Ruby sat in the doorway to his room and watched her brother thrash and murmur in a strange kind of half sleep. There was something about it—his gritted teeth and the flatness behind his eyes—that made him seem more than just sick. Ruby couldn't shake the feeling that she was watching him do battle with something greater, raging inside him in time with the storm outside.

It wasn't until dinnertime that they finally decided it would be best to take him to the hospital, after Dad had tiptoed in to sit by his side and Simon had failed to recognize him, howling like he'd been visited by some kind of ghost.

And so now Ruby stood at the window and watched as Dad carried Simon to the truck, listing sideways in the rain, his head bent low over his son. Mom waited just inside the doorway, her coat flapping around her knees like a poorly secured tent, and she brushed the hair from her face and motioned for Ruby to follow.

"It's okay," she said. "It'll pass."

Ruby wasn't sure whether she meant the fever or the weather, but it was the combination of the two that sent her heart up into her ears, a thumping rhythm that nearly swallowed the sound of Mom's voice. A piece of newspaper blew in through the front door and settled itself against the wall, and Ruby nudged at it with her toe, feeling very small in the face of the weather.

Mom looked impatient now; Dad had started the truck, and the beams from the headlights struggled to reach them through the rain. But still, Ruby just stood there. Because it seemed more than just coincidence or timing. There was something about it—the escalating storm and the rising fever—that made a kind of sense to her, though she couldn't have said why.

Maybe she was crazy. Maybe it was only a storm.

But it certainly didn't feel that way.

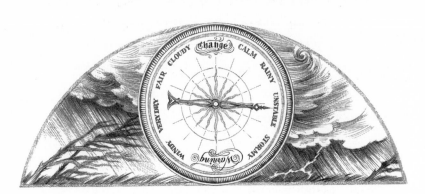

five

Just outside the emergency room waiting area, there was a small hallway with three vending machines. Ruby stood rattling the coins in her hand as she tried to decide what to get. After an hour-long wait, Simon had finally been admitted, but only Mom was allowed to go back with him. When he realized it was dinnertime, Dad had fished $2.37 in change from his pocket and sent Ruby off in search of some snacks.

As she scanned the rows of candy, someone stepped

up behind her, and Ruby had already started to move aside when she realized it was the strange man from earlier.

"Milk Dud?" he asked, holding out a box.

"Rule number one," she said with a frown. "Don't take candy from strangers."

"What's rule number two?"

"No guests in the barn."

One side of his mouth inched up into a smile. "I'm fairly certain I was bunking in with at least a handful of mice," he said. "So it seems like you have a pretty generous open-door policy."

"Yeah, well, we don't have any traps big enough for *you*."

He looked amused. "How's your brother?"

"How did you know...?"

"Not important," he said. "How's he doing?"

She shrugged. "Okay, I guess."

"Any strange visitors?"

Ruby raised her eyebrows. "Stranger than you?"

A nurse pushed past with a cart of food trays, and Ruby flattened herself against the vending machine to let her by. Once the hallway was empty again, the man stuck out his hand.

"Let's try this again," he said. "I'm Otis."

"Otis?"

"Otis Gray."

Ruby stared at his hand, hesitating a moment before finally taking it in hers. It was cool and rough as paper, but his grip was gentle.

"I'm Ruby," she told him, and he smiled.

"I know," he said. "I've come to ask for your help."

In spite of herself, Ruby couldn't help feeling flattered. This, however, didn't last long.

"Your brother's very special," Otis said as Ruby followed him around the corner and toward the doors that led to a courtyard in the center of the hospital grounds.

"Yeah, I know," she said shortly, and Otis shook his head.

"No," he said. "You don't."

He shoved the metal bar on the double doors, ducking a bit beneath the frame. It was still raining, though not nearly as hard as before, and so they stood beneath an overhang amid an array of scattered twigs and fallen leaves, debris from the sudden storm.

They were the only ones in the courtyard, and Ruby realized she should probably be nervous. But for some reason, she found herself trusting Otis. There was something sincere in the way he'd asked for her help, and despite the oddness of their encounter by the windmills earlier, and the fact that he'd been hanging around in their barn—or maybe because of these things—she was curious about what he had to say.

"Have you ever noticed anything strange about your brother?" he asked, leaning back against the railing, his arms folded across his chest.

"Strange how?"

Otis pulled his hat from his back pocket and smoothed it out. "Does he ever have bad dreams? Does he get sick a lot?"

"I don't know," Ruby said. "Not any more than I do."

"Ah," he said. "But does anything ever *happen* when he does?"

Ruby shook her head impatiently.

"What about today?"

She bit her lip and looked off toward the trees that lined the little garden.

Otis smiled. "So you do know."

"I don't," Ruby said so suddenly it surprised her. "I don't *know* anything. I just...today, when he...and the storm...it was like something..."

"Very good," he said, looking pleased. "I knew I was right about you."

Ruby was desperate to know what he meant, but she forced herself to swallow back her questions, and waited for Otis to explain.

"You have to understand that there are certain people who are..." he began, then trailed off, looking uncertain. He reached up and placed the hat on his head, then left his hand there, as if he'd forgotten to reclaim it. "There are some people who are just different, and your brother—"

A thought struck Ruby then, one she hadn't considered before. "There's something wrong with him, isn't there?"

"No," Otis said quickly. "Not like that. I'm sorry. I know I'm not doing a great job here, but I've never really done it like this before."

"Done *what*?"

He stood up a bit straighter and took a deep breath. "The timing of all this—it's not a coincidence. Simon's fever and the storm? They're connected."

Ruby felt a little flutter of recognition inside her, because as strange as it sounded coming from this mysterious man, hadn't she been thinking the very same thing?

Otis tilted his head, gauging her reaction before pushing ahead. "Your brother..." he began, then paused and cleared his throat. "Your brother is one of a very small group of people in the world who have the ability to influence the weather."

It seemed to Ruby that he was speaking much too fast, and she closed her eyes and played the words back in her head, one at a time, making sure she understood what he was saying.

"What's that even supposed to mean?" she asked, letting her eyes flutter open again. "That he has superpowers or something?"

"Not exactly," Otis said with a small smile. "More like an enhanced sensitivity to the elements. Simon's a Storm Maker."

Ruby narrowed her eyes at him, shaking her head. "No way," she said, surprised by the force of her voice. "That's crazy."

Otis raised his eyebrows as if to say, *Is it?* and something about his expression—so perfectly composed, so maddeningly patient—made her want to scream.

"This is stupid," she said through gritted teeth. "I'm going back inside."

With a small shrug, Otis stepped aside to let her pass,

but even though Ruby meant it—even though all she wanted to do was walk back into the hospital and pretend none of this had happened—she found herself rooted in place, unable to leave just yet.

"There's no such thing as a Storm Chaser," she said, her fists balled at her sides. "He's just a regular kid."

"Storm *Maker.*"

She glared at him. "Why don't you leave us alone?"

"I'm here to help," Otis said simply. He used his hat to mop up the puddles on one of the benches. Ruby sank down numbly, her head buzzing.

"I don't believe you," she said, peering up at him.

"Yes," he said quietly. "You do."

She shook her head.

"If you didn't believe me, you wouldn't be so upset. If you really thought it was so ridiculous, you'd be laughing the whole thing off."

"Ha," Ruby said, forcing a laugh that emerged roughly, like a bark. "Ha."

"Look, I know how this must sound, and I realize you have no good reason to believe me," he said. "This isn't how things are normally done. Usually, the person would be told directly, and in my experience, they always already have some sort of inkling."

Ruby's eyes were fixed stubbornly on her feet, but she couldn't stop herself from asking the question: "What sort of inkling?"

"Spontaneous dust clouds," Otis said, sitting down beside her. "Sudden wind gusts. Scattered showers. Freak snowstorms. Nothing major, because nobody's that powerful when they first flare up. It's all just reactionary weather at that stage, the result of dreams or illnesses, things like that. They can't really control themselves at first, so it's all a bit haywire, but it makes them pretty easy to spot. I'd say a good thirty percent of all weather anomalies turn out to be rookies."

Ruby had no idea what he was talking about, but she couldn't help thinking of all the times this summer when the dogs had shied away from Simon, as spooked and skittish as they were during thunderstorms. Or a few weeks ago, when he'd struck out during his baseball game, dropping his bat and kicking at the ground so angrily that when a strong breeze had blown through, swirling the dirt from the baseball diamond into little tornadoes, it had almost looked to Ruby like he'd summoned it himself.

"Stop," she said to Otis. "Please."

There was a twitch just below his left eye, the first sign of any impatience. "I wish there were an easier way to tell you this, and I wish we had more time to do it gradually, but I'm afraid we don't." He looked at her carefully. "I know I wasn't wrong about you. Whether you want to admit it or not, I have a feeling you understand exactly what I'm telling you."

Ruby ducked her head, but didn't answer. Because Otis was right—she should have been laughing or shaking her head or turning to leave. But instead, her chest had tightened and her head felt light, and she had to remind herself to breathe, because as crazy as it was—and it *was!*—there was a small part of her that believed him even so.

Just this morning, her brother had managed to short-circuit both a toaster and a truck for absolutely no apparent reason, and somehow Ruby knew—almost as if she'd always known it—that what Otis was saying could very well be true.

"I wouldn't be burdening you with this if it weren't

incredibly important," he was saying now, an urgency to his voice.

Ruby took a deep breath. "Fine. Simon can control the weather," she said, testing out the words, struggling to keep them from coming out as a question.

Otis smiled at her encouragingly. "Not quite yet," he said. "And it's really more a matter of *stabilizing* the weather. Our job is to protect people from the elements: storms and weather systems and natural disasters. But yes. Simon will be able to do all that one day, too."

"Then why are you telling *me* this?" she asked. "Why not him?"

He stood up again, folding and unfolding the poor battered hat in his hands. "You have to understand that Simon's a bit . . . delicate . . . at the moment."

"Delicate how?" she asked, glancing back at the hospital building.

"The youngest Storm Makers we've ever seen have all been of age — at least twenty-one, and usually more like twenty-four or twenty-five. Simon's case is completely unprecedented. Usually when people start to flare up, they're old enough to control themselves. At least once they learn how. But someone as young as Simon could be very dangerous." Otis began to walk back and forth in front of the bench. "You saw what happened today. He gets a fever and six power lines go down in the next town over. A man was almost killed when a tree fell on his car."

Ruby's eyes were wide. *"Simon did all that?"*

"It wasn't his fault. Our job isn't really to *cause* weather, despite our name; it's more to help control it, to keep a balance. But until you learn to do that, accidents can happen. So we need someone he trusts, someone who understands him, to help him through this."

Ruby shifted uncomfortably; she and Simon weren't as close as they used to be. "Why not tell our parents?"

"This is really secret stuff. Nobody's supposed to know. Not even you. Besides, I've never dealt with a minor before. I'm trying not to make this too complicated. You have to understand, Simon could be very, very powerful."

"He's just a kid," Ruby said again, still not quite convinced.

"Storm Makers get stronger as they get older. Starting this young could mean he'll be one of the best we've ever seen, at least once he learns to control himself. Simon has very real potential, which a lot of people will be very interested in."

"Like other Storm Chasers?"

"Storm *Makers*," he said. "And yes."

Ruby looked down at her hands. "But why Simon?"

Otis stopped pacing and stooped down in front of her. "You mean, why not you?" he asked gently, and she nodded, her cheeks burning. She knew there were far more important things to be worrying about at the moment, but she still couldn't help feeling like the last one picked in gym class.

"There's no way of knowing," Otis said, patting her shoulder a bit awkwardly. "We've rarely had two in a family before, so it doesn't seem to be genetic. And we've had all sorts of different people—plumbers and accountants and even a duke once. There doesn't seem to be much logic to it."

Ruby nodded, not really sure what to say. She felt like her mind was being pulled in too many directions, stretched far beyond what it was used to.

"I'm afraid I have no good answer for why Simon can do this, and I have no idea why it's started while he's so young. But none of that's important at the moment. All that matters right now is that Simon needs you."

"Why would he need *me*?" Ruby couldn't help asking,

the words coming out thickly. She blinked hard to keep from crying, not out of jealousy or envy or even fear— though it was all those things, too—but because she could feel the world changing fast around her, like all she'd known to be true was suddenly slipping away.

But Otis didn't answer. Instead, he arranged his hat on top of his head and then stood for a moment, peering out at the sky to the west, which had turned a brilliant shade of orange. The evening was cool now, the heat of the morning gone with the storm.

"What happens when—" Ruby began, but Otis held up a hand, cutting her off.

"There'll be time for more questions later," he said, his eyes still trained on the sky. "But for now, we need to go see your brother."

"How come?"

"Because," Otis said, turning back toward the hospital, "I have a feeling I'm not the only one looking for him."

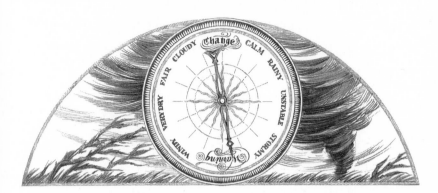

six

THE MOMENT THEY STEPPED into the hospital, Ruby's knees seemed to lock. She took a deep breath and tried to calm whatever it was that was fluttering inside her. Otis paused when he realized she was no longer following him, and though she could detect a hint of impatience in the expression on his lined face, he stood very still and waited until she'd gathered herself enough to move forward again.

They'd been gone only ten minutes, fifteen at most, but

the world felt irrevocably different to Ruby now. It wasn't so much like standing on the edge of a cliff as it was like pausing before a locked door; there was no way of knowing what might be on the other side.

Together, they wound past the vending machines and the restrooms, and suddenly they were at the door to Simon's room. Otis blinked a few times, as if surprised to find himself there so soon, and Ruby cleared her throat.

"He'll be okay, right?" she asked, her voice very small.

Otis nodded. "He will," he said, and then he said it again: "Of course he will."

This, she realized, was what she had needed to hear, and whether or not it was true didn't matter as much as believing that it could be. She straightened her shoulders.

"Ready?" Otis asked, and Ruby nodded, trying to seem more certain than she felt. Because if everything he said turned out to be true, then she had no idea what to expect. Would Simon look different? Would he *be* different? Would he be as scared as she was? Would he tell her, even if he was?

Ruby was the first to go in, just in case anyone else was already there, doctors or nurses, Mom or Dad. She took a deep breath as she nudged open the door, but when she peered around the corner, there was only Simon, asleep on the hospital bed and looking pale and drawn and about as small as she'd ever seen him. Otis stepped in behind her, and there was a long silence in the room as they stood frozen like that, only the beeping and whirring of the monitors to fill the space.

Ruby waited for Otis to say something, to wake Simon up and explain to him about what he was, what he might be—about the Storm Makers and the rules of weather and the fallen trees in the next town over—but the quiet only lengthened.

She glanced over at him, wondering what was wrong, but he simply remained there, staring at Simon as if he'd never seen a boy before.

It took her a moment to realize that the look on his face was *awe*.

Otis was looking at her brother with sheer amazement, and of all the strange and incredible things that had happened that day, this struck Ruby as the oddest of all.

After a moment, he gave his head a little shake and shifted his gaze back to Ruby. "Would you mind going back out to the waiting room?" he asked, his voice low. There was something solemn about him now; all the briskness of earlier had given way to something more reverential. "Simon and I are going to need some time to talk, so maybe you could help keep your parents occupied for a little while."

Ruby swallowed hard, trying not to look as stricken as she felt at being asked to leave. She wanted to stay and see Simon's face when Otis told him, to hear more about what it meant to be a Storm Maker. The thought of sitting in the waiting room with Mom and Dad while Simon learned all the secrets of the world was almost too much to bear.

"But can't I—"

Otis didn't even shake his head. He didn't have to. All he did was look at her, his gray eyes searching, and she could sense an urgency that hadn't been there before. She pressed her lips together, hesitating, and then nodded.

He reached into his back pocket and produced the half-eaten packet of Milk Duds. "If they ask where you've been, tell them you got lost on your way back."

Ruby took the crumpled box, glancing once more at her sleeping brother. She wondered how he'd take the news. She wondered if Otis would tell him things only other Storm Makers could know. She wondered how it was possible to be twins, yet so unequal in every way.

"Hey, Ruby?" Otis called softly, just as she was about to turn and leave. "It's only the beginning, this." His voice was weary, and something about it made her throat go tight. "There'll be other battles, and we'll need you for those."

And then, before she had a chance to ask what he meant, he pulled something from the inside pocket of his jacket and in one practiced motion tossed it her way. The object went pinwheeling through the air, small and shiny as a coin, and when she caught it, Ruby could feel the cool weight of the metal in her hand.

At first glance she thought it was a pocket watch, but when she looked closer, she saw that it was actually a kind of barometer, the edges ringed with words: *fair, stormy, cloudy, windy, rainy, unstable, calm, very dry.* On the bottom, quite ominously, it said *warning*, and above that, at the very top, where the twelve would be on a clock, was the word *change.*

"Hang on to that for me, okay?"

Ruby nodded. "And let you know if there's a warning?"

Otis smiled. "Let me know if there's a change."

With that, he turned back to Simon. Ruby stared at the barometer for another moment, running her thumb over the smooth back, where an *O* had been etched into the metal, the same one that she'd found on the silver button. Then she slipped it into her pocket and stepped out into the hallway.

All alone now, she traced a path back toward the waiting room where she'd left Dad earlier, in the company of a dozen or so other people, each of them looking as miserable and exhausted as the next, staring unseeingly at month-old magazines.

But this time she stopped short at the doorway, ducking back so that she was half-hidden by the waxy leaves of a fake plant. Dad was in exactly the same spot, and Mom had joined him. But now, sitting beside them, was a handsome man in a pin-striped suit who didn't look a bit like a doctor. He looked younger than Otis, but had the same easy confidence, like he was in possession of something more than everyone else around him. He had one leg crossed over the other, and something about the way he was speaking to her parents—with such familiarity that they may as well have been old childhood friends— made Ruby bristle.

"Oh," Mom said, looking up. "Here's our other one now."

Ruby stepped out from behind the plant, trying not to

look sheepish. As she did, the man's eyes settled on her. They were so dark that it was almost like they weren't a color at all.

"Your parents were just telling me about your brother," he said, knitting his hands together. "I'm sorry to hear he's under the weather."

Ruby had been staring at the floor, but her eyes snapped up at his choice of words.

"He's doing much better," Dad was saying. "It's just a bad viral infection, so they're getting some fluids into him, and we should be able to get out of here soon."

"Where have you been?" Mom asked, but when Ruby opened her mouth to answer, no words came out. She was still staring at the man, who cocked his head to one side, his eyes giving nothing away.

"Getting food," she said, holding up the box of Milk Duds. "But I forgot something."

"Yeah, you forgot mine," Dad joked.

"Right," Ruby mumbled, backing toward the door. "Be right back."

Once clear of the waiting room, she broke into a run, weaving past nurses and doctors, narrowly missing a gurney as it was pushed out of an elevator. By the time she made it back to Simon's room she was breathing hard, and when she pushed open the door, she was surprised to find it as silent and still as when she'd left.

Simon was still fast asleep and snoring lightly, one of his hands balled at his side, the other laid flat against his stomach. And beside him, Otis was sitting on a chair pulled up near the bed, his hat in his hands, his head bowed. He held a small blue piece of paper between two fingers and was twisting it absently.

"You didn't wake him?" Ruby whispered, and without looking at her, he shook his head.

"Everything's going to be different for him," he said, his voice breaking just slightly. "Everything." He leaned forward in the chair. "I thought I'd let him rest for a few more minutes."

Ruby took a couple of steps deeper into the room. "He's going to be fine," she said quietly. "We get to take him home tonight. But Otis..."

He swiveled to look at her, his face expectant.

"It's just that out in the waiting room," Ruby began, suddenly less sure of herself, "my parents were talking to this guy...."

She waited for Otis to ask what he looked like, what he'd said to her, what he'd been doing there. Instead, his shoulders sagged, and he rubbed his eyes.

"You remember the field where we met?" he asked after a moment.

Ruby nodded.

"Good," he said, rising to his feet. He put his hat on and took a long look at Simon, then handed Ruby the slip of paper.

"Wait," she said, stepping between him and the door. "Where are you going?"

But once again, there was no response. He simply rested a hand on her shoulder, just for a moment, and then he was moving past her and out the door, and there was nothing for Ruby to do but watch as he walked back down the long hallway.

Her mouth was dry as she stood there, unsure of what to do. She took a step forward, as if to follow him, to make sure everything was okay, but then she glanced back at Simon, and something about his face—so solemn in sleep—made her want to stay. She turned to the door again and was still paused there, paralyzed with indecision, when something hit her in the back of the head, then went skidding across the floor. Ruby stooped to pick up the pen before turning around.

"Hi," Simon said with a grin, and despite the tube in his arm, despite the hospital gown and the ashen color of his face, Ruby couldn't resist tossing the pen right back at him. It went wide, bouncing off the table, and she laughed, rushing over to the bed.

"Hi yourself," she said, unable to disguise her relief. "You look terrible."

"I feel better," he said.

Ruby had forgotten about the blue slip of paper still clutched in her hand, but Simon noticed it immediately and reached out to grab it before she could move away.

"Don't," she said quickly, trying to snatch it back. But he held it high in the air with one hand, using the other to keep her away. Ruby glanced at the door, hoping that Otis might walk in, but instead it was their parents who appeared, both of them incredulous at the scene before them: Simon shrinking back against his pillow, Ruby trying to pry his fist open one finger at a time.

"Ruby, let him rest," Mom said, hurrying over to the bed.

"They've only just said he could go," Dad said with a laugh. "If you break his wrist, we'll be here all night."

Ruby slid off the bed, shooting Simon a look, but Mom already had him buried in a hug, running a hand through his messy blond hair. A moment later, the doctor walked in with his chart, and a nurse arrived to unhook Simon's IV. There were instructions given and prescriptions written, and all the while, Ruby kept her eyes on the door, waiting and watching and hoping for it to open one more time.

When at last it was time to leave, after Simon had gotten dressed and Mom and Dad had signed all the insurance forms, they all walked out together. Ruby hung back, searching the length of every corridor, wondering if Otis would appear. But he didn't, and she wasn't sure whether to be worried or relieved.

Simon dropped back to join her, unfolding the blue paper in his palm. Once he read it, he looked over with a face like a question mark.

"What?" Ruby asked, trying to see what it said.

Simon frowned. "Meet who?"

She took the paper from his hand and read the words, which were scrawled in tiny letters across the page.

MEET ME AT SUNSET TOMORROW.

Ruby looked up at him, unsure how to answer. Her conversation with Otis felt like something she'd imagined, like maybe he'd never really been there at all. But there it was on the page: instructions for whatever it was that would come next. A meeting in an empty field. A lesson about the weather. A warning for her brother.

"Meet who?" Simon asked again, but when Ruby opened her mouth to explain, she realized she had no idea where to even begin. After a moment, she laughed.

"The Wizard of Oz," she said, and Simon gave her a look like maybe *she* was the one with the fever before skipping off ahead of her again.

Ruby was just about to crumple the piece of paper when she noticed that something else was written on the back, and her heart beat fast as she read the words.

CHANGE IS COMING.

She wasn't at all sure she wanted to find out what that meant.

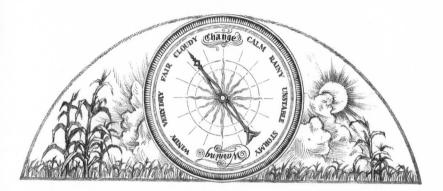

seven

ON THE WAY HOME, Simon fell asleep in the car, so when they pulled into their drive—the broad beam of the headlights sweeping across the darkened fields—Ruby nudged him gently.

"We're home," she said, and he blinked a few times, still groggy from his medication. He looked at her sleepily, his eyes not quite focused, and she had a sudden urge to tell him everything. But there would be time later.

Once Dad had parked the truck out front, he came

around to Simon's side and opened the door, ready to carry him in. But Simon scowled and hopped out by himself, fighting back a yawn.

"I'm fine," he said, as Mom eyed him with concern. He looked paler than ever in the moonlight. "Really."

They trooped silently inside, greeted by the dogs, the two of them running mad circles around Dad and avoiding Simon, who headed upstairs to put his pajamas on. Ruby had just wandered into the kitchen when she heard the front door open and then close again, and the sounds of Mom and Dad stepping out onto the porch, their footsteps hollow on the wooden slats.

She crept over to the window, looking out at the two dark forms. They were standing very close to each other, both facing out across the fields. Through the screen she could hear them speaking, quiet murmurings of thanks that Simon was okay. There was a long silence, and then Mom pulled in a breath.

"So," she asked, "how bad was it?"

"It doesn't matter," Dad said quietly. "It rained today, right?"

Mom walked over to the edge of the porch and sat down on the top step. "It's not like we can depend on that, though," she said, and Ruby could hear the weariness in her sigh. "The crops aren't enough. I think we know that now."

"We'll be fine," Dad told her, his voice firm. "It won't be long before I finish the TGI, and you were so close with that painting of the barn...."

Mom patted the stairs beside her, and Dad took a seat. "This was just an experiment," she said, "and if it doesn't work out, then—"

"It will," Dad interrupted forcefully.

She nodded. "And what if the rain doesn't come back?"

"If the rain doesn't come back," Dad said, dropping his head, "then I don't want them to know how close we are to losing this place."

Mom turned to him sharply. "How close are we?"

Instead of answering, Dad pulled a folded piece of paper from his pocket, which Mom took from him and began to read.

"He didn't even have any X-rays," she murmured. "How can it be so much?"

The question went unanswered, and Mom leaned her head on Dad's shoulder. They sat there like that in shared silence, and even through the screen, Ruby could feel the unfamiliar chill in the air, a long forgotten coolness that whistled through the corn and laced its way into the house.

A few minutes later, when they finally stood to come back inside, Ruby hurried over to feed the dogs, her mouth chalky as she filled the glinting bowls.

"Aren't you about ready for bed, too?" Dad asked when he saw that she was still up. The screen door bounced shut behind Mom, who rearranged her face into something more cheerful when she noticed Ruby.

"Yeah," she said hoarsely, turning to leave. Mom reached out to give her a hug as she walked past, smoothing her hair and then kissing her on the forehead.

"Thanks for all your help," she said. "Simon's lucky to have such a great sister."

Ruby nodded, worn out by all that had happened that day. There were so many questions still unanswered, so many things she still didn't know, and—worst of all—nothing to do but wait for Otis to show up again.

It seemed there would be no end to the things she could find to worry about tonight—huge things, terrifying things—like whether the man in the waiting room had been looking for Simon, too, and why Otis had disappeared so suddenly, and whether her brother was going to be all right.

But what worried her the most was this: Simon had made it rain.

He'd gotten sick, and the skies had opened up.

Her brother, who ate ketchup straight out of the bottle and wore the same socks for days at a time, had apparently done the impossible.

And that changed everything.

Once she'd brushed her teeth and put on her pajamas, Ruby sat on her bed and pushed back the curtains, looking out at the barn, which stood silent and glowing, its chipping paint mottled beneath the yellow moon.

After the morning's storm, it was hard to believe how quiet the sky could be, but it was now vast and still and flaked with stars. She wondered if it was someone's job to do just this, to close up shop at the end of the day, tuck the edges of the night sky in around the fields like they were putting the world to bed. It seemed a peaceful thing, a job for someone watchful and calm, and Ruby thought it might be something she'd be good at.

After a moment, she closed the curtain and swung her feet off the bed, tiptoeing across the hall to Simon's room.

He was already asleep, making soft snuffling sounds, one foot poking out from under the sheets. Ruby leaned against the doorframe, her eyelids heavy, her mind still busy.

There are days where time splits down the middle, and before and after no longer bear any resemblance to each other. Ruby already knew that this was one of those days—that everything had already changed, and that tomorrow she'd be faced with the unwelcome task of moving forward, whether she wanted to or not.

But for now, she stood there and watched Simon sleep, the questions welling up inside her, the knot of fear in her chest pulling itself tighter. There was no way to know why he'd been chosen, or what would happen as a result. All she could do for now was go to sleep, and let tomorrow come.

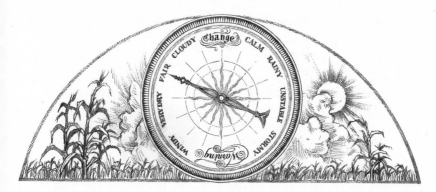

eight

WHEN RUBY LOOKED OUT HER WINDOW the following morning, she was surprised by how much damage the storm had done. Most of the fields to the south looked as if they'd fallen victim to some sort of stampede, and the only trees in sight—two old elms that stood like sentinels on either side of the front door—were badly torn up, their branches littering the ground below.

It took her a moment to remember all that had happened the night before, and the thought was slow to take shape in her mind: that it was *Simon* who was responsible for all this. Her skinny, rumpled brother, who had to lean with all his weight against the barn door to get it to open, had single-handedly inflicted all this destruction.

Ruby yawned and pushed back the covers; she hardly remembered grabbing a blanket last night, but she'd needed it for the first time in a month. She fished the barometer out from the pocket of yesterday's shorts, peering down at the little swaying needle, which was now pointed to *fair*. She still wasn't exactly sure what she should be looking for — what she should be *hoping* for — but after yesterday's storm, *fair* seemed just fine to her.

The light from the window fell in angled squares across her bedroom floor, and she padded through them in her bare feet, wondering if Simon was up yet. She pulled on a pair of shorts and a T-shirt, then hurried out into the hallway, where she saw through the open door that his bed was empty and unmade.

Downstairs, Mom and Dad were in the kitchen, reading about the storm in the newspaper. Dad waved a piece of toast at her as she walked in, but Ruby had more important things to worry about than breakfast.

"Where's Simon?"

"Barn, I think," Mom said. "He was up early."

"And he's feeling much better," Dad said, wafting the toast beneath Ruby's nose.

She grabbed an apple from the bowl on the table. "Back in a bit."

Outside, the world still looked as if it were drying out, the sky shot through with silver, the ground soft and damp. When she reached the barn, Ruby heaved open the door and then stood there for a moment, letting her eyes adjust. Simon was lying on the pile of hay in the back, his head propped on his arms as if he were stargazing. But the only thing to look at was a collection of cobwebs on the pitched ceiling of the barn, and a small jagged hole in one corner that Dad had been meaning to fix for a year now.

"Hey," Ruby said, stepping into the wedge of light made by the open door. "How're you feeling?"

Simon rolled his head to one side and squinted at her from across the long floor of the barn. Between them, Dad's workbench and various instruments littered the open space, and Ruby stepped carefully around them.

"Better," Simon said quietly. "I guess."

He certainly didn't *look* better. As Ruby took a seat

beside him on the hay, she could see that his face was still thin and drawn, and there was a slight creasing at the corners of his eyes that perhaps only she could detect.

Simon had always moved through life with such ease, and he'd settled into the farm much quicker than Ruby had. Almost as soon as they'd arrived in Wisconsin last year, he'd tried out for the town's junior baseball team, quickly becoming their starting pitcher. But by the time school started, Ruby had realized that just because her twin brother was a baseball star didn't mean she got to dodge all the standard new-kid issues, too. Especially since she was the type who preferred books to baseball, who was good at science and not so good at small talk.

Early on, Simon made an effort to include her, but Ruby quickly grew tired of trying to keep up with his new friends, who were only ever nice to her in a tolerant sort of way. It had all just seemed like further evidence that she and Simon were growing apart.

But it also made it all the more alarming to see him like this now, the usual confidence behind his eyes replaced with something like worry.

"You okay?" she asked, and he shrugged.

"I didn't sleep much last night."

"Me neither," Ruby said, leaning back.

They sat in silence, watching the wind in the doorway whip the puddles into miniature whirlpools. A spider crawled across the bale of hay beside Ruby and she studied it for a moment, trying to figure out what to do next.

In the light of morning, everything Otis had told her yesterday seemed completely ridiculous. There was simply no good way to say it: that a man who'd been lurking in their barn had appeared on a hay wagon, foretold her brother's illness, then showed up at the hospital and claimed Simon could control the weather.

The thought of saying that out loud, of giving voice to something so completely insane, seemed to Ruby like admitting she was as crazy as Otis was.

But what if he was right?

Beside her, Simon yawned, pulling a stick from the bale of hay and jabbing it absently into his other hand. "I had the weirdest dream last night," he said. "There was this guy in my room at the hospital...."

Ruby swiveled to face him. "What?"

"He was talking about clouds or something. Storm clouds, maybe? I can't really remember."

Ruby took a deep breath, waiting for him to continue.

"He was just sitting there, like he belonged in the room, and talking and talking and talking, and I couldn't wake up."

Ruby wasn't sure what made her ask the question, but it seemed important somehow. "Were you scared?"

Simon shook his head. "Not really," he said. "I mean, it wasn't a nightmare or anything. I just wanted to know what he was trying to tell me."

Ruby bit her lip. "Was his name Otis?"

"How would I know?" he asked, looking annoyed, and when she didn't answer, he tossed the stick of hay and stood up. "It was only a dream."

"Simon," she said, and he paused, lowering his gaze to meet hers. Ruby took a long breath. "What if it wasn't?"

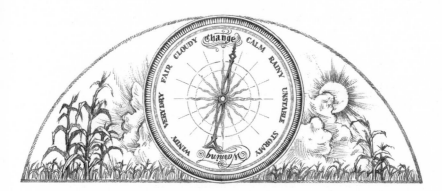

nine

ABOUT A MILE FROM THE HOUSE, there was a small pond surrounded by a grove of narrow trees. It sat on the edge of their property, a patch of green woods sprung up from the yellow farmland like a desert oasis, and they walked there now in silence, tracing a route along the western fields.

The edges of the water were swollen from the previous night's rain, and one of the trees had been split clear down the middle by lightning, part of it fallen at an angle to create a kind of steeple. Ruby walked a circle around it, running a hand along the rough bark.

"So?" Simon said, planting his feet and raising his eyebrows. She'd promised him answers once they were here, but once again, Ruby had no idea where to begin.

After a moment, she reached out and tapped the splintered bark of the tree with her palm. "I think you did this."

He shook his head. "I haven't been down here in weeks."

"Simon."

"What?" he said stubbornly. "I *haven't*."

Ruby took a few steps closer. "That guy in your hospital room? It wasn't a dream. I brought him there."

Simon was looking more and more confused, and Ruby couldn't really blame him. Maybe this was a mistake after all. Maybe she *was* as crazy as Otis.

She looked at the broken tree once more, the fallen limbs, and then back at her brother, whose hands were on his hips in a gesture that fell somewhere between irritation and defiance. It seemed impossible that he could have been the one to do this. That his fever could have downed a whole tree. A *tree*.

How would he ever believe her, when she wasn't even quite sure she believed it herself?

But then he kicked at the dirt, and the wind picked up, plucking dried leaves from branches and sending them flying, and Ruby's eyes widened.

"*That*," she said, pointing at the ground. "I think you're doing it now."

"Doing *what*?" he asked, glaring at her. "This is stupid. If there's something you want to tell me, then tell me. Otherwise, I'm going back up to the barn."

Ruby took a deep breath. "I think..." she said, then hesitated. "I think you can control the weather."

Her heart thudded in her chest as she waited for Simon to respond, to laugh at her or storm away or demand more of an explanation. But to her surprise, he did none of these things. Instead, after a long moment, he simply shook his head and let out a breath.

"Well," he said with a grin.

Ruby stared at him. "Well, what?"

"The way you were acting, I thought it was going to be something really awful."

"I don't think you get it...."

"I do," Simon said, and Ruby was struck by how calm

he was, and how certain he sounded. She'd been prepared to defend herself, to have to convince him. That
morning, she'd slipped the button into her pocket, and
she still had the barometer, too; she was carrying them
around with her like some kind of proof that Otis had
been there after all. She'd thought she would need evidence. She'd thought she would need to make a case.

But she'd been wrong. Simon appeared to be absorbing
this information with roughly the same amount of astonishment reserved for Mom's daily announcements about
what was for dinner. Ruby stared at him as he paced
back and forth along the edge of the water, apparently
deep in thought.

"I knew there was something strange going on," he
was saying. "I mean, think about the dogs. Haven't you
noticed how weird they've been around me?"

"Yeah, but..."

"And the toaster yesterday?"

Ruby nodded, not sure what to say.

"I mean, if it's true," he said, "then that would explain a
lot."

Ruby walked over to the pier where they kept the little
rowboat tied up. She kicked off her sandals to let her bare

feet dangle in the water, and after a moment, Simon joined her.

"So you knew?" she said quietly, and he shook his head.

"Not exactly. But something's been weird lately."

"For how long?"

"Not long," he said. "Maybe since school let out, since our birthday. Not long."

"Why didn't you say anything?"

"Would you have believed me?"

Ruby shook her head. "I'm not sure I even believe it now."

"Me neither," Simon said with a grin.

"That note you found yesterday?" she said, and he nodded. "It's from this guy named Otis Gray."

"The guy from my dream."

"Right," Ruby said. "Well, the guy from your hospital room, anyway. I saw him come out of the barn yesterday, and then I ran into him when I went out on my bike. He knew you were sick."

Simon bent his head, peering down at the water. "What else did he say?"

"That there are these people who can control the

weather," she said. "They're called Storm Makers. And you're one of them."

"Wow." He exhaled, fighting back a smile. Ruby could tell that however amazed he was, however impressed, he was trying hard to play it cool. But it wasn't working.

"This isn't a game, Simon," she said, sweeping an arm at the trees behind them. "All that damage? It's because you got sick. Whatever this is, you need to figure out how to get it under control."

"Jeez," he said. "Can you give me a minute here?"

"Fine, but don't be an idiot about this, okay? It's not a magic trick. It's real."

"I almost got electrocuted twice yesterday," Simon said, annoyed. "I obviously get that it's real."

"Fine," Ruby said.

"Fine," he shot back.

Neither of them said anything for a moment. Simon picked a splinter of wood out of the edge of the dock, and Ruby leaned over and searched for fish in the muddy waters.

Finally, Simon cleared his throat. "Look, just because you're not—"

Ruby scowled. "Not what?"

"Nothing."

"Just because I'm not one, too?" she said, struggling to her feet. "I should've known you'd be like this."

Simon stood up. "Like what?"

"Even worse than you've already been lately."

"What's that supposed to mean?"

"Nothing," Ruby said. "Otis is coming back tonight, and hopefully he'll explain about everything then."

"Great," Simon said, shoving his feet back into his flip-flops. "I'll tell him you say hi."

Ruby glared at him. "I'm coming, too. You don't even know where it is."

"Fine," he said, turning to walk back to the house.

"And you better be in a good mood."

He paused. "Why?"

"Because," she said, hurrying past him, "I really don't want to have to ride out there in the middle of a tornado or something."

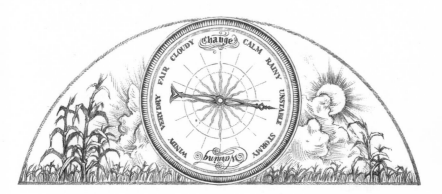

ten

BY THE TIME they made it back up to the barn, much of their anger seemed to have melted in the sun. Though he was about four paces ahead of her, Simon dropped back as they neared the house, which was his way of apologizing. Ruby reached over and punched his shoulder, which was hers. There were too many possibilities to discuss, too many things to marvel over; this was simply too big for them to stay mad at each other for long.

As they ducked into the barn, Dad looked up and

waved a wrench in greeting. "Anyone want to keep me company?"

"No," they both said at once, laughing.

Simon grabbed a couple of mitts and a baseball, and for once, Ruby didn't argue. They trooped back out into the heat together, zigzagging between the puddles on the gravel drive, which were already drying up again.

Behind the house, they spread out, and Simon tossed the old baseball in her direction. They played in silence for a while, like actors going through the motions, pretending things were normal, though they were both keenly aware of the hours still left before they were due to meet Otis.

"I wonder how much you can do," Ruby said, stooping to pick up the ball after it had fallen out of her mitt. "I mean, do you think it's just rain showers and stuff? Or, like, tornadoes and hurricanes?"

Simon wiggled his eyebrows at the sky. "Abracadabra."

Ruby looked up, half expecting a sudden hailstorm.

"See?" he said with a shrug. "The only thing I'm good at so far is frying toasters."

Ruby laughed. "But you're *really* good at that."

He took a little bow. But when he straightened again,

his face was serious. "Why didn't Otis stay and talk to me yesterday?"

"I guess he had to go."

"Go where?"

"I don't know," she said truthfully. How could she tell him about the man in the waiting room, about the fact that there might be other people after him? Especially when she didn't know anything for sure? Tonight, Otis could explain everything. In the meantime, there was no sense in worrying Simon.

"Hey, I bet you could learn to make it snow," she said, and his face relaxed into a grin.

"I'd make every day a snow day," he said. "No more school."

"And no more rain delays for your baseball games."

"And no more of this *heat*," he said with a groan, tilting his head back and laughing at the high ball of sun in the sky. Ruby smiled, too. It was easier this way, imagining a blizzard in July or a tropical Christmas. It was far simpler to ignore the darker threats and immediate dangers, to get lost in the magic of it, the impossible gift that had fallen into their midst.

Around noon, the day began to grow even hotter, and

when they passed Dad on their way back to the barn, he was scowling so hard at the sky that he barely noticed them.

"Maybe I should help him out and try to make it rain again," Simon said under his breath, and though Ruby knew he was half joking, she still remained quiet. It wasn't fair not to tell him about the conversation she'd overheard the night before, about how bad things really were with the farm. But there was a part of her that was afraid to do it.

Because what if he *could* make it rain again?

Ruby knew she was awful—she was mean and horrible and pathetic—but there was a small and miserable part of her that couldn't help rooting for the farm's failure. Especially if it meant going back to the way things used to be.

And so she kept quiet.

Without their exactly agreeing to it, Ruby realized they were both avoiding Mom and Dad. At lunchtime, Simon ducked into the kitchen and grabbed their sandwiches before Mom had time to do more than ask how he was feeling, and they spent the rest of the afternoon dodging Dad as he cleaned up after the storm. It was almost like how things used to be between the two of them, moving as a unit, everything in silent accord.

When Mom finally called them to dinner later, Simon and Ruby exchanged a glance before walking slowly toward the house. They both knew this wasn't something to share with their parents—it was much too fragile and far too important—but Simon had never been particularly good at keeping secrets.

Ruby opened her mouth to remind him, but Simon held up a hand. "I know, I know," he said. "Not a word."

In the kitchen, Dad was busy setting the table—usually the twins' job—and Mom was carrying over a huge bowl of spaghetti and meatballs. Ruby saw there was a small plate of cupcakes with green frosting on the counter.

"What's the occasion?" she asked, and Mom smiled as she pulled out her chair.

"We thought we could use a treat after last night."

"Exactly," Dad said. "We're just glad Simon's back to normal."

Ruby nearly choked on her water, and Simon shot her a look.

"And," Dad said, leaning forward and braiding his

fingers together in the way he always did when trying not to give something away, "your mother sold her painting today."

"*Mom!*" Ruby said, jumping up to give her a hug. "Congratulations!"

"That's awesome," Simon said, digging into his pasta. "Does that mean we don't have to worry about money anymore?"

Mom and Dad glanced at each other, and Ruby slipped back into her seat.

"It wasn't a big sale," Mom explained gently. "Just the first."

"Which is really exciting," Dad said, reaching to place his hand over hers. "And the start of many more to come."

Simon stabbed a meatball with his fork. "Awesome," he said again.

"Who bought it?" Ruby asked, and Mom beamed.

"The bank in town, actually. One of the women who works there saw it when she came by last week, and she's going to hang it in her office there."

Ruby looked up. "Someone from the bank came by?"

"Just a routine visit to pick up some paperwork," Dad said quickly.

Simon—completely oblivious—dropped his fork with a clatter, then stood to grab the basket of bread. They all stared as he piled several slices on his plate.

"Jeez, Simon," Mom said. "Dad should be doing a scientific study on *you*."

"Normal Eating Habits of the Twelve-Year-Old Male," Dad joked, and Simon looked up from his plate, his chin red with pasta sauce.

"Exactly," he said. "*Normal*."

⚡

It was just before dusk when they wheeled their bikes from the barn. The mosquitoes were out in full force, and Simon slapped at his knee as they set off together, moving with a kind of unspoken urgency. At the end of the drive Ruby coasted ahead, leading them to the left, following the same route she'd taken just the previous morning, though it seemed much longer ago.

The windmills looked different at this time of day, bright against the fading colors of the evening sky. Simon had slowed down and was staring up in quiet awe, and Ruby felt a kind of peace overtake her at the sight of them. She hoped that someday someone would look at an invention of her dad's and feel the same way.

When they rounded the bend, she stood up on the pedals, trying to catch a glimpse of the hay wagon, looking for the familiar shape of Otis's hat. She hopped off the bike and let it clatter to the ground, then ran the rest of the way between the crops. But as she drew closer, she couldn't escape the sinking feeling that was starting to surface, and by the time she reached the hay wagon, she knew it was true.

Otis wasn't there.

Ruby spun around to face Simon, who was a few steps behind.

"Are you sure this is when he said to meet?"

"You saw the note," she said, aware of the rising panic in her voice.

"Well, are you sure this is the right place?"

She nodded stiffly. She hadn't realized how much she'd been counting on seeing Otis again, hadn't even paused to consider that he might not return. And now it was as if something inside her had collapsed, like the wind had rushed right out of her. She sat down in the dirt, still muddy from yesterday's rain, and rested her forehead on her knees.

"Hey," Simon said, sitting down beside her. "It's okay. He's probably just late."

"He's not," Ruby said, her voice choked. "He would've been here."

The evening had darkened a shade, and the crows in the field had gone quiet. A rabbit darted between stalks of corn and paused when it saw them, nose twitching, before running off again. Above them, the windmills continued their steady rotation, always moving, but going nowhere.

"What now?" Simon asked, and his voice sounded so unlike him, so unsure, that it took everything in Ruby not to cry.

"Maybe he meant tomorrow night," she said without much hope.

"Then wouldn't he have said so?"

"Yeah, but just maybe..."

Simon stood up and brushed off the back of his shorts. The sky was growing rapidly darker, and they both knew they'd be in trouble if they didn't start for home soon. They walked their bikes across the uneven ground, the tires bouncing over rocks, and when they'd made it out to the road, they stood there for a moment and looked back, reluctant to give up. But nobody was there and nobody was coming.

They were all alone.

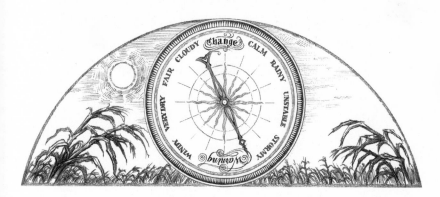

eleven

THE NEXT MORNING, they all drove into town to deliver Mom's painting. But when they arrived at the bank, Dad handed Simon and Ruby each a five-dollar bill.

"This might take a little while," he said. "Can you guys entertain yourselves for a bit?"

"What could possibly take so long?" Ruby asked. "You walk in, you hand over the painting, you walk out."

"Ruby," Mom said, a warning tone to her voice. "We'll find you when we're done, okay?"

"Don't spend it all on candy," Dad said, and then they pushed open the doors to the old stone bank building, leaving the twins alone outside.

"Candy?" Simon suggested, but Ruby shook her head.

"Follow me."

It was already hot out for so early in the day, the sidewalks baking in the morning sun. Ruby led them around the corner, past the general store and her least favorite antique shop and the place that sold dresses only a grandmother would wear.

"We're going back to the mechanic's?" Simon said when there was nothing ahead of them but the squat gray building that sat on the last corner in town. "How come?"

Ruby didn't answer him, and when they'd crossed the oil-stained driveway and were standing before the open door of the garage, Daisy's head emerged from beneath the hood of an old blue sedan that looked as if it had seen better days.

"You two again," she said, wiping her forehead. Her eyes settled on Simon. "Come to barbecue another car?"

He flushed, rocking back on his heels.

"We're waiting for our parents," Ruby said. "Can we watch?"

Daisy brushed a strand of blond hair from her eyes,

leaving a streak of grease near her temple. She put her hands on her hips and sighed. "I prefer to be alone."

"We want to know how all this stuff works," Ruby said, and Daisy eyed her carefully.

"What stuff?"

Ruby gave her an innocent smile and gestured toward the car. "Car stuff."

"Is that so?"

"Yeah," Ruby said, meeting her gaze. "I bet we could learn a lot from you."

Daisy tossed Simon a rag. "You can try helping me again," she said. "But this one is mine. So stay away from the battery."

"It's yours?" Simon asked, his nose wrinkled. The car must have been at least twenty years old, and the paint was orange with rust in places, giving it a speckled look, like an Easter egg. There was a huge dent in one of the back doors, a cracked taillight, and a broken window. "It looks like a lost cause."

"I like lost causes," Daisy said, gazing at it with pride. "Just wait. I'll have it up and running again in no time."

As she and Simon set to work, Ruby looked on. "You know, Simon was in the hospital the other night."

"You were?" Daisy asked, her face unreadable, and Simon nodded. "I'm sorry to hear that."

"Yeah, the night of the storm," Ruby continued, aware that she was speaking a bit too loud. "He was feeling a little *under the weather*. But hopefully it won't *flare up* again anytime soon."

Daisy started, bumping her head on the open hood of the car. From down the street, the church bells began to toll, and a few birds that had been perched in the shadow of the building scattered, their wings flapping loudly. "I think you guys should probably get going," she said, wincing as she brought a hand to her forehead. "Your parents must be looking for you."

"Can't we finish this first?" Simon asked, but Daisy was still looking at Ruby, who took a few steps closer.

"You know, don't you?"

"Ruby," Simon said, suddenly aware of her tone, the challenge in it.

"She *knows*," Ruby said again.

Daisy folded her arms. "I have no idea what you're talking about."

"He's one of them," she said, thrusting a finger at Simon, who made a strangled noise.

"Ruby."

Daisy reached for a spray bottle on the nearest shelf, then began cleaning the windshield of the car. Her face had clouded over, and she scrubbed furiously at the spots on the glass. "You don't know what you're talking about," she said as she worked. "And I've got customers coming soon."

"I'm not wrong," Ruby insisted. "I saw your face when the battery got struck the other day."

Daisy had been running a rag along the wiper blades of the car, but now she paused, shaking her head. "He's too young," she said, so softly that they almost missed it. When she lifted her chin, her eyes met Ruby's, and there was a long silence as they stared at each other across the garage.

Finally, Ruby grinned. "I was right."

For the first time since they'd arrived at the garage, Daisy's composure seemed on the verge of crumbling. She blinked a few times, then shook her head again.

"Otis said he's the youngest one ever," Ruby explained, and Simon took a step toward her.

"I am?" he said, at the exact same moment that Daisy dropped the bottle she'd been holding. It rolled underneath the car, the liquid inside sloshing back and forth.

"You met Otis?" she asked, her voice trembling. Her

face had gone pale, and her green eyes were as round as two coins. She opened her mouth to say more, but there were footsteps behind Ruby, and they all turned to see Mom and Dad walking up to the entrance. Simon stood frozen beside the car, as if afraid to move, and Daisy and Ruby exchanged a long look.

"I hope these two grease monkeys weren't bothering you," Dad said, placing one hand on Ruby's shoulder and offering the other to Daisy, who shook it stiffly.

"Not at all," she said. "In fact, they've been very... helpful."

"Well, they do a lot of this kind of mechanical stuff back home," he said with unmistakable pride.

Daisy nodded politely, and there were a few beats of silence before Mom glanced down at her watch. "Well," she said. "I guess we should be—"

"Maybe they'd like to work here," Daisy said, the words emerging in a rush. She looked as surprised as the rest of them by her offer. "I mean, if they're not too busy this summer, and they want a job, maybe they could come by and help out from time to time. It'd be minimum wage, but they could learn a lot—"

"*Yes,*" Simon and Ruby said at once.

Mom and Dad exchanged a look, and Ruby could almost see the whole conversation unraveling between them— *more responsibility, good opportunity, character building, pocket money*—and after a moment, Mom gave Daisy a little nod.

"School's out already," she said, "so that would be fine, if they're up for it."

"We are," Ruby said brightly.

"Great," Daisy said. "Whenever they're ready to start, then."

"How about tomorrow morning?" Simon suggested, and when everyone seemed to agree to this, he pumped his fist triumphantly.

As they all turned to go, Daisy lifted a hand to wave good-bye. "Stay out of trouble till then, okay?" she said, echoing her parting words from the last time, and Dad laughed and tousled Simon's hair. But Ruby didn't have to turn around to know that it wasn't a joke at all.

On the way back to the farm, Dad talked about how proud he was of Mom for selling her painting, and Mom talked about how proud she was of Simon and Ruby for getting their first summer job, and all the while, the twins sat in the back of the truck and looked out their separate windows.

Later that evening they rode out to the windmills again, but there was none of the urgency of the night before, and neither really expected that Otis would be there. So when they pulled up to the hay wagon, they weren't surprised to find it empty.

"You shouldn't have trusted him," Simon said, his voice gruff. "And maybe we shouldn't trust Daisy, either."

"What choice do we have?" Ruby asked.

Simon seemed unable to think of anything to say to this.

This time, they hadn't even bothered getting off their bikes, so they simply turned around and headed toward home again. The windmills grew small behind them as they pedaled, and Ruby steered with one hand, using the other to pull the barometer from her pocket. Even though the evening was silent and calm, the arrow was pointed to *stormy*. She shook it once, and the needle bobbled beneath the curved glass.

But when it came to rest again, it was in the exact same place.

twelve

Simon didn't often fall behind, especially on his bike, so on the way home from the windmills Ruby was surprised to find herself out ahead and alone, nothing but wheat fields on either side of her. When she braked to look back over her shoulder, Simon was stooped beside his bike, examining the deflated rubber of the front tire.

"Must have been a piece of glass in the road or something," he said with a groan.

Ruby dismounted, too, and together they began to

walk the bikes up the dusty lane, the spokes clicking loudly in the quiet evening.

"This is gonna take *hours*," Simon complained. Each time the tire rotated, it made a sort of scraping sound, and after a while Ruby grew used to the odd rhythm of it. It was comforting, in a way, out here where there was nothing else around for miles.

The sky above was a dusky gray; not yet dark, but not fully light, either. The fields around them were planted with wheat, the brown stalks almost ready for harvest and nearly as tall as both Simon and Ruby, so that it almost felt as if they were walking through a tunnel. There was sure to be a sunset off to the west somewhere, and the crickets had just started to emerge, the sound of their chirping echoing through the crops.

"Do you think he's gone for good?" Simon asked, and though Ruby knew he was talking about Otis, she couldn't quite bring herself to answer. After a few minutes of silence, Simon tried again: "Are we going back again tomorrow night?"

Ruby shrugged. "He must have a good reason."

"How do you know?"

"I just do," she insisted.

"Well, I wish he'd been able to teach me a few things before skipping town," Simon said, squinting up at the sky. Using one hand to hold the bike steady, he waved the other vaguely. "I keep trying to make some weather, but nothing seems to work."

"Maybe Daisy can teach you something tomorrow."

"You really think she's one, too?"

"Come on," Ruby said. "You were there this morning. You saw how she reacted. There's no way she's not."

Simon nodded. "Well, at least we know where she works. That makes it a lot harder for *her* to abandon us."

"Otis didn't abandon us," Ruby said, not quite sure why she was defending him. She was as disappointed as Simon; maybe even more so. But she couldn't bring herself to give up on Otis just yet. "He'll be back," she said. "I know he will."

Just ahead of her, Simon stopped short.

"Is that him?" he asked, pointing down the road, which was so long and straight and flat that it looked almost endless, cut off by nothing but the horizon itself. And in the middle of it, about a hundred yards away, stood a man in a black suit.

Ruby opened her mouth, but found that her breath was

caught in her throat. The moment they paused, the man began to walk toward them. It was definitely not Otis, but he had the same airiness about him, like he might just as easily have been walking to work in a big city somewhere. There was nothing in his manner that suggested he was on an empty country road, the wheat leaning this way and that all around him.

As he approached, Ruby realized it was the man from the waiting room at the hospital, the man whose presence had somehow made Otis disappear. And now here he was, bearing down on them. She stood stock-still, unable to move. But when she glanced over, she was surprised to find no trace of fear on Simon's face.

His eyes were wide and his lips just slightly parted, and there was an eagerness about him that made him seem like a little kid again. As the man drew closer, Simon readjusted his grip on the handlebars of his bike and shifted nervously from one foot to the other.

"I don't mean to alarm you," the man called out when he was nearly there. He lifted a hand in a gesture halfway between a salute and a wave. His suit was black, and his shoes were shiny, and his hair was so perfect that he looked almost like a cartoon character, with dark eyes and a strong jaw and a smile that was infuriatingly white.

"You must be Simon," he said when he was close enough, reaching out to shake his hand and ignoring Ruby entirely.

Simon nodded. "And this is Ruby."

The man slid his eyes over to her and inclined his head.

"We met at the hospital," she reminded him, but he chose not to acknowledge this.

"Are you Otis?" Simon asked.

The man let out a laugh like a cough. "Am I Otis Gray?" he said with a thin smile. "Hardly."

Simon looked over at Ruby, not quite getting the joke.

"I'm Rupert London," the man said, drawing himself up to his full height. "Chairman of MOSS."

"Chairman of *Mouse*?" Simon asked, and Rupert London flexed his jaw. He pulled a card from his pocket and handed it over. Ruby leaned in and saw that there was nothing but a little storm cloud and an address printed on the card.

"I'm the Chairman of the Makers of Storms Society," he said. "And I've come all this way to see *you*."

His voice seemed to imply that this was some kind of

great honor; it was so full of pretentiousness that Ruby couldn't help rolling her eyes. But Simon was beaming up at the man as if he'd just been knighted.

"Wow," he said. "I mean, thanks."

London nodded solemnly. "You're the talk of the Society right now," he said. "There are a lot of people back at our headquarters in Chicago who would love to meet you."

"Too bad we live up here, then," Ruby chimed in, but London ignored her.

"I don't know how much you've heard just yet," he continued, pivoting so that he was facing only Simon, his back to Ruby. "Or how *dependable* your sources have been. But not only have you revealed yourself to be our newest Storm Maker, you're also the youngest ever recorded. And that makes you pretty special. So we're all very excited to see what you can do."

Ruby could see Simon absorbing all this, the word *special* landing squarely across his face, which broke into a smile. "Yeah, Ruby met Otis the other day, and he told her that, too. But we haven't seen him since."

"Well," London said, "do you mind if I walk with you, then? Perhaps I can be a bit more enlightening than our friend Otis."

Without bothering to look at Ruby, Simon nodded, and the two of them started off ahead of her, Simon's bike clanging with each step he took. The sky had darkened another couple of shades, and it was starting to get harder to see. In the distance, Ruby heard an engine start up, probably a tractor in a far-off field, and she wished they were closer, or that a car would drive by.

There was something about Rupert London that felt wrong to her. She supposed it was no less creepy to show up at the hospital than it was to hide out in their barn, but for some reason, she'd trusted Otis immediately. Rupert London, on the other hand, made her feel utterly powerless.

When she caught up, London was telling Simon more about the Society.

"Thousands," he said strolling with his hands behind his back. "There are thousands of us. And not just here, but all over the world."

"And you're in charge of them all?" Simon asked.

"Many of them," he said. "Each country has its own separate Chairman, and we each preside over all the Storm Makers in our regions. But everyone knows who's the most powerful."

"Who?" Ruby asked innocently, and London narrowed his eyes at her before turning back to Simon.

"Before I was elected Chairman, I was the Director of the Department of Severe Weather for the Western Time Zone," he said, strolling with his hands behind his back. "In charge of blizzards, hailstorms, tornadoes, and general storms."

Simon paused. "Stopping them, right? Not making them?"

"Of course, of course," London said breezily. "A Storm Maker usually excels in one particular area, though sometimes it takes a while for that talent to emerge. It's not that they can't manage the others, but someone who is especially proficient in hailstorms doesn't tend to be as useful when it comes to tsunamis, if you see what I mean."

Simon nodded sagely. "So yours was . . . ?"

"I've dabbled in everything," London said with a smile so falsely modest that Ruby almost rolled her eyes again. "It's like with athletes. Most tend to specialize in one sport, but every once in a while, someone comes along who just seems to be able to play them all."

"And that's you?" Simon asked, his eyes glinting.

"That's me."

Ruby cleared her throat. "And what's Otis's specialty?"

Without looking over, without taking his eyes off her brother, London inclined his head. "Your sister's friend Otis once worked in my time zone, too. He was in charge of heat-related disasters. He was supposed to be skilled in fires and droughts." His voice had gone thin and reedy, and he paused for a moment before continuing. "And before that, he was one of our best Trackers, which is probably why he was able to find you so quickly. Otis was always quite good at locating rookies. He had something of a sixth sense for these things, which must be why he was lured back into the fray when he caught wind of you."

"Why, what does he do now?" Simon asked, and Ruby skipped forward a few steps, eager to hear.

"I'm afraid he's no longer with the Society," London said, looking off into the fields. "Not every Storm Maker feels the need to work for the greater good. They're still responsible for following our rules, of course, but there are those who would rather strike out on their own than be part of the Society. Otis had a bit of a breakdown a few years back. And the poor man's become something of a crackpot ever since."

"He's no crazier than you," Ruby said, and for the first time, London turned to face her, his eyes flashing.

"I'd take care to mind your own business," he said. "The only reason you're privy to this conversation is because Otis has already shared confidential information with you, and there's no taking that back."

Simon stiffened, then slowed until his stride was even with Ruby's, their shoulders nearly touching. "We're twins," he told London. "We tell each other everything."

Ruby smiled at him gratefully, not just for defending her, but also for lying; it had been a while since they'd told each other everything, but in that moment, it was nice to believe it was still true.

"Yes, I know," London said to Simon, his voice a bit gentler now. "Which is why we're making an exception in this case. Normally, it would be Storm Makers only. There are strict punishments for any sort of leaked information."

Simon pulled ahead again. "Like what?"

"Oh, I wouldn't want to bore you with talk of such things, but let's just say we have ways of reminding our members to stay in line," he told them. "Nobody likes to wake up and discover they can no longer make so much as a drizzle."

Simon looked awed. "So what sorts of things can you do? What will *I* be able to do? Can you show us?"

London paused in the middle of the road, which was now nearly dark. A breeze wound through the fields, and Ruby shivered in spite of the heat. She leaned against her bike, wishing they were home right now, wishing Otis had shown up, wishing none of this had ever happened. The back of her neck prickled as London turned around.

"What would you like to see?"

Simon shrugged. "Anything."

It happened in a flash. With a quick jerk of London's head and a crack that vibrated straight down through Ruby's toes, the sky lit up with orange. Ruby felt the heat before she saw the fire, which had leapt from a patch of wheat to their left, burning high and bright, making the rest of the world darker by comparison. The stalks popped as they burned, and the smoke made her eyes water as the flames danced in the sky, illuminating their faces.

"Stop," Ruby said, her voice choked. "Please stop it."

Simon looked dazzled by the display. For a moment he stared at it with a kind of horrified awe, but at the sound of Ruby's voice, he ran forward a few steps, then turned back to London.

"Those are somebody's crops," he said. "Make it stop."

London bowed his head and, with a twirl of his finger, Ruby felt a great wind at her back, the force of it propelling her forward a few steps. She sucked in a breath as she saw its source: a small tornado about a hundred yards away, moving sideways through the wheat and then jumping the road in a swirl of dust, barreling straight into the fire.

The flames seemed to get snapped off by the wind, twisted up and lost in the vacuum of air, and what was left of the burned crops was torn up at the roots, chewed and swallowed and spit out again by the funnel.

Ruby's eyes stung from the nearness of it, from the wind whipping at her hair. There was nowhere to duck and nowhere to hide; all she could do was watch, stunned, as it began to die out again, the air falling flat all around them, leaving a wide patch of land stripped bare, littered with the charred remains of the wheat. She spun around, furious.

"How could you do that?" she asked, surprised to find that there were tears in her eyes. "That's someone's land. You're supposed to protect people from the weather, not use it as a weapon."

"It was a demonstration," he said, but Ruby had the sense that it was more than that. There was a meanness to the act, a disregard that frightened her. She and Simon had spoken of rain clouds and snow days like this was all some great source of amusement, but standing now beside the smoking ruins of the wheat, she realized this was no longer a game.

"Now," London was saying. "Let's see what *you* can do."

Simon lifted his gaze from the road, but it was Ruby he looked at first. There was something in his eyes that she hadn't often seen before, and she realized with a start that he was scared, too.

"I can't do anything," he admitted.

"Of course you can," London said with a smile. "I heard about your fever."

"But I haven't been able to do anything since then," Simon said. "At least not on purpose. I was thinking maybe if someone could teach me..."

"Some of it can be taught, but most of it is instinct," London said, reaching into his pocket. He pulled out what looked like a stopwatch, but Ruby realized it was a barometer. Unlike the one from Otis, though, there were simply numbers around the edges. "So go ahead," he said. "Make it rain."

Simon flashed her a panicky look, and Ruby took a step forward.

"We need to get home," she said, trying to sound braver than she felt. Her voice wobbled, but she squared her shoulders and stood her ground. "Thanks anyway."

London laughed a humorless laugh. "This won't take long. I just need to see it for myself."

"I can't," Simon said miserably, tilting his head to the sky. The road remained dry and dusty, and the last embers of the fire were still dying in the wheat. "Maybe I'm not who you think I am."

London pressed his lips together. When he spoke, his voice was low and ragged. "Make it rain," he repeated. *"Now."*

Ruby watched as Simon began desperately mouthing something at the sky, but nothing was happening and nothing was coming, and she glared at London, a knot of anger twisting itself tighter inside her.

When she followed Simon's skyward gaze, she thought fleetingly of all that she'd learned in science class, about · how impossible it would be to replicate something as complicated as this, the chemical composition of rain, the way it moves through the atmosphere. She pictured water vapor and condensation and weather fronts, and as she did, the anger evaporated and there was only the domed sky and her brother's prayer, and her own aching wish for Simon to succeed, and in that one brief moment, Ruby closed her eyes and, to her surprise, felt the first raindrops fall over her gently, like a mist, like a blessing, like a curse.

Simon let out a whoop, and Ruby blinked. It was only a dusting, but it felt like a downpour, and it smelled like spring, and she let the water slide down her forehead and fall off the end of her nose.

Simon was grinning now, doing a little rain dance, and when she turned back to London, there was a look of immense satisfaction on his face. He snapped shut the barometer and walked over to Simon.

"Well done," he said, placing a hand on his shoulder. "That's some fine work for a rookie. Especially one your age."

"Thank you, sir."

"I hope you'll come down to see us in Chicago very soon. There's a lot I could show you down there. A lot for you to learn."

"I'd like to," Simon said, "but I don't know...."

"No, I understand," London said, but the smile remained frozen on his face. He scanned the disappearing horizon for a moment, as if deep in thought, then turned back to them. "What a drought," he said, shaking his head. "I'd hate to see it continue."

Ruby felt the words like bullets, each one hitting her dead in the center of her chest.

"But if you can't make it down," London said, his voice becoming abruptly cheerful, "I'll be back up here to check on you soon."

The rain was already letting up, and the road was almost completely dark. Simon bent to pick up his fallen bicycle, then looked up at London. "When?" he asked.

"Soon enough. Before the twenty-first, anyway."

Ten days, Ruby thought, the words like an alarm.

"What's the twenty-first?" Simon asked, but London didn't answer. Instead, he lifted a hand once more, then started off down the road in the opposite direction from which he had come. For a long time, Ruby and Simon simply stood there with their bikes, the smell of smoke still heavy in the air, watching as he was swallowed up by the darkness.

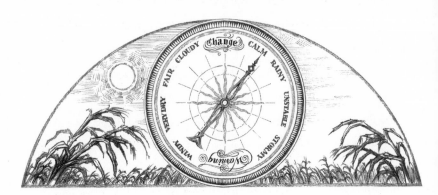

thirteen

RUBY WOKE WITH A START THE NEXT MORNING, her bed swaying like a boat at sea. For a moment, she thought maybe she was dreaming, but when she opened her eyes, it was to find Simon bouncing on the end of the mattress in his bare feet.

"About time," he said as she propped herself up on one elbow and squinted at him.

"What're you doing?"

"I had the craziest dreams last night," he said, taking

one more jump before flopping down onto the bed. He sat with his legs dangling over the side, twisting at the covers with his hands.

Ruby yawned and turned to the window, pushing aside the curtain. At the sight of the farm—all those fields of wheat, the acres of dry crops like so much tinder—she felt herself jolted back to the night before. Her stomach twisted at the memory, and she scanned the horizon, trying unsuccessfully to spot the burned-out section.

When she turned around again, Simon's eyes were bright.

"All night," he said, his voice tinged with excitement. "All night I dreamed about making it rain."

Ruby tossed aside the covers and stood up. She wasn't sure what to say to this; her own sleep had been dreamless, just as it always was, nothing but a colorless background, a reliable static. And for once, she was grateful for this. She couldn't think of anything worse than for the events of last night to have followed her into sleep. They'd been bad enough while she was awake.

"And not just that," Simon was saying, trailing her as she headed out into the hallway and down the stairs. He lowered his voice as they approached the kitchen, where the smell of bacon and eggs drifted out into the foyer. "The fire, too. And the twister."

Ruby stopped on the second-to-last step, spinning to face him.

"Dreams like those, you usually wake up and they're gone," Simon said, his face aglow with the excitement of it all. "But this one was actually real, you know? It actually happened." He shook his head. "Amazing."

Ruby held herself absolutely still. She wasn't sure how to tell him there was nothing amazing about it, that if anything, the word he should be using was *terrifying*.

Standing there on the stairs, she could hear the bacon sizzling in the frying pan, and she was suddenly right back in that field, the heat on her face, the crackle of the crops going up in flames, the acres and acres of empty darkness pressing in all around them.

No matter what he'd said last night, Ruby didn't trust Rupert London in the least. But how could she explain that to her brother, who had listened so raptly, who had been so eager, who was practically trembling at the memory of it even now? He'd made it rain last night. He'd raised his arms, thrown his head back, and made it *rain*.

And there wasn't much she could say to compete with that.

*

After breakfast, Dad drove them into town for their first day of work at Daisy's garage. His eyes kept sliding over to Simon, who was buckled beside him in the front seat. At breakfast, both of the twins had been unusually quiet— Simon lost in thought, Ruby anxious and worried—and Mom had decided it must be because Simon still wasn't feeling well.

"Maybe you shouldn't go this morning," she'd said, resting her palm against his forehead. "Maybe it's too soon."

But Simon shook his head, forcing her to pull her hand away. "I'm fine," he said, looking desperately at Ruby, who shrugged and gave him a look that said plainly, *You can make it rain, you can handle Mom.*

Simon had ended up doing the dishes in an effort to prove he was in good form, his eyes fixed on the fields beyond the window. Ruby didn't have to ask what he was thinking about.

Now, wedged into the back of the truck, she tried to

put her own thoughts in order. There was so much she needed to ask Daisy, so many things she wanted to know, and as they neared town Ruby hoped the garage would be empty, that there would be no customers, that all the cars in town would choose today to behave themselves.

When they pulled up in the driveway, she was relieved to see that this was the case. There was nobody there but Daisy, who was already at work inside the open garage. She was wearing overalls, her long hair tied back in a messy ponytail, and from where she was standing in the middle bay — a wrench in one hand, a rag in the other — she glanced over at them, but didn't wave.

"Can you let us out?" Simon was saying as he jiggled the door handle on the passenger side, where the lock had a tendency to stick. But Dad was clearly in no hurry.

"Your very first day of work," he said. "I feel like I should've brought a camera."

"Dad," Ruby said impatiently from the backseat. "Come *on.*"

"Don't you want any fatherly wisdom?" he asked. "Some sage advice from your old man?"

Simon lunged across the front seat and hit the unlock

button himself. "I think we're all set," he said, pushing open the door. "But thanks."

"Yeah," Ruby said, climbing out. "We've had twelve whole years with you, which has pretty much prepared us for anything."

"Okay, okay," Dad said with a grin. "I'll pick you up in a couple of hours. Don't drive off in anyone's car or anything, okay?"

As he pulled away, Ruby trotted after Simon, who was several steps ahead of her. Now that they were there, she was unaccountably nervous. What if this really was just a regular summer job? What if there were no answers, no advice, no acknowledgment of what was happening to Simon? What if they just spent the morning learning about lug nuts and tire jacks? Ruby wasn't sure she could bear another disappointment like that. Not after what had happened with Otis.

Up ahead, Daisy had set aside the rag and was watching them approach, tapping the wrench against her hand in a steady rhythm. The twins hurried up the rest of the drive and into the cool of the garage, and without saying anything — without even a hello — Daisy turned to walk over to the far wall, where she flipped a switch.

With a groan, all three garage doors lurched toward the ground, the gears grinding, the metal clanging. Just before they closed and the sunlight disappeared altogether, Daisy slipped underneath the nearest one, ducking out of the garage and leaving the twins standing there alone in the dark.

Ruby took a step closer to Simon, who was breathing loudly in the blackness. Her heart was thundering in her chest, but she just stood there, too stunned to move.

"Do you think this was a trap?" Simon asked. "Maybe she works for Otis or something."

"If anyone's trying to trap us, it would be your pal London."

They were silent for another moment, at a loss for what to do next, until a door at the side of the building was thrown open. A wedge of sunlight fell across them, and Daisy appeared as a silhouette.

"Sorry," she said. "Forgot to put the *Closed* sign up on the office door."

They blinked at her as she grabbed a flashlight from one of the shelves and clicked it on and off three times to test it.

"Follow me," she said, weaving between toolboxes and

tires and the great hulking cars in the middle of the garage, until the beam of light fell across the outline of a square in the floor near the back. There was a rope attached to a metal loop at its center, but otherwise, it was easy to miss in all the clutter. Daisy wrapped the string around her hand and leaned back, struggling to open the heavy trapdoor.

Ruby stepped up to the edge and peered down, but there was only more darkness.

"Ready?" Daisy asked, brushing a strand of hair from her eyes.

Simon and Ruby exchanged a glance. Ready for what?

But as her eyes focused, Ruby saw that there was a ladder along one side of the shaft. Daisy handed her the flashlight, swung her leg over, and began to lower herself one rung at a time.

"Couldn't we at least leave the lights on for this part?" Simon asked, his eyes following her nervously.

"No need," Daisy called up. She was halfway down the chute by now, and it was becoming harder to see her. "There are lights down here. Besides, it's a waste of energy." She paused, the tinny sound of her footsteps on the ladder falling silent. "You guys coming?"

Simon dropped to his knees, looking down. "Are you going to kill us?"

There was a long silence, and then Daisy began to laugh. "The mechanic in the auto shop with the wrench, huh?" she joked, and Simon frowned.

"I'm serious," he called back down as they heard Daisy's feet hit the ground with a smack. Ruby pointed the flashlight down the chute, but there was nothing to see; Daisy had moved away from the opening. Crouching beside Simon, she turned the light toward his face, which looked eerie in the dark, his forehead creased with worry.

"Come on," Daisy's voice floated up from below. "I promise not to kill you."

"That's what the killers *always* say," Simon pointed out, inching closer to the edge. "How do we know for sure?"

Down below, they could hear a series of beeps and whirs, and then the opening of the tunnel was illuminated by a brief flash of light before falling dark again. Simon leaned forward.

"Guess you'll just have to take your chances," Daisy called up, and with that, Ruby tucked the flashlight under her arm, placed a foot on the ladder, and stepped into the blackness.

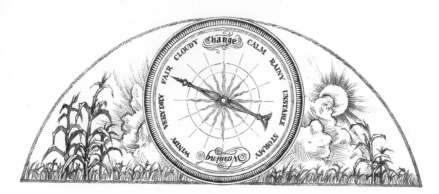

fourteen

By the time Ruby was halfway down the ladder, Daisy had switched on a light, so when she hopped off the last rung and spun around she was able to see her surroundings clearly. Even so, she just stood there, taking it all in, until Simon was nearly to the bottom of the ladder himself. He took a swipe at her shoulder with one of his legs, attempting to nudge her out of the way.

"Wow," Ruby said, still rooted in place. "Do you do this with all your summer employees?"

From where she was examining what looked like a radar screen, Daisy smiled. "Just the ones with potential."

The room was about the size of Ruby's bedroom, but it looked more like their basement, the walls made of gray concrete, with exposed pipes and beams forming a lattice across the ceiling. There were three plush couches in the middle of the room, each a different color—purple, green, and pink—and all arranged to face one wall, which looked like the command station in a newsroom.

"So this is where they host The Weather Channel," Simon said with a grin, standing in front of the many screens that were hung on the wall like paintings. One showed a gathering storm over the Atlantic; another glowed with a tangle of brightly colored charts and graphs; and a third displayed the local forecast for their area over the next one hundred days. Simon's eyes were wide as he walked from one to another, his doubts about Daisy clearly giving way to awe over all the technology. But Ruby was most interested in the other wall.

Behind the couches were rows of bookshelves wedged shoulder to shoulder across the entire width of the room. But other than a row near the bottom, where there were a few ancient-looking almanacs, there were hardly any books at all.

Instead, the shelves were lined with some of the most curious instruments Ruby had ever seen, strange and incredible tools: glass baubles and wind chimes, cracked timepieces and whistles, and more thermometers than Ruby had ever seen before, the mercury in each reading something entirely different from all the others.

There were two glass jars stacked on top of each other—one with a dandelion inside, the other with a puffball—and as she watched, the dandelion began to wilt, and the seeds of the puffball started falling to the bottom of the jar. Ruby blinked, surprised, before moving on to what looked like a model of a waterfall, though it had slowed to a mere trickle, the few drops of water pooling in a metal pan at its base. She craned her neck to peer at the back of it, to see what the trick was; there must be a switch, or a tube, or something. But it was as if the water came from nowhere at all.

"What is all this stuff?" she asked, peeking into a box filled with compasses of various shapes and sizes. Beside that, there was an odd-looking machine with a pressurized spout, which blew a little puff of steam as she watched, the miniature cloud drifting halfway across the room before evaporating. Ruby stared at the spot where it had been, her mouth open.

"Is it all yours?" Simon asked, and Daisy shook her head.

"Some of it is," she said. "And some of it is just old junk that used to be my dad's. I haven't had the heart to throw it away."

The far wall was decorated with maps of all kinds, many of them yellowed and curling, and above that, the pipes on the ceiling were strung with globes that bobbed and dangled like Chinese lanterns. As she walked over, Ruby nearly tripped over a box filled with weather vanes, most of them rusty, the figures at the top—pigs and chickens, whales, and even one very lost-looking giraffe—pointing in all sorts of directions.

"So, you don't just fix cars, then," Ruby said, and Daisy smiled.

"This stuff is really more of a hobby," she said. "I haven't had any real use for it in years."

Simon frowned. "How come?"

Daisy didn't answer. She crossed the room, then

stooped beside a black box in the corner. On top of it sat three little jars, all of which had—to Ruby's astonishment—tiny bolts of lightning inside, the lines of electricity flickering like captured fireflies.

As Daisy tugged on the handle to the box, Simon took a step closer. "What's that do?"

"It's a pretty amazing piece of technology, actually," Daisy said, turning around with a can of soda in each hand. "It keeps drinks cold."

Simon's cheeks reddened, and he accepted the Coke with a sheepish grin. Daisy grabbed a third, then led them over to the couches, sitting down on the green one and folding her legs beneath her. Ruby was eager to keep looking around, but she took a seat on the pink couch anyway, leaving Simon the purple one.

"So," Daisy said, pulling back the tab on her soda. "Anything you two want to tell me?"

Simon looked at her levelly. "You first."

Ruby frowned at her brother, astounded by his boldness, but Daisy just nodded, as if she'd expected as much. "Fair enough. What do you want to know?"

"You're a Storm Maker?"

She nodded again, though Ruby noticed the way she

gripped her soda can a bit tighter, her knuckles whitening. "Yup," she said. "Flared up when I was twenty-four."

"How old are you now?"

"*Simon*," Ruby muttered, but Daisy only smiled.

"It's okay," she said. "I'm thirty."

"So you must be really good," Simon said. "You get better as you get older, right?"

"I'm not *that* old," Daisy said. "But that's true, up to a point, and I used to be good. I suppose I'm a little bit out of practice these days."

Simon sat forward. "So what can you do?"

"What can *you* do?" Daisy asked in return, and Simon— who had clearly been waiting for this question—sat up a bit straighter.

"I made it rain last night."

Daisy's face didn't change, though her eyes registered a brief flicker of surprise. On one of the screens, a monitor began to beep, and one of the blue lines spiked before falling flat again. "That's impressive," she said with a little nod. "Was it proactive or reactive weather?"

Simon frowned. "What does that mean?"

"Did you make it yourself, or was it in response to something—illness or emotion, something like that?"

When Simon only stared at her in confusion, Daisy tilted her head. "Someone *has* explained all this to you, right?"

Simon's eyes traveled over to meet Ruby's, and then they both turned back to Daisy, who stood up and began pacing around the little table at the center of the couches. "Unbelievable," she said. "I mean, if it's true what they're saying, and nobody's even bothered to properly explain—"

"What are they saying?" Ruby asked, and Daisy paused to look at her.

"That he's the youngest one ever. Which means he has the potential to become the most powerful ever. Most Storm Makers don't flare up till their early twenties. The handful who started earlier—eighteen or nineteen— have turned into the most formidable Storm Makers in history. And if Simon has such a huge jump on *them*, who knows what he could do one day."

"When did Rupert London flare up?" Simon asked, and Daisy froze. Her whole body stiffened, and she swiveled to face him slowly.

"You know about Rupert London?"

"He came to see us last night."

"London himself?" Daisy asked, frowning. "Are you sure it wasn't someone on his behalf? There are representatives for this sort of thing, you know, Trackers to bring in rookies. Ryan Doherty heads up this region, so it could've been him. Or maybe you're thinking of Brian Ascher? He's the Director of Storms, so maybe he was up because of the—"

"No," Simon said firmly. "It was London."

Daisy sank back down onto the couch.

"He showed us what he can do," Simon continued. "He made a fire out in the fields, and a tornado, too. It was kind of awesome."

Ruby shook her head. "It was kind of *awful*," she said, angry. "He burned down people's crops in the middle of a drought. We were standing right there, and he wrecked them. Just like that. Isn't the whole point of this thing to help protect people? That's what Otis said, anyway."

Daisy was watching her now with interest. "What else did Otis say?"

Ruby told her the whole story, how she'd first noticed him in the barn, how he'd appeared in the fields. She told her about the start of the storm and his warning about Simon, and about how he'd shown up again at the hospital and then disappeared just as quickly when London had arrived.

"He promised to meet us the next night," she said, trying to keep the hurt out of her voice. "He said he'd be back."

Daisy nodded. "But he wasn't."

"Right," Simon said. "But London *was*."

Ruby glared at him openly, her arms folded across her chest.

"Did he say where he was going?" Daisy asked after a moment. "Or what he was planning to do?"

"Otis?" Ruby asked, then shook her head. "No."

"What about London?"

Simon nodded. "He was going back to headquarters in Chicago. And he wanted me to go down there, too." He cut his eyes over to Ruby, who was holding her breath. A part of her had been hoping Simon would have forgotten this particular detail, but she could see now that the idea had taken root inside his head. "He said there's a lot he could teach me. That he'd take me under his wing."

Ruby wanted Daisy to tell him that the idea of going down to the Society's headquarters in Chicago was completely ridiculous, not to mention dangerous, but Daisy only leaned forward, her face serious. "Did he say if he'd be back up here at all?"

"Yeah," Simon said. "Sometime before the twenty-first."

Daisy's head snapped up, her face suddenly ashen. "The twenty-first?" she said quietly. "Are you sure that's what he said?"

Both Simon and Ruby nodded. Across the room on the bookshelves, the dandelion was now just a bud, and the puffball was nothing but a stem. On top of the refrigerator, the lightning flashed in the jars.

"Why?" Simon asked. "What's the twenty-first?"

Daisy's eyes were very far away, and the room was quiet but for the hum of the radar screens and the soft sound of rain falling inside the various bottles. Ruby waited for an answer, but as the minutes ticked by, she realized there wouldn't be one. Just like when Simon had asked London the very same question the night before, there was only silence.

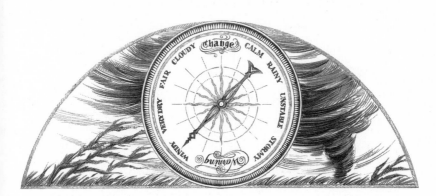

fifteen

LATER THAT AFTERNOON, Ruby wandered into the barn to find Simon glowering at the ceiling. She crept up to stand beside him, following his gaze, but there was nothing except beams and rafters and a bird's nest.

"What are we doing?" she asked after a minute, her chin still angled.

"Trying to make it snow."

Ruby nodded, resisting the temptation to suggest he start with rain. It was about a million degrees in the barn, but of course, it didn't surprise her at all that Simon would skip right to snow, attempting one impossible thing on top of another.

"It's not going very well."

"No," she agreed, holding out a flattened palm. "I guess not."

With a sigh, Simon broke his staring contest with the ceiling and walked over to sit on one of the bales of hay. Ruby joined him, resting her elbows on her knees.

"Just be patient," she said, watching as he twisted a stick of hay between two fingers. "Daisy said she'd help you."

"Yeah, but London said it can't all be taught." He threw out his hands again, like some sort of magician, setting loose a few pieces of hay. But there was still no sign of any rain; there was only the stillness of the barn, and the light footfalls of the cats in the loft above them. Simon sighed again. "Maybe it can only happen when he's around."

Ruby frowned. "That's ridiculous."

"It's not any more ridiculous than any of the rest of this," he said. "You just don't like him."

"Why would I?" Ruby asked, glaring at him. "Why do *you*?"

"Because," Simon explained in a tone that made Ruby grit her teeth. "Because he chose me."

"*He* didn't choose you."

"Then who?"

Ruby opened her mouth, then closed it again. She didn't have an answer; whatever was happening to Simon was nothing short of a mystery. But the one thing she knew for certain was this: Rupert London was no fairy godmother. She was sure of it.

"Simon," she said finally, "he's just using you. Did you ever think that maybe he was the one who made it rain last night, and not you?"

Simon narrowed his eyes. "Why would he do that?"

"I don't know," Ruby said. "To make you think you have potential? To make you believe it's all real? I have no idea. All I know is that I don't trust him. Not at all."

"It was me," Simon said under his breath. "I felt it happen."

Ruby sighed. She wasn't sure what to believe anymore.

It could have been Simon or it could have been London or it could have just been nature itself, a strange coincidence, a quirk of timing.

"Fine," she said. "But I still think he's using you. You didn't get to meet Otis. So I guess I can see why—"

"It has nothing to do with Otis or anyone else," he said, sliding off the hay bale. "London thinks I'm special. He thinks I have great potential."

"So does everyone else," Ruby insisted. "So does Otis. So does Daisy. So do I."

Simon stood with his arms folded across his skinny chest, his eyes bright, and for a moment he was just her brother again, all the smugness stripped away. When he spoke, his voice was very small. "You do?"

"Of course," she said. "Of course I do."

"Then why does it feel like you wish all this hadn't happened?"

Ruby dropped her eyes, not sure what to say to that. He was right; she *did* wish this had never happened. The enormity of it all didn't feel magical or dazzling. At least not to her. These people showing up at the farm, setting fire to the fields, capturing weather in jars like it was something that could be controlled, like it was some kind of weapon—it frightened her.

They were both silent for a moment, and then Simon began to walk toward the double doors at the other end of the barn.

"Simon," she called out, and he paused. "You did it once. You'll do it again."

He squared his shoulders, but didn't turn around. "Of course I will," he said, his voice drifting back over his shoulder. "London said so."

They didn't see each other again until dinnertime, though Ruby guessed Simon probably spent the afternoon off in one of the fields, trying to coax a hailstorm out of the sky. When he slid into his seat at the table, he looked pale and tired, and the hint of arrogance she'd seen earlier had disappeared again. Her eyes slid over to the window, where even this late in the day the heat still hung over the cornfields like gauze, making everything wavy and indistinct. It wasn't hard to guess that he'd been unsuccessful.

As she walked over with the last of the dishes, Mom grabbed an envelope from the pile of mail on the edge of the kitchen counter and dropped it in front of Simon. "This came for you earlier," she said. "Who do you know in downtown Chicago?"

Simon flicked his eyes over to Ruby, who craned her neck to see what was on the envelope. The address was handwritten in elegant cursive, and in the corner where the return address was supposed to be, there was only a small logo of a storm cloud, the same one she'd seen on the back of London's business card.

"Can I be excused?" Simon asked, and without waiting for an answer, he shoved the envelope in his back pocket and sprang up from his chair, startling the dogs as he hurried out of the kitchen. Mom stared after him with a baffled look, and Ruby studied her plate intently.

"I bet I know," Dad said, leaning back in his chair, and Ruby's stomach tightened with worry. But he only grinned. "I bet he's got a girlfriend."

"If he does," Mom said, shaking her head from side to side, "then she deserves some kind of medal. That kid is getting weirder and weirder."

Ruby let out a long breath. "You have no idea."

When she found him in his room later, Simon was sitting cross-legged in the middle of the floor, which was littered with dirty socks and baseball equipment. The envelope was lying on the rug beside him, jagged at the top where it had been torn, and Simon was busy twirling a finger at the floor, as if drawing circles in the air.

"Tornado?" Ruby asked, and he smiled sheepishly.

"No luck."

"I'm pretty sure that's a good thing," she said. "Mom doesn't even allow the kittens in the house. I don't think she'd be too happy about a tornado." She bent to hand him a plate covered in tinfoil, then nudged a baseball mitt aside with her toe so that she could sit down beside him. "So what was it?"

He molded the foil into a little ball, then tossed it into the garbage can near his desk—a perfect shot. "See for yourself."

Ruby pulled the envelope closer, surprised at the weight of it. When she turned it upside down, a small silver pin in the shape of a storm cloud fell into her palm.

"It's from London," Simon said, a defensive note to his

voice. He held up a small card lined with neat handwriting, the same emblem at the very top of the page. "This is what you're supposed to wear," he said, then added, "if you're a Storm Maker."

Ruby put the pin gently back into the envelope, then handed it over to Simon. Something about the gift unnerved her. "Lucky you," she said, trying to keep her voice neutral.

But if Simon noticed the edge to her words, he said nothing. He just turned back to the plate of cold chicken in front of him. And so after a moment, Ruby stood to go, leaving him there on his own, attempting to conjure tornadoes out of thin air.

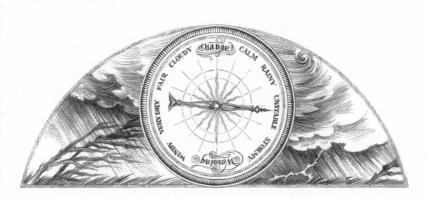

sixteen

At Daisy's the next morning, Ruby was unable to sit still. She wandered around the edges of the room, poking through the boxes of rusted equipment, while Simon lay back on the purple couch, droning on about his weather-making difficulties like a patient in a therapist's office. From the green couch, Daisy was frowning.

"Not even a few drops?" she asked. "Maybe some wind?"

Simon shook his head, and Ruby rolled her eyes.

"We're in the middle of a drought," she said. "Can't we just blame him for that?"

Daisy rose from the couch and picked up a teapot, which had been boiling on top of what looked like a regular coaster.

Ruby took the opportunity to peek at the barometer, keeping one hand cupped around it as she drew it from her pocket. She wasn't sure why she hadn't shared it with Simon yet, but it reminded her of Otis, and there was something reassuring in that. For once, Ruby wanted something for herself. Simon could have his pin from London; this was better.

Most of the time, there was nothing to see, anyway. Pretty much whenever Ruby examined it, the needle pointed to *very dry*, which was hardly a surprise. But right now, she saw that it was angled toward *unstable*. She glanced around the room, then rocked back and forth on the balls of her feet, as if testing the floor. But it was the same as the ground was anywhere: steady and unchanging.

She slipped the barometer back into her pocket.

"I'm afraid the drought isn't you," Daisy was saying as she poured a cup of tea. "I'm pretty sure that it's..."

"What?" Simon asked.

Daisy bit her lip. "I just heard they're working on it down at headquarters."

Ruby made a face. "Yeah, well, maybe if they knew what they were doing down there, all these farmers wouldn't be losing their crops."

"Ruby," Simon warned, but Daisy just waved a hand as she emptied the pot of tea into the last mug.

"I don't disagree," she said. "It's not the most well-run place at the moment."

"Because London's in charge?" Ruby suggested, ignoring the dark look Simon shot her way.

Daisy just sat back down with her mug in her hand and didn't answer. After a moment, she turned back to Simon, leaning forward as if she was about to say something. But just as suddenly, she froze, her mouth falling open and her face going abruptly pale.

"Where'd you get that?" she asked quietly, and Simon followed her eyes down to his shirt, where the little storm cloud glinted under the lights strung from the ceiling.

"London sent it to me," he said proudly, puffing out his chest to show it off. "It came in the mail yesterday. It's a Storm Maker thing, I guess." He paused, his brow furrowed. "Hey, shouldn't you have one, too?"

For a long moment, Daisy said nothing, though her eyes were still caught on the pin. The color had risen to her cheeks, and she looked so feverish, so completely stricken, that Ruby sat forward to ask whether she was okay. But before she had a chance to say the words, there came a rattling sound from above.

It started out quietly, like a tinkling of bells, and then grew more insistent, until Ruby could feel it beneath her feet as well: The earth was moving.

All at once, everything seemed to be happening both very fast and very slow. Ruby's eyes met Simon's from across the room, and she saw the same panic that must have been evident in her own wild glance. But it took another few fleeting seconds for it to really register, the word flashing through her head like an alarm—*earthquake! earthquake!*—before she slid off the couch and onto the ground, scraping her knees as she was jolted sideways by the force of it.

Above her, Daisy was still sitting absolutely still, her face frighteningly blank, but Simon had dropped down as well, both of them trying to hold on to something as the floor shifted this way and that. The jars lining the shelves were providing a kind of manic background music, clanging and singing, until finally they began to fall. As each one shattered, the tiny bits of weather inside disappeared in puffs of mist.

The world tilted, the radar screens went dark, and the refrigerator shimmied across the floor. Twenty seconds, thirty seconds, forty. It felt like a lifetime and no time at all. Ruby was thrown sideways into the table, and her fingers scrabbled uselessly against the smooth concrete floor as she tried to steady herself. One of the TV screens was wrenched from the wall with an awful ripping sound, and it crashed to the ground near Simon's leg, the metal frame splintering.

The lights went out and the thick walls of the basement room seemed to groan and heave. Ruby closed her eyes and ducked her head against the debris that rained down around her, the weather vanes and the compasses, the barometers and the funnels, each of them turned into

tiny weapons. The floor was still rolling beneath her, and she tucked herself against the couch, which had slid toward her despite its bulk. Then she closed her eyes, held her breath, and waited.

Even when it was over, even when the world had righted itself again, Ruby stayed curled up beside the couch. When you get off a boat, you can still feel the waves beneath your feet, and it was like that now in the darkened basement. It was an odd sensation, not to trust the very floor on which she stood, but there it was.

Simon's footsteps near her head sent shock waves through her; she felt like a tuning fork, hyperaware of motion and noise. She lifted her head to see his outstretched hand, and allowed herself to be pulled to her feet again. A generator must have kicked in, because the lights flickered back to life, so she was able to survey the damage; broken glass and fallen objects and cracks in the walls, some as fine as spiderwebs, others big enough to reach inside.

When her gaze finally fell on Daisy, it was to find her sitting with the same stunned expression she'd worn before the earthquake.

"I'm sorry," she murmured, her face ghostly pale. "I'm really sorry."

"We should get outside," Simon said. "In case there's an aftershock."

Daisy rose to her feet, but she was shaking her head. "There won't be," she said. "That was my fault. But we should still get out of here, in case anything's unstable."

Ruby stared at her. No matter what rules had changed in the past days, no matter what she'd already seen, it was impossible to believe that this tiny blond woman could have just made the earth move so violently.

"That was you?" Simon asked, his mouth open, and despite the scrapes on his hands and the bruise blooming on his knee, Ruby could detect a note of admiration in his voice.

But Daisy didn't respond. She stood beside the ladder and waited for them to climb up first, and when they were all at the top she paused, gazing down at the broken room below before closing the hatch. Simon flipped the light switch in the garage, and they could see that there were some overturned oil cans and a few fallen tools, but the damage was mostly confined to the basement.

Daisy looked visibly relieved. "I'm glad we were underground," she said, walking over to the side door. "It would've been much worse if I'd been up here."

Ruby followed closely behind, eager to get outside and away from anything that could fall on her. Despite what Daisy had said, she still didn't quite trust that these moments of calm wouldn't give way to more shaking.

"What happened?" she asked when they were all three standing in the daylight again, the sky a blue so bright that it made them squint. Daisy dropped down heavily on the grass that bordered the driveway, and Ruby and Simon joined her. The three of them sat cross-legged, as if ready for a picnic, their hands still trembling and their chins tilted skyward to soak up the blinding sun.

"I'm sorry," Daisy said again. "That shouldn't have happened. It's just—"

"Reactionary weather," Simon supplied.

"Right," she said. "My specialty is earthquakes."

Ruby couldn't help laughing as she pictured the needle on the barometer: *unstable*. "You don't say."

"When that kind of thing happens, when the weather is a result of something else—emotions or illness, stuff like that—it goes right to your default mode," she said. "So for me, if I don't keep a lid on what I'm feeling— *boom*. The ground moves."

Simon shook his head. "Wow."

"But I'm supposed to know how to keep it under control," she said. "You're not supposed to perform any kind of major weather movements at all, unless it's sanctioned by MOSS or it's some kind of emergency, or else you can get in trouble. It's just that I'm out of practice, and when I saw that pin..."

Ruby glanced over at Simon's shirt, but he'd clapped a hand over the little storm cloud. Daisy rubbed her forehead. The color had returned to her cheeks, but her eyes were too bright and somehow very far away.

"I stopped wearing mine a long time ago," she said. "After my dad died."

"How come?" Simon asked.

"It's the official emblem of the Society, but it just didn't mean the same thing once he was gone. And after a while, I guess I couldn't bear it."

Ruby sat forward, waiting for her to continue.

"My dad was a Storm Maker, too," Daisy said quietly. "It's extremely rare to have two in one family; there've only ever been a few instances of it. He's the one who taught me all this." She waved a hand at the garage, indicating the cars and tools beyond. "And most of those gadgets downstairs were his. He always loved working with metal, and when he first flared up and discovered he had a gift for conjuring storm clouds, he made himself a pin like that."

Simon moved his hand and held the pin away from his shirt, examining the contours of the metal, the rounded edges of the cloud and the little bolt of lightning that stretched beneath it.

"When he was chosen as Chairman—"

"What?" Simon asked, looking up. "Your dad was Chairman?"

Daisy nodded.

"Before London?" Ruby asked.

"Yes, right before," she said. "He made that pin the official emblem of the Society. Every new Storm Maker gets one in a ceremony."

"How come I didn't get a ceremony?" Simon asked, but Ruby was far more interested in hearing about Daisy's dad.

"What happened to him?" Ruby asked.

Daisy brushed a strand of hair out of her eyes, suddenly looking very young. "He died," she said simply. "Four years ago, he had a heart attack. It was right after one of the big storms down on the coast. Hurricane season is always really stressful, and we took a lot of hits that year."

"I'm sorry," Ruby said. "About your dad, I mean."

Daisy gave her a watery smile. "Thank you," she said. "I was working at headquarters at the time. I'd worked my way up to Associate Director of Land Movement, but I left after that. I had to get away from it all. So I came up here to take over the garage, which is what my dad had always wanted to do when he retired."

"Well, this seems like a nice thing, too," Simon said doubtfully, as if trying to imagine why someone would choose a greasy auto shop over the glamorous headquarters of a secret society.

"You didn't think about staying?" Ruby asked.

Daisy shook her head. "Not even for a minute."

"Why not?"

"Because," she said after a long moment, "that was when Rupert London took over."

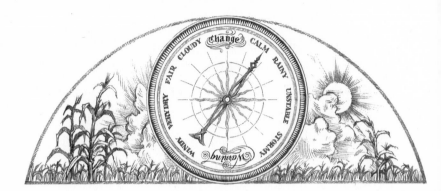

seventeen

WHEN THEY SHOWED UP at the garage the following morning, Daisy was nowhere to be found. There was no note on the door, no message for them anywhere, only the CLOSED sign that hung behind the dusty glass window of the office. The twins stood there looking at it for what seemed like forever, their backs to the driveway, until they finally heard the engine of the truck go quiet.

Simon was the first to turn around. "She's not here," he

said to Dad, who was leaning on the car door and squinting at them across the blacktop.

"Maybe she's late," Dad called out, but Simon shook his head, giving Ruby a wordless glance. But it was there all over his face, as plain as if he'd said it aloud: *I knew this would happen. We shouldn't have trusted her. I told you so.*

He turned to pound on the door, making the glass rattle in its frame, and then he muttered something under his breath and headed for the truck, leaving Ruby all alone.

It was nearly noon; the garage should have opened up hours ago. But even so, it seemed to Ruby that if she stood there long enough, Daisy might come trotting around the corner, her long hair tied back beneath a bandanna, her hands smudged with grease. On the street, a red car drove past in a rush of noise. The church bells rang out from the other side of town, and above them, the high ball of sun bore down on the sizzling asphalt.

But there was no sign of Daisy.

With a sigh, Ruby walked back to the truck. Simon was already belted in the front, which meant she had to climb in through the driver's side. As he helped her in, Dad gave a little shrug.

"I bet she has a good reason," he said. "I wouldn't worry. She probably just had an appointment or something. Or maybe she's under the weather."

From the front seat, Ruby could see Simon raise his eyebrows. "Yeah," he said. "Maybe."

When Dad turned over the ignition, the truck started with a small sputter, and they all fell silent as they eased out onto the road, leaving the garage behind. Ruby turned around to look out the back window, feeling the full weight of this latest abandonment. It was the worst kind of disappointment. First Otis, and now Daisy.

Once again, they were truly on their own.

These people might be good with weather, she thought as they drove away, *but they aren't great with promises.*

†

For the next couple of days, it was almost easy to believe that none of it had happened at all. The morning after Daisy disappeared, they woke to find that the heat that had plagued them for the past month, that had settled over the county like a heavy blanket, had finally lifted. It was the middle of June, but the air smelled of springtime, cool and sweet. Even the dogs felt the change, the two of them zigzagging through the newly planted cornfields like puppies after a month spent dozing in the unwavering sun.

One morning, Mom dragged her easel out onto the porch, where she set to work on her newest painting, and when Dad returned from a trip into town, the worry that had been etched across his face all summer seemed to have lightened.

"I think the corn looks perkier already, don't you?" he asked, walking over to kiss the top of Mom's head. He was talking about the very field she was painting, and even though most of her palette was composed of muted browns, in that moment, the idea that she might soon be using shades of green seemed entirely possible.

Simon and Ruby were playing cards on the steps of the porch, half listening as Dad gave Mom the gossip from his trip to town—someone's wife was pregnant, and someone's husband was sick; a farmer lost a cow to the heat—but they didn't look up until he mentioned the mysterious loss of a half acre of Orville Thompson's wheat crop.

"Apparently, a lot of it was burned," he was saying. "And the rest of it is all chewed up. It's just this perfect little square of destruction. Strangest thing."

Simon's eyes met Ruby's over their cards, but neither said a word.

"Oh," Dad said, glancing over at them. "And I drove by the garage on my way there. It's still all closed up. I asked around town to make sure Daisy's okay, but nobody seems that concerned. I guess she's always done this sort of thing; she just takes off from time to time. It sounds like she has family in Chicago or something."

Ruby nodded stiffly. It had, of course, crossed her mind that Daisy might be working with London. What else could explain not just the earthquake, but also her sudden disappearance right as the drought started to improve? But in the end, there was too big a part of Ruby that wanted to believe in her, and how could her instincts be *that* wrong?

"We'll check again soon," Mom was saying. "I'm sure she won't be gone long."

This time, though she could feel his gaze, Ruby refused to look up at Simon. Instead, she studied her cards intently, shuffling through her pile, a shrinking collection of unappealing maneuvers.

But by mid-afternoon she'd managed to push every-thing from her mind again. It was the kind of day that could make you forget about the weather entirely, and it seemed possible to Ruby that she could go on pretending forever.

After all, Otis might never come back, and who knew when Daisy would show up again. And as for Rupert London, even if he *were* to return, it would just be for long enough to realize that the night of the rain was nothing more than a fluke, and he'd have no choice but to leave them alone again. They could spend the rest of the summer swimming in the pond and riding their bikes and helping Dad out in the barn.

And if it did rain, it would just be because of a storm passing through. And if did snow, it would only be because it was winter.

There would be nothing more to it than that.

After lunch, Ruby stepped outside to call the dogs in, rat-tling a bowl of kibble. It didn't take long for them to come bounding around the side of the house, their red tails fanning the air. But when she stooped to pet them, Ruby's hand brushed against one of their collars, and she felt the cool touch of metal where there was usually only leather.

To her surprise, when she pulled the wriggling dog closer to look, she found a small pin in the shape of a storm cloud. Her heartbeat was loud in her ears as she unfastened it with shaking fingers. She cupped it in her palm, then whistled for the other dog, who sat beside her as she examined his collar, where she found a second pin.

She looked over at Simon's bedroom window, hesitating for a moment. But then she closed her fingers around the two pins in her hand and, without waiting, without even really thinking, she took off toward the barn at a run.

The doors were open enough for her to slip inside, and she stood there quietly until her eyes had adjusted to the darkness. And when they did, she almost laughed out of sheer relief. Stretched out on a pile of hay, his hat resting over his eyes, a stick of straw in his teeth, was Otis. And across the open floor of the barn, sitting before a mess of wires and tools, her head bent in concentration, was Daisy.

They hadn't forgotten them after all. Daisy hadn't been on London's side. Otis hadn't left them behind. There they were again, right there in the barn.

Ruby couldn't help smiling as she opened her hand and held out the pins. "So," she said, looking from one to the other. "Did the dogs get a promotion?"

Otis sat up with a grin. "Not exactly," he said. "But you did."

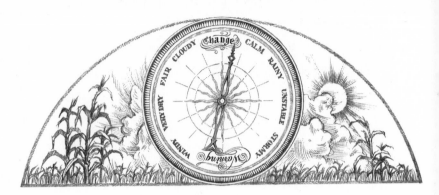

eighteen

As THEY MADE THEIR WAY down to the pond later, Ruby was almost afraid to look over at Simon. She was sure the expression on his face would be something between anger and annoyance. He'd been up in his room when Ruby had thrown open the door, insisting he come with her.

"Where?" he'd asked, looking skeptical. But Ruby had refused to say, and now, as they picked their way through the wheat together, the late-afternoon light falling across the fields at a slant, his jaw was hard and set. He slid his eyes in her direction, but she only pursed her lips and shook her head.

"You'll see," she said in answer to his unasked question.

When they neared the grove of trees that rose up from the surrounding flatness like a mirage, Ruby slowed a bit, a thought occurring to her.

"Be nice, okay?" she said, and Simon shortened his stride to match hers.

"To who?"

"Just please," she said. "Be nice."

Simon opened his mouth to ask again, but they were moving through the thicket now, the soft sounds of the water ahead of them, and before he could say anything, they came across the two figures on the dock.

Otis was leaning against the railing in a rumpled three-piece suit, his long arms folded across his chest as he regarded Simon with the smallest hint of a smile. There was a stillness to him that reminded Ruby of a deer, the way they could be absolutely motionless yet also quivering with a kind of electricity.

Simon had come to an abrupt halt, and Ruby saw his eyes light briefly on Daisy—who had been sitting on the edge of the pier, and who now rose to her feet with the graceful movement of a ballerina—before his gaze returned to the tall stranger.

"Otis?" Simon asked after a moment. His face was still neutral, but it was not without effort; Ruby could tell he hadn't yet made up his mind how to react.

"I am indeed," Otis said, walking over to greet them. When he was close enough, he extended a hand, which Simon made no move to take. "We met once before, actually, but you were unconscious."

Daisy, who was a few steps behind, couldn't help laughing at this, but Otis didn't smile. He was looking at Simon with the same unwavering gaze that Ruby had seen in the hospital, the same sense of quiet amazement.

"I'm sorry I couldn't stay," he said. "I would've liked to introduce myself, but—"

"What are you doing here?" Simon asked, and though Ruby could see a flicker of hurt behind Otis's eyes, he only blinked.

"It was the soonest I could make it back."

"From what?" Simon demanded, his voice charged. "If I'm so important, then why do you all keep leaving? Why hasn't anyone stuck around long enough to tell us anything that actually matters?"

Otis only inclined his head, apparently waiting for Simon to continue.

"You turn up in our barn, and then at the hospital," Simon was saying. "And you try to get my sister to be on your side...."

Ruby opened her mouth, but Otis shook his head at her, just barely. Simon was pacing now, and he swiped a loose branch from one of the trees and began whisking the air with it like a conductor.

"And then you don't even bother to show up when you said you would," he said, pausing to turn around, his eyes narrow. "You know who *did* show up?"

Otis nodded. "Rupert London."

"Yeah," Simon said. "And he told me you're nothing anymore, that you're all washed up now."

This time, it was Daisy who moved to say something, but Otis stopped her with a hard look, and Simon watched them, tapping the stick against the palm of his hand.

"So why should I believe anything you say?"

All four of them stood there without speaking for a long moment as the water went still in the pond and a crow called out above the fields. Simon was practically trembling, his knuckles white around the stick. Ruby swallowed hard, waiting for Otis to defend himself, to set Simon straight, to spill all the long-held secrets they'd been waiting for. But he only stepped forward and put a hand on her brother's shoulder.

"Come on," he said. "Let's take a walk."

With the sun low in the sky, the figures ahead of them were silhouettes, blue-tinged against the gold of the horizon. As they walked, Otis bent himself to one side like a misshapen tree, leaning to listen to Simon, who looked tiny beside the soaring figure to his right. A great quiet had come over the fields. This was Ruby's favorite time of day, when the breeze tickled the crops with a rustling like music, and the sky grew soft and pale.

She and Daisy hung back, following Otis and Simon from a distance as they traced the edge of a field, the only place where there was enough room to walk side by side. Ruby trailed her fingertips along the wheat, which now rose nearly to her shoulders. She suspected Daisy was waiting for her to speak first, but Ruby wasn't sure where to begin. She wanted to know what Otis and Simon were talking about up ahead, but she couldn't quite bring herself to voice this.

"Ask me," Daisy said after some time had passed.

Ruby tilted her head. "Ask you what?"

"Anything you want. I know you've probably got a million questions."

"Fine," Ruby said with a little nod. "Where'd you go?"

"To find Otis."

"Where?"

Daisy lowered her eyes. "California."

"Why was he there?"

She shrugged. "It's not important."

"But you said I could ask anything," Ruby insisted. "I want to know why."

"That was just where I found him," Daisy said with a sigh. "Before that, he was in Louisiana, and then Texas, and then Arizona. He meant to meet you at the windmills that night, but things were moving fast, and he needed to leave sooner than expected."

"Why?"

"Because," Daisy explained, "he was gathering information. And support."

"For what?"

"For Simon," she said simply, looking ahead. A sudden breeze stirred the wheat, and Ruby shivered. "I'm sure that's what he's telling your brother now, too," Daisy continued. "How he's been reaching out to other Storm Makers, the ones less directly involved with the Society, and those who have fallen away from it completely. Otis has been talking to all of them, telling them about Simon, about what it means to have found him."

"What does it mean?"

Daisy stopped walking, and Ruby was struck by how serious she looked. "When my father was Chairman, the Society was there for a reason. You know how doctors have that mantra, 'First, do no harm'? It's supposed to be like that. Our job description has always been to maintain control of the environment—not to make or stop weather, necessarily, but to keep everything in balance."

"How?"

"All sorts of ways," she said, and Ruby fell in step beside her as she began to walk again. "Reducing hurricanes down along the coast, where they get hit hard year after year. Or trying to slow the effects of global warming. Things like that."

Ruby looked around at the dry fields. "Stopping droughts?"

"Lessening them, anyway," Daisy said with a nod. "But things are different now. And Rupert London..."

"Let me guess," Ruby said quietly. "He doesn't care much about helping people."

Daisy bowed her head. "That's true," she agreed. "And if that were all, I'd still think he was irresponsible and hard-hearted."

"But that's *not* all," Ruby said, her voice flat.

"No," Daisy said. "It's not."

Up ahead, Otis and Simon had stopped walking, and now stood facing each other. Even from a distance, Ruby could see that Simon was shaking his head, and that his shoulders were hunched.

"Nobody ever wants to believe the worst," Daisy murmured, and Ruby answered without thinking.

"I already do," she said. "After seeing him destroy the field that night, I don't think anything about London could surprise me."

Daisy sighed. "His philosophy is actually pretty simple. Completely backwards, but still pretty simple," she said. "He believes that since people are ruining the Earth with their big cars and oil spills, their endless garbage and high energy consumption, that we shouldn't bother to help them anymore. He thinks they should get what they deserve, and we shouldn't try to steer their hurricanes off course or slow their tornadoes. He believes that nature should have a chance to fight back."

Ruby nodded.

"He's not the only one who feels that way, of course. But he's the only one who's taken it a step further."

"How?"

Daisy's face was drawn. "Rather than slow the destruction, or even just stand aside and do nothing, he believes that Storm Makers should actually be helping it along. Teaching everyone a lesson. It's the reason I left the Society, and why I didn't want to be involved anymore. I mean, if my dad could have seen—"

"But you are now," Ruby interrupted. "You're involved again. Because of us."

Daisy hesitated a moment, then nodded. "I guess I needed some time to catch up. You have to realize how fast everything changed. My father died, and London took over. Otis disappeared, and the fire—" She stopped abruptly, sucking in a breath. "Never mind. All I'm saying is that I realize now that I was wrong. Simon showing up, and Otis coming back—it's helped me understand that you can't hide from this kind of thing, you know? It's like the weather itself. Sometimes you just have to face the storm."

"I guess," Ruby said, fishing a tissue from her pocket, which she held out as an offering. But Daisy shook her head, wiping her eyes roughly with the back of her hand instead.

"I'm not crying."

Ruby lowered the tissue again, nodding agreeably.

"I never cry," Daisy said with a little scowl, and despite the way her eyes were shining at the moment, Ruby believed her. Daisy seemed tough in ways that were impossible to imagine, ways that could only be a result of things seen and survived.

As they neared the others, it was clear from Simon's expression that they were talking about the very same subject. Except where Ruby had been stunned, Simon seemed to be defiant, his face set stubbornly, his eyes flashing.

"He wouldn't," he was saying as they approached, his voice echoing across the empty space between them. "There's no way."

Otis was about to say something, but Ruby walked up beside her brother. "Come on, Simon," she said gently. "You saw him that night, too. It wasn't all magic and fireworks. It was horrible."

Still, Simon continued to move his head mechanically from side to side. Ruby pictured his face the night London set the field on fire, how he'd looked on in such awe. Now it was as if a part of him was still trying to hold on to that, and even Ruby couldn't entirely blame him. Because hadn't it been the same when she'd been counting on Otis to return? Hadn't she, too, been clinging to a kind of desperate belief in something larger than herself?

Simon looked up miserably. "He said I was the future."

"You are," Otis said. "Just not in the way he thinks."

"There hasn't been a Storm Maker powerful enough to take him on in years," Daisy said, her eyes drifting over to Otis, who looked away. "Maybe ever."

"London has the Society on his side, but only because they're intimidated," Otis explained. "There are plenty of others out there who are furious about the direction he's been going, and that's what I've been doing this week—talking to them, telling them about *you*."

Daisy was beaming at Simon. "You're the youngest Storm Maker ever. Do you know what that could mean?" she said. "You've given everyone a reason to hope again. And it's been a really long time since we've had that."

Otis looked at her over the rims of his glasses, his eyes soft. "Since your dad was Chairman."

"And since you were part of the Society," she said with a smile.

The sky had faded to purple now, and the stars were beginning to emerge in the twilight. Beside Ruby, Simon let out a breath of air.

"So you see?" Otis said with a small smile. "You're the one we've all been waiting for. You can help us make things right again."

When Simon finally spoke, his voice was heavy. "Then I'm sorry to disappoint you."

"You haven't—" Daisy began, but Simon cut her off.

"I have," he said quietly. "Because there's no way I can possibly be the most powerful Storm Maker ever."

They were about to say more when Simon shook his head.

"I can't be," he said. "Not when I can't make any weather at all."

He kept his eyes turned to the ground, as if afraid of their reaction, but Otis only swept an arm out over the darkening fields.

"Where do you think we're going?" he said with a smile, and Simon looked up in surprise. "It's time we had our first practice."

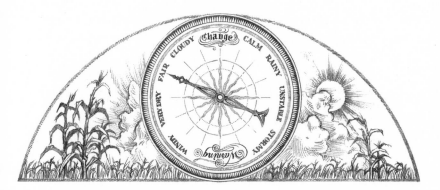

nineteen

WHEN RUBY AND SIMON APPEARED in the kitchen the next morning, Dad dropped his doughnut in mock surprise.

"I don't think I've ever laid eyes on you two at this hour," he said. "I hardly recognize you."

Mom handed them each a piece of toast. "I'd probably be incorrect to assume you're up at five AM to help me with chores."

"Yes," Simon said with a matter-of-fact nod. "That would be incorrect."

"So, what, then?" Dad asked, and Ruby shrugged.

"Couldn't sleep, I guess," she said.

Across the table, Simon grinned at her.

They were still yawning as they stepped outside later, the dogs following closely at their heels as they made their way down toward the pond. The night before, she and Simon had stayed up talking until late, and he'd fallen asleep curled at the foot of her bed, the way he used to when they were younger. When the first pieces of sunlight had come through the curtains this morning, Simon had sat up—his blond hair sticking up in the back, his eyes still sleepy—and smiled at her in wonder.

"Wow," he said, and Ruby had nodded. She understood exactly what he meant.

Lately they'd been feeling like a couple of Ping-Pong balls, batted this way and that, hopeful and excited one moment, terrified and anxious the next. It was an odd mixture of fear and wonder, this weather business; at times, all they could think about was the miracle of rain, and at others, like last night, they were reminded of the grim odds against them, the battles still to be waged, and it was then that the doubt crept in again.

But this morning was bright with promise, and it

seemed to Ruby that she and Simon were once again on the same team. And that had always—*always*—made everything better.

When they neared the trees, the dogs wandered back toward the farm and Simon and Ruby trotted the rest of the way, crashing through the branches to find Otis and Daisy waiting for them on the dock.

"You're late," Daisy pointed out.

"We brought doughnuts," Ruby said, handing over a brown paper bag.

Daisy grinned. "You're forgiven."

Ruby and Daisy sat cross-legged on the dry grass near the edge of the pond as Otis and Simon got to work. The night before, they'd all stood in the dark field and watched Simon try to make it drizzle without any more luck than he'd been having on his own. Otis had paced back and forth, offering tips like a baseball coach, readjusting Simon's hands, suggesting mental exercises—*Picture the rain cloud!*—and just generally shouting encouragement.

"It's not all magic," he'd said. "It's about tuning your mind to the exact weather phenomenon you're attempting to conjure."

Simon had looked at him blankly, then wiggled his

fingers at the sky one more time without any sort of results. After that, they'd called it a night.

Now they were working on wind. Simon was perched on the edge of the dock, eyeing the glassy surface of the pond.

"Just a slight breeze is all you need to start," Otis was saying, but when Ruby craned her neck to look at the water, the only movement she saw was the ripple of the minnows below. Simon threw his head back in frustration, blowing out an exaggerated sigh.

"You just need to—" Otis began, but Simon cut him off.

"*You* do it," he said, his voice full of challenge. "Let's see you do it."

From where she and Ruby were sitting near the edge of the pond, Daisy narrowed her eyes as she watched the scene before her. Simon drew himself to full height, straightening his scrawny shoulders, waiting. But Otis only took a step back to lean against one of the rails of the pier.

"You're the one..." he said, then hesitated; there was a catch in his voice. "You're the one who needs to know all of this."

Simon seemed to deflate somewhat, and he bowed his blond head, his shoulders once again curved. "I can't."

Beside Ruby, Daisy sat absolutely still, her forgotten doughnut dangling from one of her fingers. Her blond hair was whipping around her face, stirred by a breeze that apparently none of them had created.

"I know this isn't easy," Otis said. "But think of it like baking a cake."

Simon gave him a wary look.

"You don't just fling everything into a bowl and hope for the best. There's an order to things, a correct way of doing it. And if you don't follow the steps, then no cake."

"Simon's worst nightmare," Ruby couldn't resist muttering under her breath, and her brother shot her a look.

"Fine," he said, turning back to Otis. "How do I do it, then?"

"First you need your ingredients," Otis said, running a hand absently through his salt-colored hair. "So say we're aiming for rain. What would we need?"

"Water," Simon said dully.

"Water *vapor*, actually," Ruby chimed in, and beside her, Daisy bobbed her head.

"Exactly," said Otis. "Water vapor. Moisture. Condensation. Like with a cake, the ingredients in the atmosphere have to be just right for rain."

Simon blinked up at the milky sky through the branches of the trees. "But if it's not already there, how do you make that happen?"

"Ah," Otis said, his face splitting into a grin. "That's where the magic comes in."

"But how?" Simon asked, looking frustrated again. "You can't just say that part of it is magic and then not tell me how to do it. That's like telling me to just start juggling. I have no clue how."

"Storm Makers don't flare up unless they're ready," Otis said. "So much of it is just instinct, and that part will kick in soon." He flashed Simon a little smile, but Ruby didn't think he looked completely convinced. "Until then, we just need to practice."

"But practice *what*?" Simon asked, his voice tight. "Practice imagining rain? Staring at the sky? Thinking about weather?"

"I know it's hard to understand," Daisy said, crossing her legs and sitting forward. "It's hard to explain, too. It's like—" She furrowed her brow in concentration, trying to come up with an example. "It's like tying your shoe," she said finally. "You had to learn how to do it once, but now it's just automatic. You don't think about it at all. Your fingers just fly, right?"

Simon nodded.

"So that's why it's hard for us to give you specific instructions," she said. "It's been so long that for us, our fingers just fly."

With that, she twirled a hand above her head, and the trees around them shuddered, a few stray leaves sailing to the ground, before everything went still again.

Daisy grinned. "The science is important," she said, "but the magic is what makes it all come together, and it's not something that's easy to teach. It's something that's inside you."

"Exactly," Otis said. "And now we just need to find a way to get it out."

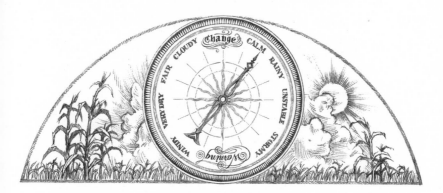

twenty

LATER, AS SIMON AND OTIS CONTINUED TO PRACTICE, the day around them quiet and still and completely uncooperative, Daisy finished off the last of the doughnuts, licking the powdered sugar from her fingers. When she was done, she turned to Ruby.

"So who's building an energy converter out in your barn?"

Ruby raised her eyebrows. "You could tell that's what it was?"

"Of course," she said. "It's a great idea."

"It's my dad's invention. It's part of the reason we moved up here."

"Oh yeah?"

"It's not really working out, though," Ruby said, unable to hide the catch in her voice. "And if it doesn't..."

Daisy raised her eyebrows.

"Then I guess maybe we move back," Ruby admitted, pulling at a few blades of grass. "Which wouldn't be the worst thing, you know? I mean, Dad could be a science teacher again, and Mom could go back to work at the flower shop. And we'd get to live in the suburbs again, instead of out here in the middle of nowhere. And..."

"And?"

"And then maybe we'd just be normal kids again," Ruby said, raising her eyes.

Daisy reached out and placed a hand on hers, just briefly, before taking it away again. She shifted her gaze out past the water and the trees, through the small thicket where the golden fields peeked through. "I'm afraid it doesn't work that way," she said. "Simon is what he is. It has nothing to do with geography."

Ruby was silent for a moment. Her brother was now

crouched like a frog on the wooden panels of the dock, staring down at the water with a fierce intensity.

"You know, I was the opposite of you," Daisy said, leaning back. "We lived up here when I was little, my dad and me, and then we moved down to Chicago when I was about your age."

"How come?"

"He got a big job with the Society," she said, smiling. "And it would've been a mighty long commute."

"Did you always know he was a Storm Maker, your dad?"

"Not at all," Daisy said, shaking her head. "You're a complete exception to the rule. Usually even the families never know."

"So what did you think he was?"

"He was a mechanic," she said. "That was his first love. We used to spend hours out in our old garage together. I knew he was fascinated by the weather, too—always keeping an eye on the sky, obsessing over the satellite pictures on the news—but I didn't find out until much later, when I flared up myself. As a kid, I never could have imagined he had this whole secret life as the Secretary of Hailstorms down at headquarters."

"But he always planned to go back to being a mechanic?"

Daisy nodded. "He did," she said. "But that's the thing. It's not like a job or a hobby or a piece of clothing you can just take off whenever you feel like it. You can't ever give it up entirely. It's a part of you, being a Storm Maker. You don't have to be all that involved with the Society, but you still have to play by their rules. At least until you fade out."

Ruby glanced over. "Fade out?"

"It's like anything else," Daisy said. "After a certain point, the older you get, the weaker you become. Think of it like a baseball player; one day you can throw a hundred-mile-an-hour pitch, and the next, you start to feel a weakness in your arm. Eventually you'll barely be able to make it out to the pitching mound at all. Happens to everyone. Even Storm Makers. Eventually, you can't make a single raindrop."

Ruby thought about this for a moment. "Is that what happened to your dad?"

"No," Daisy said, shaking her head. "He was still pretty powerful when he died."

"How did he become the Chairman?"

"He was chosen."

Ruby wanted to ask more questions, but it was clear that the conversation was over. Daisy was brushing grass from the back of her jeans, and her eyes moved out over the pier, where Simon was still facing down the water.

As Ruby watched, there was a sudden stirring of wind, and the surface of the pond began to move out in waves. They were tiny at first, mere ripples that grew larger as they reached the banks. Simon looked so surprised he nearly fell off the dock, but Otis was frowning at Daisy, who laughed as she joined them.

"Sorry," she said with a grin as the water began to settle again, swaying gently near the edges of the pond. "But even the fish were getting bored."

Simon groaned in frustration.

"Let me take a shot at this," Daisy said to Otis, who nodded. As Ruby hoisted herself onto one of the railings along the pier, Simon shot her a desperate glance, then turned to face Daisy with a look of utter defeat.

"It's hopeless," he said. "I can't do anything."

"That's where you're wrong," she said, pacing around him. "Because I've already seen you nearly electrocute yourself, and you broke a window in my house with that fever storm of yours."

"Fine," Simon said, shoving his hands in his pockets. "Then I can't do anything on command. Are there Storm Makers who turn out to be duds?"

Daisy shook her head. "Sometimes people lose their abilities, but not when they're just starting out," she said. "Stop being so hard on yourself."

"How do people lose their powers?"

"Sometimes due to age, sometimes due to other circumstances," Daisy said vaguely. "But that's not important right now."

Simon, however, refused to be deterred. "What kinds of other circumstances?"

Daisy hesitated, and when she finally spoke, her voice was soft. "Down at headquarters, there's this machine."

"Daisy," Otis said. "Don't."

But she ignored him. "It's called the Vacuum, and it basically saps you of all your abilities to make weather. The longer you're in there, the more power you lose."

Ruby and Simon were both speechless.

"It's supposed to be used only in emergencies," Otis told them, his voice as weary as a teacher's. "Like during the Snowball Riots of the late 1800s, and the Waterlogged Uprising in 1972—things like that. It was meant to help control those who used the weather to cause damage."

"And now," Daisy said, "it's controlled *by* those who use the weather to cause damage."

"But that's not important right now," Otis said, removing his hat to run a hand through his graying hair. "And it has nothing to do with Simon."

"True," Daisy said. "At the moment, we need to figure out how to get you to cook up some weather."

"What if I can't?"

"Every Storm Maker has to start somewhere," Daisy said. "Rupert London might now be powerful enough to cause a massive avalanche, but there was a time when he couldn't even blow the seeds off a dandelion, and that's when he was a whole lot older than you are."

Simon looked skeptical. "How big an avalanche?"

"Big," Daisy said. "The kind that's made by a completely unprecedented earthquake beneath a mountain range near a ski resort." She seemed to trip over the word *earthquake*, and Ruby couldn't help wondering whether she'd told Otis about her own mishap at the garage the other day. But it was clear that her mind was elsewhere now, and she lowered her eyes as she told them the next part.

"The kind that's big enough to kill more than a hundred people in one fell swoop."

"I remember that," Ruby said. "It was just last year, right?"

"March twentieth," Otis and Daisy said at the exact same time.

"London did that?"

Otis nodded, but said nothing. He was watching Ruby with watery eyes, his face impossible to read. He looked as if he were arriving at a decision of some sort, and she thought of the barometer tucked away in her pocket and felt suddenly desperate to ask him what sort of change they were waiting for, and how to know when it might be coming. But Daisy had already turned back to Simon.

"Let's see what you can do, kid," she said, reaching out to spin him by the shoulders, maneuvering him toward the end of the dock. For a moment, Ruby was worried she was going to push him off the edge, but instead she whispered something in his ear. The two of them directed their gazes at the water.

Otis and Ruby watched as the pair of towheaded figures eyed the murky pond, the brackish water flecked with leaves and algae. Ruby held her breath, expecting to feel a breeze on the back of her neck, a gust of wind, anything. But several minutes passed, and still nothing happened.

"Forget it," Simon said, turning around again. "This isn't working." His face was pale from effort, and he slumped against the railing of the dock. "Maybe I'm not the person you're looking for. Maybe there's been some kind of mistake."

Ruby looked from Otis to Daisy, waiting for one of them to assure him this was untrue, to tell him he was wrong, to explain that these things simply took time.

But nobody said a word.

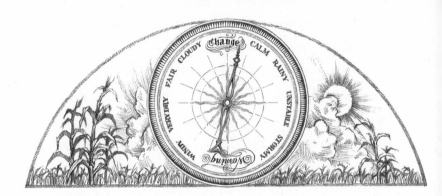

twenty-one

Ruby had been assigned lunch duty, and for once she didn't mind missing out on the action. As the morning wore on, Simon had started to look increasingly miserable, and the pressure had grown almost unbearable. She was more than happy to escape.

When she returned to the grove with another brown bag, this one full of sandwiches and chips and cans of soda, the others were all sitting on the edge of the pier.

They were each facing in a different direction, occupying all three sides of the dock, their feet hanging off the edge. But Ruby could see that they were talking even so, and when she was close enough to hear, she realized that the conversation was about the night Rupert London showed up.

"And then he just asked to see what you could do?" Otis was asking. He pivoted as Ruby approached, her sandals loud against the wooden slats of the pier.

"More like *ordered* him," she said, dropping the bag. "He didn't exactly say please."

Simon gave her a pained look.

"Well, he didn't," Ruby said, sitting cross-legged as she began to unpack the picnic lunch. "I know you want to think you were buddies that night, but he was awful to you. And even worse to me."

"Yeah," Daisy said, swiveling around to grab a sandwich. "London's not a huge fan of non–Storm Makers. And the fact that you actually know what's going on with Simon must be driving him nuts."

"So what happened next?" Otis asked, the lines on his face creasing. "What did you do?"

Simon shrugged. "I made it rain."

Daisy and Otis exchanged a look. Ruby nodded, as if to confirm the story.

"So what was different then?" Otis asked. "Was there anything you did that night that you're not doing now?"

Reaching for a bag of chips, Simon shook his head. "I don't think so."

Otis turned to Ruby.

"Well, there was a lot of pressure," she said. "He was sort of yelling at him. And it was scary to think what might happen if he *didn't* make it rain."

"So maybe we should just be shouting at him more," Daisy said, making a face that was meant to be menacing, but which fell somewhat short due to the streak of peanut butter on her cheek. Simon laughed as Daisy winked at him. Ruby was smiling, too, but when she glanced over at Otis, he looked troubled.

They kept at it all afternoon, moving from the basics—rain and wind—to things that were more difficult—lightning and snow, funnel clouds and frost—until the light had shifted to the other side of the trees, the day slipping by without any results at all, and Simon finally sank to the ground and flung out his arms and groaned.

"This is useless," he said. "Why don't we just try again tomorrow?"

"Because tomorrow is already June nineteenth," Otis said grimly. "We're running out of time."

"Till what?" Ruby asked.

"Till June twenty-first."

"I know," she said, gritting her teeth. "But what's June twenty-first?"

Otis didn't bother to answer. He seemed deep in thought, pacing the rough trail that led back into the fields with a look of indecision, until at last he raised an arm for them all to follow, and they began the long walk back up to the farmhouse together, the day's lesson apparently over after all.

They cut through the wheat, which was soft and dry and nearly ready to be harvested, walking single file: first Otis, then Simon, then Ruby, and finally Daisy at the back. As if to mock them for their earlier efforts, there was still no breeze at all, the air heavy and still, and so Ruby could hear quite clearly as Simon asked the same question that had been on her mind for days.

"So, if London is so bad, who let him become Chairman in the first place?"

"Nobody *let* him," Otis said gruffly. "He was chosen."

These were the exact same words that Daisy had used when talking about her father earlier, and Ruby found herself straining forward to hear what else Otis had to say, nearly clipping Simon's heels in the process. But the looming figure at the lead fell silent, plunging ahead through the crops without turning around.

"There's a compass." Daisy's voice came from behind them, and Simon and Ruby both stopped, whirling around to listen. Otis paused, too, his face dark. "Not all Storm Makers are involved with the Society. Everyone has to follow certain rules, of course, but they don't all have weather-related jobs. Some of them are doctors and lawyers and teachers."

"And mechanics," Ruby said softly.

Daisy smiled. "And mechanics," she said. "But when it comes to being the Chairman, it doesn't matter. You could work at headquarters in a position of power, or you could be a plumber from Oklahoma who happens to have a knack for defusing tornadoes. It could be anyone, and Storm Makers come from all over the country to see if they might be the one."

"How would they know?" Simon asked.

"Because of the compass. It's this enormous thing that's hundreds of years old, and it's kept in a room that's normally closed off. But every four years, any Storm Maker who thinks they might possibly be the next Chairman — whether they make a pilgrimage to see the compass or already work in the halls of headquarters — is allowed to take a turn circling around it. For most people, the compass remains where it is: pointing north. But for the chosen person, the needle follows, spinning as they walk the circle." She paused. "Four years ago, it spun for London."

"And that's it?" Ruby asked. "Even though he's so terrible, everyone just listens to a stupid piece of equipment that's probably broken?"

Otis turned his flinty gaze in her direction. "Nobody could have known what Rupert would be like once he took power," he said. "And even if they had, it's still a piece of our history. Part magic, part science. It's the way things have worked for centuries."

"Why four years?" Simon asked. "It's not like he's the president."

"No," Daisy said with a smile. "The president couldn't make it snow."

"Four seasons in a year, four years in a term," Otis explained. "It's been that way for a long time. London has actually been there a little bit longer, because of..."

Daisy met his gaze. "Because my dad died a few months before the end of his term," she told them. "But it's due to spin again very soon."

Otis nodded. "Though I have a feeling Rupert isn't quite ready to leave yet."

"Why don't they just kick him out, if he's so terrible?" Simon asked.

Daisy smiled. "It's not exactly a democracy. He holds a lot of power. Let's just say he can be very..." It took her a moment to find the right word. "Persuasive. He threatens his followers with the Vacuum, promises to damage their home cities if they don't do as they're told. And even without all that, he's still one of the most powerful Storm Makers we've ever seen. So even if he *did* step aside as Chairman, he'd still be dangerous. But with the whole Society at his disposal, with all his influence and power, it's so much worse."

Not far from them, a flock of crows startled, scattering into the pearly sky in a burst of noise and feathers.

"So where does Simon come into this?" Ruby asked,

moving around her brother so that she was now peering up at Otis. "If Storm Makers get more powerful as they get older, then what could he possibly do to help now? I mean, you saw him out there." She turned to her brother. "No offense, Simon. But you're a pretty terrible Storm Maker at the moment."

He grinned sheepishly. "Can't argue with that."

Ruby turned back to Otis. "And if London is so bad, then why don't you just stop him yourself?"

Even from a few feet away, Ruby could sense Otis tensing up. He pulled his crumpled hat from his pocket and shoved it on his head, blinking a few times. Finally, he met her eyes.

"Because," he said, turning around again, "I'm not enough."

They all stood there as he began to walk away, until Daisy gave Ruby and Simon each a little nudge, and they trotted to close the distance between them. Falling back into single file, nobody seemed quite sure what to say, and they continued on in silence until the farmhouse grew near and Otis paused again. There was something thoughtful in his expression when he turned to them, and something sorrowful.

"To tell you the truth, I'm less worried about the change in power right now," he said. "At this very minute, London is preparing for his next strike, and it's my responsibility to figure out a way to stop him." He looked at Simon and Ruby. "And it's *your* responsibility to trust that I'll find a way to do that."

"But how can I help fight if I can't even make it rain?" Simon asked.

"There's not going to be a fight," Otis said, the lines around his mouth deepening again. "Just think for one moment about what that would mean."

Daisy put a hand on Simon's shoulder. "Thunder and lightning. Hailstorms and hurricanes."

"All it would take is one tornado ricocheting off a massive storm front to cause more destruction than London could ever dream of doing on his own," Otis said. "It would be catastrophic. Which is just what he wants."

Ruby lifted her eyes to meet his. "So how are we gonna beat him?"

"That," Otis said with a hint of a smile, "is something I'm still working on. But in the meantime, we practice. And we keep our eyes open. Because I have no doubt

212

that they're out there, keeping an eye on us, too." As he spoke, he tilted his head to the west, and sure enough, when they shifted their gazes out across the endless fields, there was the faintest smudge of black, a shadowy figure against the darkening line of the horizon. Ruby let out a little noise of surprise and took a step closer to Simon, who stared at Otis.

"They're watching us?" he asked, his voice sounding very small.

"Of course," Daisy said. "You didn't think London would head back to Chicago without keeping tabs on his newest star, did you?"

"I thought..." Simon said, then trailed off. "I don't know."

"So that means they know you're here," Ruby said, and Daisy nodded. "Which means they know what you're planning?"

"That would be tough," Otis said, grinning for the first time in what felt like hours. "Since I don't even know that myself." When he saw Ruby's stricken look, he reached over and placed a hand on her shoulder, the way he had that day in the hospital, a whole lifetime ago. "Don't worry," he told her. "I'm working on it."

After dinner that night, Ruby walked out to the barn with Dad. Ever since the day of the storm, she hadn't been spending nearly as much time with him, and he was eager to show her the progress he'd made on the invention. But her mind was still back in the cornfield, her head swimming with Otis's words.

I'm not enough, he'd said. And what if that was true?

She'd waited for him to come back, to instruct them, to save them, to tell them what to do. But even with all they'd learned in the past few days, there were still so many questions. If they weren't preparing for a fight with London, then what? And if Simon wasn't the key to some great battle plan, then why was everyone so interested in him?

As she and Dad crossed the gravel drive, the dogs streaked ahead of them, twin shadows in the gathering darkness. The air throbbed with the sound of crickets, and the sky above the fields was dimming.

Dad followed Ruby's eyes out across the horizon. "Soon we'll be going in the opposite direction," he said, and when she looked at him blankly, he smiled. "Longest day of the year coming up," he explained. "After that, it'll start getting dark earlier again."

"Right, I forgot."

"Yup," Dad said. "June twenty-first."

Ruby stopped abruptly, her mouth falling open, but Dad didn't notice. He was still making his way toward the barn, his voice trailing behind him.

"Summer solstice," he was saying to no one in particular. "Longest day of the year."

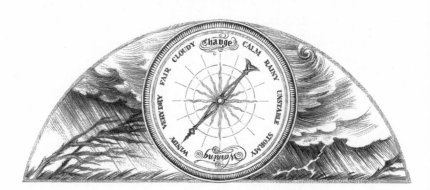

twenty-two

LATER, RUBY PAUSED while brushing her teeth, her head cocked to one side. She reached out with her left foot to kick open the bathroom door, listening for the sound of Simon's voice, which was drifting up the stairs from the foyer.

"Yeah, tomorrow at Ben's house," he was saying. "And we'll probably sleep over there, too."

Toothbrush still in hand, Ruby tiptoed across the hallway and peered over the banister. There was an edge to

Simon's voice that she found suspicious, and this was the first she knew of any plans with his friend Ben. The last she'd heard, they were supposed to practice with Otis and Daisy again tomorrow.

"It's fine with me," Dad said. He was sitting on the bottom step, pulling off his work boots. Mom was leaning against the front door, nodding at Simon.

"As long as it's okay with Ben's mom," she said.

Ruby leaned farther over the railing, her blond hair falling across her face. "As long as what's okay?" she asked, her mouth still full of toothpaste. All three of them looked up at her.

"Simon's spending the day with some friends tomorrow," Dad said.

"And probably the night, too," Simon added a bit too quickly.

Ruby raised her eyebrows at him, but he looked away. She wiped her mouth with the back of her hand and frowned.

"So you get to hang with me, you lucky duck," Dad said, laughing at the expression on Ruby's face. "Maybe we'll head into town, run some errands, see if Daisy's back yet."

Ruby ignored this, afraid to give anything away. "It's just that I was planning to go with Simon, too," she said, turning to her brother. "Didn't you tell them?"

Simon's face clouded over. "No," he said, his voice strained. "I thought we'd agreed you *weren't* gonna come. Since it's all guys and it's not really your kind of thing, anyway."

Ruby had no clue what he was talking about, but his gaze was burning a hole through her for reasons she couldn't begin to understand, and something was telling her to press on. Below her, Mom and Dad were clearly waiting for an answer as to why she so desperately wanted to hang out with her brother and his friends, something she usually avoided. Her mind raced to come up with a reason, to figure out what Simon was planning, but nothing came. A dribble of toothpaste fell off her brush and onto the carpet beside her bare foot. She tucked her hair behind her ears and cleared her throat.

"Allison and Erika are gonna be there, too," she said, ignoring Simon's frantic look. "Remember?"

"Ben's sisters are into baseball?" Mom asked, sounding dubious.

"*You're* into baseball?" Dad said, even more skeptical.

"Of course I am," Ruby said with a conviction she didn't quite feel.

"Okay," Mom said. "If you'd rather play baseball than hang around here, it's fine with me. A little strange, but fine. As long as it's okay with your brother."

Ruby turned to look down at Simon, but all she could see was the top of his head. They all waited for him to respond, the silence filling the foyer. In the next room, one of the dogs barked twice, then fell quiet again.

"Fine," Simon said eventually, without lifting his head, and Ruby had the feeling he was agreeing to more than just her tagging along, that something far more important than baseball had been settled here. "Ruby's coming, too."

"Glad to hear it," Dad said, clapping his hands on his knees and then rising to his feet. "But that's tomorrow. For now, lights-out."

"How about ten more minutes?" Ruby asked, eager to talk to Simon alone.

"How about two?" Dad said, and she grinned.

"I'll take it."

She hurried back to the bathroom to rinse off her toothbrush then jammed it into the cup holder at the edge of the sink. By the time she emerged again, Simon had already slipped into his bedroom and shut the door. Ruby knocked a few times, leaning against the wooden frame, but there was no answer, so she gave up and headed back to her own room. But when she heard his door creak open nearly an hour later, long after lights-out, she threw back her covers, tiptoeing out of bed and into the hallway.

Simon groaned when he saw her, looking like someone caught committing some sort of crime. Even from upstairs, they could hear Mom and Dad talking quietly in the kitchen, so he silently motioned for Ruby to follow him into the bathroom. Once inside, she hoisted herself up onto the counter, her legs dangling against the cabinets, and he pressed the door shut and then turned to face her.

"So I'm guessing you're not actually playing baseball at Ben's tomorrow," she said, and he nodded, his face solemn. Ruby curled her fingers around the edge of the counter; she suspected she already knew the answer to her next question, but she felt she had to ask it anyway: "So where are we going instead?"

"Chicago," Simon said, slumping back against the door.

Ruby nodded. So he hadn't forgotten. "I guess we're probably not going to see the sights."

"No," he said with the faintest hint of a smile. "Not quite."

"What if Mom and Dad find out?"

Simon rolled his eyes. "Never gonna happen," he said, and Ruby had to admit he was probably right. Their parents had been so distracted by their own separate projects lately, not to mention the looming money troubles that were threatening the farm, that they barely noticed where the twins were these days. "We'll say we're working at the garage tomorrow, and getting picked up right from there."

"But they think Daisy's still gone."

He grinned. "Not after we fake a phone call from her in the morning."

"Well, what about Otis?" she asked. "Are we gonna tell him?"

Simon shook his head.

"Why not?" Her voice was unintentionally loud; it pinballed around the tiny bathroom, and Simon put a finger to his lips, then slid down the door until he was sitting on the tiles, his knees drawn up to his chest.

"Because he'd want to come, too," he said. "Or he'd tell us not to go."

"Probably for good reason."

Simon lowered his eyes. "I need to see London again."

"Why?" Ruby asked, giving him a hard look. "What do you think that's gonna help?"

"I don't know yet," he admitted. "But he obviously wants me to come down there, and I figure maybe if I could just talk to him..."

"Talk to him?" Ruby said doubtfully.

Simon shrugged. "Maybe if he realizes I can't make weather, he won't care about me anymore. If he doesn't think I'm special, maybe he'll stop whatever he's planning."

Ruby gave him a hard look. "Come *on*."

"What?" he asked, a bit too innocently, but she could see that his ears had gone pink, a sure sign of guilt.

"It's something more than that," she said. "It's got to be. Otherwise, this makes no sense. Why would you want to walk right into his hands? I mean, we have no idea what he wants you for, and there are about a million ways this could go wrong. What if he wants to hurt you?" She paused, tracing the edge of the sink with her finger. "Us. What if he wants to hurt *us*?"

Simon bowed his head. "I just..."

"What?"

"I just feel like I need to do *something*," he said after a moment. "All we've been doing is wasting time. I'm not getting any better, and Otis and Daisy aren't helping. I haven't made even a single raindrop since they started practicing with me. And London—he said he could teach me."

Ruby stared at him. "Teach you what? How to destroy people's fields?"

"It's not like that."

"It's exactly like that," she said, sliding off the counter and folding herself onto the floor beside him, her back against the bathroom door. "I know you're frustrated, but I don't think going to see London is the answer."

Simon didn't look convinced. "He makes things happen," he said, his voice cracking. "And right now, it just feels like all we're doing is waiting around."

"Yeah," Ruby said quietly. "For June twenty-first."

"Exactly," he said. "Whatever that is."

"It's the summer solstice," she told him. "The longest day of the year."

"I know that," he said with a little scowl.

"So remember when Daisy mentioned that earthquake

earlier?" she asked. "They said it was March twentieth. *Last year.*"

"So?"

"So that's the vernal equinox," she explained. "The spring solstice."

Simon's face was still blank.

"And two years ago, there was that crazy blizzard on December twenty-first," she said. "The one that killed a whole bunch of people in the Northeast."

"And?"

"And *three* years ago," she said, "there was that awful hurricane in Louisiana that hit on September twentieth. I checked. That's the fall equinox."

Simon looked skeptical. "So you think London did all that?"

"I know it seems a little far-fetched, but why else would they be so worried about June twenty-first?" she asked. "He's only been Chairman for four years. So you see? He's been planning disasters every year, moving forward in the calendar each time." She held up her fingers and ticked them off as she spoke. "Fall equinox, winter solstice, spring equinox."

"So all that's left is the summer solstice."

"Exactly," Ruby said, watching her brother closely, trying to read the expression on his face. It was obvious that London had some sort of grip on him; he was like a plume of smoke, obscuring Simon's view of things, and Ruby wasn't sure how to get him clear of it. But beneath all that starry-eyed wonder, she knew there was someone who still cared about the same things she did.

They were both quiet for a moment, and when Simon looked up, his face was tinged gray with worry. "Do you think he's planning something around here?" he asked, and just like that, he came back to her. Just like that, he was her brother again.

Ruby bit her lip, trying to hide her relief. "I don't know," she said truthfully, and Simon nodded.

"Then maybe that's what we need to find out."

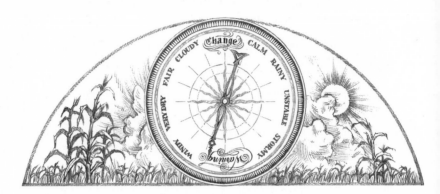

twenty-three

THE SLIP OF PAPER in Ruby's hand fluttered in the breeze from the open window of the truck as they made their way into town. She tucked it into the front pocket of her backpack and looked up at the rearview mirror, where she could see Dad's eyes roving over the brittle landscape. The dirt roads leading out of the farm were still cracked from the glare of the sun and shimmering slightly in the heat.

There was still no breeze this morning, and Ruby

couldn't help wondering if London had decided not to wait for June 21 after all, if perhaps this had been his plan all along—that rather than some sort of biblical storm, they were instead being treated to a slower kind of torture, this unrelenting and punishing sun.

As they neared town, it became clear that they weren't the only ones worn down by the weather. A few older women with makeshift paper fans hovered in the door of the general store, and a man toting a bag of grain under his arm paused to pat at his forehead with the end of his shirt.

As much time as Ruby had spent wishing to be anywhere but here, she felt a quick surge of affection for the place. She thought of the Fourth of July parade last summer, the tiny marching band tripping their way down this street, and the picnic that had followed, when Simon had gotten in trouble for launching a water balloon at the mayor's wife. She pictured the many trips to the hardware store, the two of them deliberating over the bins of candy as if it were the gravest of decisions. And she remembered when they'd first bought the farm, waiting in the cool of the bank lobby until they heard the click of Mom's heels on the marble floor, and Dad following closely behind, waving the paperwork in triumph. How happy they'd looked then, the idea of the farm still nothing but possibility, undamaged by the sun and the heat, the corn still nothing but kernels, the wheat only seeds in their hands.

Now Ruby blinked out at the dusty street and the broken signpost at the main intersection as they turned the corner toward Daisy's garage. She fidgeted with the seat belt, trying not to think of what might be ahead of them today, wishing she shared Simon's certainty that this was the right thing to do. There was clearly a part of him that was still eager to see London again, to catch a glimpse of the mysterious world he might one day inherit. But Ruby chose to believe that the bigger part of him was trying to find a way to fix everything, to avert disaster on June 21. It was a fragile hope, but a hope nonetheless, and that was the part of her brother that Ruby was following today.

"Doesn't look like she's here yet," Dad announced as he threw the truck into park near the entrance to the garage.

"She will be," Simon said.

"Want me to wait with you?" Dad asked as Ruby passed forward Simon's backpack, then grabbed her own. She'd almost given them away this morning when Mom pointed out that she forgot her baseball mitt. After all, they were supposedly being picked up by Ben's mom at the garage after spending the morning working for Daisy. It was supposed to be a day of baseball and hot dogs and lemonade, followed by a big sleepover in Ben's newly finished basement.

Only Simon and Ruby had other plans.

"We'll be fine," Simon said. "She'll be here soon." Before he slid out of the truck, he reached over and gave Dad's hand an awkward little pat. "Thanks for driving us."

"Yeah, of course," Dad said, taking off his sunglasses.

Ruby clambered up front, then fell into Dad's arms for a hug. She inhaled deeply, memorizing the scent of the soil that clung to his shirt.

"Hey," he said. "What's this for?"

"Nothing," she said, pulling away and forcing herself to grin. The lines on his forehead creased, but he only shrugged.

"Call me tomorrow when you're ready to come home, okay?"

As Ruby joined Simon on the pavement, they both nodded. Dad wiggled his eyebrows at them, put on his sunglasses, and started the car. The two of them stood there and watched him pull out of the driveway, their eyes following the truck all the way down the long ribbon of road until it disappeared in the wheat.

Once it had, Ruby let her backpack slip from her shoulder, feeling suddenly desperate. She glanced back at the garage, hoping Daisy might emerge, but they knew she was keeping it closed today so she could continue training Simon, which was exactly why they'd planned it this way. They were on their own.

After a moment, Simon bent down and picked up Ruby's backpack. His face was as serious as she'd ever seen it. "Ready?" he asked, and she nodded. But when she reached for the bag, she remembered the piece of paper inside, and she hesitated.

"It's a long bus ride," she said, slipping the note from the pocket where she'd stashed it just before Simon turned to her with a look of great impatience.

"No, it's not," he said. "It's a short bus ride, and then a longer train ride. We went over this last night."

"I'm just saying maybe I should use the bathroom first," Ruby said, fixing her eyes on the door to Daisy's office, which was set just to the right of the garage.

"It won't be open," Simon said with a sigh, but even as

he did, Ruby was already jogging across the driveway, the paper folded in her sweaty hand.

"I'm just gonna check," she called over her shoulder. She came to a stop at the glass door, where the CLOSED sign was hanging in the window, and made a show of jiggling the handle as she slipped the note into the mail slot. The night before, she'd suggested doing this very thing, but Simon had been quick to nix the idea. He didn't want Otis and Daisy more involved than they already were; he insisted that he and Ruby needed to do this on their own.

Still, when she saw the little square of white paper hit the floor on the opposite side, Ruby couldn't help feeling relieved that at least someone would know where they were.

"You're right," she said, taking a deep breath and squaring her shoulders before turning around again. "It's locked."

"No kidding," Simon grumbled, holding out her backpack as she trotted back to meet him.

Together, they crossed the pavement, moving away from the building and over to the little road behind it. At the far edge of town, just off a cracked piece of sidewalk, there was a small blue sign that indicated the bus stop, which was nothing but a green bench. The night before, Simon had looked up the schedule, and now he dug through his bag for the money he'd been saving for a new baseball bat. Ruby had tucked hers into her shoe.

After about ten minutes, it became clear that the bus was running late, and Ruby could see that Simon was growing worried. What if they hadn't read the schedule correctly? Or what if someone saw them there and told their parents? They hadn't bothered to come up with a backup plan, so certain were they in this one, but now doubts filled the space between them as Ruby paced back and forth along the sidewalk and Simon picked at the peeling green paint of the bench with a scowl.

Ruby took a moment to glance at the barometer, which she now always carried with her. For the first time, the arrow was tipped to *warning*. She swallowed hard.

Not long from now, Otis and Daisy would be arriving at the pond. Ruby closed her eyes and tried not to think about them waiting there.

"Are you sure—" she began, but Simon cut her off.

"Yes," he said. "But it's fine if you're not."

She took a seat beside him on the bench, and Simon swiveled to face her.

"You don't have to come," he said. "It's not about you, anyway."

Ruby looked away, not wanting him to see the way her eyes were starting to swim. No matter how much she tried to help, ultimately this was Simon's battle. And right then, he looked ready for it; there was an intensity about him that—despite days of witnessing otherwise—made her believe he really *could* make it storm. He didn't look like someone who needed help at all right now. But he was still her brother.

"No," she said firmly. "I'm coming, too."

It was then, almost as if she'd conjured it herself, that the bus appeared. It slowed to a noisy stop before them and the door opened with a pop and a hiss. They gave their fares to the driver, a beefy man with a rapidly balding head, and then slid into the first seat, despite the bus being mostly empty.

As they lurched away from the curb, Simon grinned at Ruby. "I can't remember the last time I sat up front on a bus."

"I can't remember the last time you sat with *me*," she said, and he looked surprised.

"I sit with you sometimes."

"Never," she said, shaking her head. "You sit with all your friends in the back, and I always sit up here and read."

"Do I?" he said forcing a too-cheerful smile. "Well, I'm sitting with you now, aren't I?"

Ruby made a face. "It's not like you have much of a choice."

The train station was only two towns over, and the bus moved swiftly along the country roads, past fields with elaborate irrigation systems working futilely against the drought, and pastures of cows huddled in knots beneath what little shade they could find, their tails flicking lazily at the flies.

When they finally arrived at a town only a little bit larger than theirs, they grabbed their bags and hopped off the bus with minutes to spare before their train arrived. In the small depot, they once again counted out their dollar bills, and then climbed on board and purchased their tickets from the conductor.

It had been a long time since Ruby had taken the train downtown. After they'd first moved, Mom had taken her on trips to the museums every couple of months.

"Count me out," Simon always said, just as happy to be left behind with Dad. But for Ruby, it was nice to be reminded that there was a whole world beyond the edges of the farm. They'd flip a coin to see who got to pick the museum, and Mom would inevitably choose the Art Institute. But when it was Ruby's turn, she never failed to pick the Museum of Science and Industry, the great domed building filled with locomotive engines and enormous swaying pendulums, space shuttles and robots and submarines.

And at the end of the day, when they'd return to the farm, she'd sit out in the barn and tell Dad what she saw, using her arms to demonstrate the size of the planets, the way an abacus works, the width of the trees in the rainforest exhibit. She loved those days, a kind of lifeline to the real world. But it wasn't long before the trips became less frequent, and then eventually, they stopped going altogether.

She wished now that their destination could be a museum instead of the unknown headquarters of some still slightly unbelievable and potentially terrifying organization. For now, it was easier not to think about what awaited them, to pretend this was just another holiday trip, a day in the city with her brother.

The motion of the train was making her eyes feel

heavy, and Ruby decided it was okay to close them for a minute or two. But when she opened them again, it was to find trees streaming past instead of crops. They were so green, so lush and bright and alive, that she thought for a moment she must be dreaming. It had been a long time since she'd seen anything so brilliant.

"Looks a little different down here, doesn't it?" Simon asked from beside her, and Ruby yawned.

"Where are we?"

"Not far from home, actually."

She looked at him sideways. "Still?"

"No, I mean the old one," he said with a rueful grin. "We're pretty far from Wisconsin. You were asleep for a while."

She settled back into the orange cushion of the train seat, resting her head against the window, watching the world slide past. Soon the houses began to give way to bigger structures, blocky and imposing, and the green trees were replaced by billboards. If she pressed her cheek all the way up against the window, Ruby could see the skyline in the distance, the staggered buildings nothing but silhouettes against the noonday sun.

She turned to Simon, about to ask if he had the address

ready, but as she did she saw that he was pulling London's business card out of his pocket. The corners were bent, and there was a piece of lint clinging to the edge, but they could clearly read the address beneath the logo of the little storm cloud.

"Should we go there right away?" Ruby asked as the train drew closer, shadows falling across their faces as they moved in and out of tunnels. "We could grab some food first or something, maybe take a walk...."

"Ruby," Simon said. They both knew she was stalling.

She dropped her chin. "I know."

"It'll be okay," he said as the train pulled into the darkened corridor of the station, the lights of the car flickering on. As they slowed to a stop, the passengers around them stood to gather their belongings, but Ruby remained frozen in her seat. If there was a point at which there was no turning back, at which they began something that could no longer be undone, this was that moment.

But Simon was rising to his feet, pulling their backpacks from the racks above the aisle, and it seemed there was nothing more to do, and nothing more to say. Together, they stepped off the train and into the crowded station.

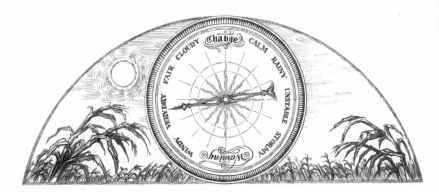

twenty-four

THE BUILDING LOOKED LIKE any other in downtown Chicago, sleek and black and endless, stretching high into the cloudless sky above them. Ruby and Simon stood on the sidewalk before it, their eyes grazing the floors upon floors upon floors.

It had taken them nearly an hour to find their way here, a journey that consisted of two local buses and several blocks' worth of wrong turns. But now that they'd arrived — their hearts lifting at the sight of the address,

which was laid out in curving metal figures above the rows of revolving doors — it seemed as much a dead end as anything else. There must be hundreds of companies housed in this building, thousands of people. The card in Simon's hand held no further instructions beyond the address itself, and it seemed wrong to just saunter in and ask the guy at the information desk on which floor they might find the secret society of people who wanted to inflict a major weather disaster upon them.

But they'd come this far, and it now seemed there was little other choice.

Once inside, they waited behind a woman looking for her lawyer's office — which turned out to be at a different address altogether — and when she was finished, the steely-eyed man behind the front desk pointed his face down at them.

"Can I help you?" he asked, looking anything but helpful.

"We're wondering what floor MOSS is on?"

He raised one eyebrow. "Mouse?"

There was a massive security guard standing at the other end of the desk, and he shifted his eyes in their direction without moving his head.

"No," Ruby said. *"MOSS."*

"M-O-S-S," Simon said, spelling it out, and the security guard's shoulders visibly relaxed.

The man behind the desk punched something into his computer, and Ruby glanced at her watch, aware that everything was taking too long; aware that Daisy had probably gone back to her shop and read their note by now, since they hadn't shown up at the lake; aware that the clock was continuing its march forward toward June 21. Now that they were this close, it seemed urgent that they keep moving—though toward what, she wasn't exactly sure—and she willed the man to hurry up and figure out where they were supposed to go.

But he took his time, frowning at the computer, hitting a few more keys, scratching his head, and then doing the whole thing all over again. Finally, he looked up.

"I'm not seeing it," he said. "What does it stand for?"

Ruby and Simon exchanged a look.

"We're not exactly sure," she lied.

"Sorry," he said with a shrug. "Then neither am I."

Outside, they let the flow of people stream all around them as they studied the card again, looking for missing clues. But it was stubbornly cryptic, nothing but a storm

241

cloud and an address, *this* address, which apparently did them no good.

"What now?" Simon asked, staring up at the building again. Ruby followed his gaze, and just as her eyes settled on the spire at the very top, she saw it: the briefest flash of light in the otherwise quiet sky. It happened so fast she couldn't be quite sure it had happened at all.

"Did you see that?" she asked Simon, who looked at her blankly.

"See what?"

"I think it was lightning."

He narrowed his eyes at the sky. "Looks pretty calm to me."

"Exactly," she said, feeling triumphant. "Which means we're probably in the right place."

"But they said —"

"Doesn't matter," Ruby said, cutting him off. She scanned the sidewalk, trying to work out where to go next, and caught sight of a man pushing a cart full of boxes around the corner of the building.

"Come on," she said, grabbing Simon's arm and hurrying him along so she wouldn't lose sight of the man. They weaved through the crowds as they followed, sidestepping businessmen on cell phones and women with strollers, until they saw him disappear into an alley. There, they discovered a separate service driveway for the building, marked with a big green sign that read LOADING DOCK.

They hung back for a moment, ducking behind a wall to watch as a man emerged from the shadows to speak with the delivery guy. He was short and broad, with unruly red hair and a patchy beard, but Ruby could see the bright glint of a silver button on each of his cuffs. After exchanging a few words with the delivery man, he took one of the boxes and turned to wait at the door for a large service elevator. When it arrived, the man swept his eyes from side to side, making sure nobody was watching, and then reached for the grate that served as the door.

As his hand touched the metal there was a spark, and Ruby stepped out from the shadows.

"Hey," she called out, and the man turned.

"Deliveries only," he said, but his eyes rested on Simon.

"We're looking for MOSS," Ruby said, and the man tilted his head to the side, just barely.

"Haven't heard of it."

"Have you heard of Rupert London?" Simon asked, and the man's face tightened.

"What's it to you?"

Simon dug in his pocket for the card and held it up. There was a flicker of recognition on the man's face, a sudden realization, and he jostled the box from one arm to the other, using his foot to hold open the elevator grate.

Without waiting for any further invitation, they hurried over to step on. As Simon passed, the man's eyes widened a little, and he shook his head as he let the grate fall shut again.

"So you're the one," he said gruffly, jabbing at a button on the panel. Simon said nothing; he just gazed at his feet.

Ruby had been expecting to be carried upward, toward the roof, where she'd seen the lightning. It seemed only logical that the offices would be near the very sky they controlled, from where they drew so much of their power. So she was surprised to feel the elevator dropping. Through the bars of the grate, she could see the numbers written on the door of each floor, and her stomach clenched with worry as they passed one after another, lower level and parking garage, basement and sub-basement, moving lower and lower into the depths of the building and away from the safety of people and daylight.

The elevator was the slowest she'd ever been on, and the man said nothing at all the whole time, didn't even turn around to face them, but instead stood looking at the door with his head slightly bowed. Simon shifted from one foot to the other nervously, and Ruby swallowed hard, wondering how much farther down they could possibly go. But then the elevator came to a stop with a loud wrenching sound, jostling them slightly, and the one dim bulb in the center of the ceiling flickered before brightening again.

"Lower level eight," the man said without turning around. He closed a beefy hand around the heavy grate and heaved it back. "Makers of Storms Society."

As the interior door swung open, Ruby blinked in surprise. Whatever she'd been expecting, it was certainly not this. If she'd thought about it at all, she would have assumed it would be a place like the room in Daisy's garage, dark and guarded and mysterious, like some kind of secret lair.

But as the door slammed shut behind them and the

elevator lurched upward again, she saw that the place spread out before them looked like nothing more than an ordinary office. It could just as easily have been a law firm or a bank. There were rows upon rows of cubicles in neat lines, harsh fluorescent lighting that gave the whole thing a yellowish tinge, and the sound of telephones going off at regular intervals.

The two of them stood there, stunned. Ruby shook her head, about to say aloud the thought that was running through her mind—that they must be in the wrong place—when a voice startled her. She whirled around to see what was clearly the receptionist, leaning across an unusually tall desk and motioning them over.

"Can I help you?" she asked when they were standing before her.

Without warning, Simon let out a little cry of surprise, moving toward Ruby so fast he nearly knocked her over.

"What's wrong with you?" she asked, but he was staring wide-eyed at the empty spot where he'd just been standing.

"It's freezing there," he said, rubbing his arms.

"Cold pocket," the receptionist said sweetly. "There's a

warm one just to your right, so be careful. What can I do for you?"

Caught off guard, Ruby was unsure what to say. This wasn't exactly how she'd imagined they'd be confronting London, by making an appointment with the reception- ist, and there was something about the sense of order to this place that was unsettling, the sheer and startling normalcy of it all. She shivered slightly, despite being several feet from the mysterious pocket of cold air.

"Um, we're looking for Rupert London," Simon said. He'd taken a step closer to the desk, though he could barely manage to see over it, his chin coming up to the top. "We have some, uh, business to discuss with him."

With a crisp nod, the woman picked up her phone and hit a single button, then hummed while she waited. Ruby and Simon each took a small step backward until they were standing beside a watercooler, which seemed to contain some kind of funnel, an internal whirlpool that was whipping the drinking water into a frenzy. From around the doorways of offices and over the tops of cubicles, people were starting to peek out at them, their faces anxious and drawn. Ruby lowered her voice to whisper to Simon.

"There's something creepy about this," she said. "Maybe we should—"

"What?" he said. "What can we do at this point?"

Ruby had no answer for this. She looked up at the woman, who murmured something, then put her palm over the phone.

"Name?" she asked, and Simon stepped forward again.

"McDuff," he said. "Ruby and Simon."

Her whole face changed then, the businesslike demeanor dissolving into a look of pure shock. She stared at them openly, the color rising to her cheeks, until a staticky sound from the other end of the phone jolted her back and she lifted the handset back to her ear and nodded into it, as if she'd lost her words entirely. After a moment, she let it slip from her hand, cradling it into the receiver, and then raised her eyes again.

"Mr. London will see you now," she said in a wavery voice, pointing down the longest corridor, which stretched back between a wall of offices and a row of cubicles. "Last one to the right."

The woman continued to watch as they turned to go, though it took Ruby a moment to begin walking. She felt as if she were in some kind of dream, where everything was just sideways of normal, where an ordinary-seeming hallway might very well lead to a trap.

On the door to every office they passed, there were little weather symbols rather than nameplates: raindrops and snowflakes, tornadoes and plumes of fire. Inside they could see charts and graphs and radar screens, much like the ones in Daisy's basement. But there were also things that made Ruby and Simon pause every so often, eyes wide. In one office, there were shelves and shelves of jars, each one filled with a different kind of miniature weather phenomenon: tiny lightning bolts and puffy rain clouds, a perfectly unmelted snowball, and even a little twister. There were no clocks on the walls, only weather vanes, and in the place where a normal office might have had a photocopier or a fax machine, there were a telescope and a small weather balloon that bobbed up and then sank down again and again like a sluggish yo-yo.

But the strangest thing of all was the people. In spite of all the professional trappings, there was an air of great nervousness about the place. Everyone seemed to scuttle rather than stroll, to lurk rather than look. And every eye in the place was focused on Simon and Ruby as they made the seemingly endless trek to London's office.

Midway down the hall, there was a solid gray door marked with a NO ADMITTANCE sign, and below it a symbol they hadn't seen before: a small circle with a single dash at the top. When Ruby paused before it, she could feel dozens of pairs of eyes on her back, and a collective intake of breath. But before she had a chance to say anything, a voice rose up from the far end of the hallway and a dark figure stepped out into the corridor.

"Well," said London with a smile so broad it whipped the breath right out of Ruby, set her heart hammering and her hands trembling. He gazed down the length of the hallway at them, his head tilted to one side, his eyes bright with interest. "So glad you could finally make it."

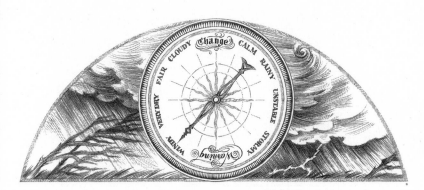

twenty-five

Ruby's FIRST THOUGHT when London gestured to a seat in his office was *This is more like it*. Because as professional as the rest of the place looked, as average and ordinary and normal, Rupert London's office was exactly what she'd been expecting. And something about this seemed to help her regain her balance.

As she sank into one of the uncomfortable wooden chairs in front of his desk, Simon sliding into the other, Ruby let her eyes wander. It was a huge room, roughly

the size of the whole first floor of the farmhouse, and sparsely decorated. As opposed to the whiteness of the rest of the office, which had about it a sort of polished gleam of productivity, everything here was covered in dark wood and burgundy wallpaper, the carpet an even deeper brown.

They were too far underground for windows, and there was only one lamp, which gave off an orangey glow that didn't quite reach all the way into the corners. While the rest of the offices seemed to be filled with the building blocks of the trade—radar screens and weather samples, various gadgets and instruments—London's shelves were mainly lined with old books.

"I've been hoping you'd visit," he said to Simon as he pressed the door shut with a click. His dark hair was immaculately combed, his suit pressed and neat. If he were to walk through the lobby of the building above, nobody would suspect he was anything but some slick lawyer or banker, a businessman with a busy day of meetings and an agenda that did not include things like implementing natural disasters.

"I take it your lessons with Otis have been somewhat less than thrilling." He looked pleased at the thought, smiling as he crossed the room. "Come to learn from the master, then?"

"Yes, sir," Simon said, avoiding Ruby's eyes.

London crooked a finger at one of the bookshelves and a wall of fog appeared, making everything behind it fuzzy and indistinct. Then he snapped his fingers and it was gone. "You've made a wise choice," he said. "There's a lot I can teach you."

As he pulled out the armchair behind the cherry desk, Ruby noticed a set of framed photographs behind him, and she felt weak at the sight of them, lined up so neatly in a row. "Like that?" she asked, pointing.

"Ah, yes," London said, spinning the chair halfway around so that he could look up at them, too. The first showed an aerial shot of the city of New Orleans in the wake of a hurricane, the waterlogged streets turned to rivers. The second was starkly different, with white snow filling the frame, the great Northeast blizzard from two years ago, one of the worst in history. And the third, which would have been beautiful had it not been so horrible, had it not killed so many people, showed an avalanche in motion, the snow tumbling down the bald face of a mountain in the Northwest, the result of the earth beneath it quaking, a jolt that turned deadly for dozens of people.

Beside these was an empty frame, just waiting for something to fill it, waiting for June 21, for the next disaster in the next city that would claim the next however many lives.

"It's somewhat of a hobby for me," London explained, like the curator of an art exhibit.

"Destroying cities?" Ruby asked in an acid tone, sounding braver than she felt. "You must be so proud."

He swiveled to face them again. "I am, actually," London said. "Not a bad collection, don't you think?"

Ruby glanced over at Simon, whose face had drained of color. Even though Otis and Daisy had told them about these, it wasn't the same as seeing the evidence displayed with pride across the wall of an office. Ruby understood how badly Simon had been wanting to cling to the idea of the wizard they'd met on the road that night, the one who promised to share all his secrets. But there was no longer any way to deny that the man before them was cruelly calculating, and when Simon's eyes met hers, they were full of panic.

Now, finally — perhaps too late — he was realizing just how wrong he'd been.

Ruby turned back to London, blazing with a sudden anger. "So a few people forget to recycle, and you go ahead and wipe out their whole town?" she asked, her voice louder than intended. "Just like that? Just for sport? How is that fair? The whole point of the Society is not to do any harm. You're the Chairman. Doesn't that mean anything?"

Beside her, Ruby could feel Simon bracing himself for the response, but London looked nothing if not amused by her outburst.

"It's just as well that you didn't end up with your brother's powers," he said with a little smile. "You'd be a chore to control."

Ruby glared at him, but said nothing.

"As for the rest of it, I have my reasons," he continued, rising from his chair. He rested both palms on the desk and leaned across it. "The only thing reliable about weather is that there's always a cause, and there's always an effect. Let's just say I prefer being the cause."

"What's that supposed to mean?" Simon asked, and London smiled thinly.

"It means that we can either be a tool or a shield," he said. "We can either get behind a storm and help it to hammer a city, or we can try to stand in its way, to lessen the winds and mute the rains. Which is what Storm Makers have always done in the past."

"So why not now?" Ruby asked, and London frowned.

"Because shields don't always work," he said. "And hammers always do."

"But that's not the point," Simon said. "You're supposed to help people. You're supposed to use your power to stop them from getting hurt, not to hurt them even worse. Why would you—"

London cut him off. "No use explaining to you, I suppose," he said, turning back to the photographs on the wall, evidence of his handiwork. "From what I've heard, you haven't been making much weather at all. Which doesn't make you a particularly effective hammer *or* a shield. But that's not important. All that matters now is that you *have* done it, and so theoretically you *can* do it. And most important, that you're incredibly, impossibly young."

"I'm not going to help you," Simon said as London lowered himself back into the chair. "I'm not."

"That makes no difference at this point," he said lightly, as if they were discussing something far more mundane, a change in scheduling or a food preference. There was a calmness to him now that made him seem far more crazy than he had even when he'd been conjuring flames out in the fields. "Everything's already in motion."

"But why?" Ruby asked, the words emerging thickly. "Why go to all this trouble?"

"Why?" London said, but there was an edge to his voice now. "I guess your new friends didn't tell you the whole story."

"Otis and Daisy?" Simon asked, and Ruby pictured the note she'd slipped through the door of the garage, just one line — *Gone to Chicago* — but more than enough to tell the whole story, if only Daisy had found it.

Please, she thought, squeezing her eyes shut. *Please let her have found it.*

London was watching them with an unreadable expression, his forehead creased in thought. After a moment, he lifted his hand and hit a button on his phone. Seconds later, the door opened with a click that made both Ruby and Simon jump.

"Summer," said London, his voice oddly bright. "May we have some tea and lemonade?"

In the doorway, the receptionist from out front had

appeared, and Ruby could see that she was practically trembling. When their eyes met, she looked quickly away.

"Yes, of course, sir," she said, then stepped out again, shutting the door behind her.

London sat back with a satisfied expression. "I figured some refreshments might be in order," he said. "After all, this is a rather long story."

"What is?" Simon asked, and London closed his eyes.

"The one about how Otis Gray killed my sister."

twenty-six

IT TOOK SEVERAL MINUTES for the tea to be poured, the office quiet but for the low hum of the air-conditioning. London stirred the pot with such a civilized calm that by the time he handed over her mug, Ruby's hand was shaking. The words he'd spoken had completely unnerved her, and they continued to rattle around in her head, filling the weighty silence.

Otis had killed someone.

It didn't seem possible. As she cupped the mug in both

hands, she pictured his face, the kindness she'd so often seen in his gray eyes. She thought of the way he'd spoken to her in the hospital that day, the stark relief she'd felt when he'd reappeared with Daisy at the lake.

But there was a distance to him, too, a sense that even when he was with them, he was also somehow entirely on his own. And what did she really even know about him, anyway? That he'd once been a great Tracker of rookie Storm Makers. That he disagreed with London's philosophy. But where had he been all these years, since he'd fallen away from the Society? What if what London had said was true? What if it turned out that Otis had been on the run for something as unimaginable as killing someone? Ruby had been so quick to trust him, to convince Simon of it, too. But what if she'd been wrong after all?

London's eyes met hers, as if he could read her thoughts. When he was finished pouring the last cup of tea, he set the pot down—the noise loud in the quiet room—and sat back in his chair. As he went to take a sip, he flinched at the temperature, and then quickly bent his head to blow on it. To their surprise, what emerged was a puff of crystallized air that seemed to hover above the mug for a moment, creating a thin sheen of ice on top of the hot liquid. Steam rose off it in a cloud before quickly disappearing.

London raised the cup to his lips once more, and this time, he smiled. "Much better," he said with a nod. "Now, to Otis. I suppose, since you've chosen to throw your lot in with him, that you're at least aware that we used to be best friends?"

Ruby sat very still, but Simon managed to shake his head.

"And you must know that he used to be married to my sister?"

Again, neither of the twins spoke. Ruby adjusted her grip on the mug.

"And, because he's your mentor—because he's taken it upon himself to insert himself into something that he has no business being involved in—he probably also told you that almost five years ago, during a forest fire that he'd been called in to prevent, he—stupidly, danger-ously, and against every rule we have—brought along my non–Storm Maker sister, who was killed by the flames because she couldn't protect herself?"

There was a long silence, in which Ruby held her

breath. London was studying them from across the desk with an odd look in his eyes; where there should be sadness and grief, there was only a burning anger. In the tightness of his mouth, the flintiness of his eyes, there was a kind of seething, and this was more frightening than all the rest of it.

Ruby swallowed hard. "Why?" she asked. "Why would Otis bring her?"

"Because," London said, setting his cup down hard on the desk, "she was his wife."

Whatever last scraps of calm had been holding him together now seemed to snap entirely, and he stood up and placed his hands on the table, his knuckles going white.

"He was my best friend, and she was his wife," he repeated, his voice choked. "And she died in a fire that was *his* job to prevent, in a place where she wasn't supposed to be." He banged a palm against the desk, rattling the china cups, rippling the tea in its pot. "Because he was always a hotshot. He always thought he was the best, that he could get away with anything."

Ruby and Simon sat frozen as London whirled around, stepping up close to the photographs on the wall, so close they must have been nothing but a blur to him.

"But he didn't get away with *that*," he said, his head bent. "And he's not finished paying for it yet."

Ruby had the sudden and ridiculous urge to comfort him then, as he stood there with his shoulders hunched, the pain in his voice breaking through all the anger. She tried to picture what had happened that day, a blazing fire and a helpless woman, smoke thick as fog and Otis trying to keep it all back like it was something that could be stopped. But as horrible as it was—and it *was* horrible; it was heartwrenching and awful—Ruby knew deep down that it was more than that: It was reckless.

No wonder London hated him.

No wonder Otis had disappeared.

There were so many questions crowding Ruby's head that she wasn't even sure where to begin: Why had Otis let his wife come with him that day if he knew he might not be able to protect her? Why did he hate London so much, when it was London who had every right to be angry with *him*? How could they let so many other people get hurt, let so many other tragedies occur, all because of an old grudge? And what did Simon have to do with all this?

But before she could ask anything, Simon spoke up.

"I don't get it," he said, and when London turned around again, his face was composed.

"What?" he asked, his voice like ice.

"She died in a fire..." Simon began, then trailed off.

Behind the desk, London stiffened.

"So wouldn't you want to be the guy who stops fires now?" Simon asked, sitting forward so that the tea sloshed in his cup. "I mean, instead of making all these other disasters, wouldn't you want to be the one to stop them? So that other people don't get hurt that way, too? Sort of in honor of your sister?"

London's eyes snapped up at this. "In honor of my sister?"

Simon nodded, but less certainly now.

"In honor of my sister," London repeated, but this time his voice was low, and it was almost as if he found this funny. He turned back to the photos and his voice drifted behind him. "I've found another way to honor my sister," he said. "My own sort of anniversary."

"A disaster on every solstice," Ruby said, having found her voice again. "We know what you've been doing."

London laughed, a high, thin sound. "I wouldn't give yourself too much credit," he said, spinning around again, motioning to the frames on the wall. "I haven't exactly made a secret of it."

"But why?" Ruby couldn't help asking. She'd set her teacup on the desk and was now gripping the edges of the chair, her hands sweaty, her muscles tense. She felt like she was in the middle of some kind of riddle, and she couldn't quite see her way to the answer.

"She died on the summer solstice, the longest day of the year," London said, stepping out from behind the desk to pace around the edges of the room, lingering near the bookshelves. "So I decided to work my way back up to this day—the grand finale, if you will. One disaster each year. And I started with New Orleans, as a tribute to our friend Otis. What better way to begin than to cause a massive hurricane in his hometown?"

Ruby's eyes trailed over to the photo of the devastation, the city underwater, the roads turned to rivers, and she shuddered.

"And then the next year, the blizzard in Boston, which is where Sophie and Otis met," he said, half turning to face them. "They were in college there together, before either of us flared up. We all were." He began to walk again, his eyes very far away. "And then last year, the earthquake in Colorado. Which is, of course, where they got married. Seemed only fitting."

"And this year?" Ruby asked, her stomach churning. She wasn't sure she wanted to know the answer.

"This year?" London said, crossing the room to stand in between the two chairs where Simon and Ruby sat, so that they had to swivel to look at him. Framed by the lights from the ceiling above, his face looked almost ghostly, and a thin smile formed on his lips. "This year is fire, of course."

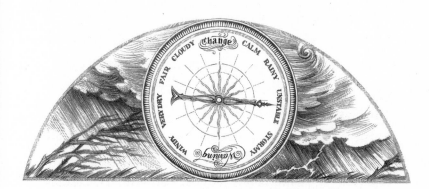

twenty-seven

RUBY FOUND A CRACK IN THE CEILING, a spidery little thread of a thing, and she fixed her eyes on that as London spoke, because it was easier that way; it was easier not to have to watch his coal-black eyes, or see the photographs on the wall, evidence of his even blacker heart. It was easier to pretend none of this was happening, none of it at all.

Every now and then, she blinked back the tears that kept threatening to spill over, but other than that, her face remained unchanged; blank and unmoving and entirely numb.

Because the things London was saying were almost too big to imagine, even in spite of all the other too-big-to-imagine things that had happened over the past week and a half.

He told them about the drought back home, how he'd ordered it earlier in the summer, even before he knew about Simon. He told them how the land was now primed to burn, a sprawling tinderbox just waiting to ignite—not just there, but in other places, too: in Texas and in Florida, in Arizona and in Iowa. And, of course, in California, where it had all started, where his sister had died, turning a promising young Storm Maker into this: a man twisted by grief and bent on revenge; a man willing to kill so many others just to make himself feel less powerless.

"A hurricane in New Orleans," he was saying, as Ruby eyed the ceiling with an intensity that matched her fear, that echoed the whiteness of her knuckles and the trembling of her fingers, "a hurricane in New Orleans is nothing compared to what I've got planned."

Beside her, Ruby could hear Simon's leg bobbing, a nervous habit that sounded loud in the quiet room, but still she kept her eyes trained on the ceiling.

"That first one was all me, though," London continued. "I hadn't gathered enough of a following for anything too elaborate yet. And though I did have some help the past couple of years, with the blizzard and the earthquake, I needed to build up to this last one. I needed the whole Society on board for the grand finale."

"So why do you need me?" Simon asked, a challenge in his voice.

Ruby was busy wondering whether Otis knew about this, and if so, why he'd wasted the past few days trying to help Simon make it drizzle, when he should have been down here putting a stop to everything. But as Simon spoke, she finally lowered her chin, letting the crack on the ceiling out of her sight, and she gazed across the desk at London, who was watching her levelly, his hands clasped in front of him.

"I *don't* need you," he said. "At least not yet. *You* came to *me*, remember?"

Ruby felt her cheeks flush at this, because it was true, and it was hard now to remember the logic, to recall why it had seemed like a good idea to agree to Simon's plan in the first place.

But here they were.

"Of course, I was going to be needing Simon soon enough for a little physics experiment, of sorts, anyway," he said. "So you're not entirely off base. But the two things are unrelated."

"What two things?" Ruby asked, but even as she did, London's eyes drifted to the wall behind her; when she swiveled to follow his gaze, she saw only a clock. There were the usual three arrows—the steady hour hand, the faithful minute hand, and a second hand that thrummed as fast as Ruby's own heart—but the outer rim was decorated with degrees rather than numbers, an *N* where the twelve should be, an *S* to mark the six.

It looked, she realized, like a compass.

And all at once, she understood what London was planning to do with Simon, why he needed him so badly despite his lack of weather skills, why Otis was trying so hard to protect him.

She knew.

It was clear that London had seen the light go on

behind her eyes, that flicker of recognition, because he smiled a slow-blooming smile.

"You're smarter than you first appear," he said. "So is that how it works? Your brother gets all the power and you get all the brains?"

"What is he talking about?" Simon asked, turning to Ruby, his eyes wide with confusion.

London laughed. "You're not exactly the prodigy everyone thinks you are," he said, then shook his head. "But no matter. As long as they keep thinking that, it doesn't make a difference." He raised his eyes and regarded Simon for a long moment. "You do at least know what a physics experiment is, don't you?"

Simon frowned at him, unsure how to answer this.

"Stop it," Ruby said. But neither of them so much as blinked; London was still waiting, and Simon wasn't saying anything, and so after a moment, she sighed. "It's a method of investigating a principle of physics."

"Very good," London said. "And let me guess which one of you can tell me what sort of instrument determines direction relative to the Earth's magnetic poles?"

Ruby felt a prickle along the back of her neck, and her

throat suddenly felt too tight, because now she knew for sure.

The silence lengthened as Simon squirmed in his chair and London leaned forward, but all Ruby could think was that she was right.

And she wished more than anything that she wasn't.

London lifted his hand, and then, as if swatting a fly, he brought it down hard against the cherry-colored desk, causing a pile of papers at one end to shift toward the edge.

"What," he began, his words measured, "is the answer?"

Ruby took a deep breath. "A compass," she whispered, and London beamed at her.

"Exactly right," he said, his eyes sliding over to Simon. "A compass. And in which direction does a compass point?"

"North?" Simon ventured, and London banged his fist against the desk again, causing the whole thing to quiver this time.

"Wrong!" London shouted. "Wrong, wrong, wrong."

Ruby looked frantically at Simon, who was scrambling to his feet. As soon as he was out of the chair, London stood, too, moving around the desk in a smooth motion, sleek and quick as a cat. In her struggle to get up, Ruby knocked over her chair, and she tripped backward on it, barely managing to stay on her feet. A moment later, she felt London's hand—cool as ice—on the back of her neck, and with his other hand gripping Simon, he began pushing them toward the door.

"The compass does *not* always point north," he continued. "It points to the one who is meant to be Chairman. And every day of every week for the past four years, it has pointed at *me*."

"So?" Simon practically spat, and the question caused London to pause long enough for Ruby to twist out of his grasp. Simon's head was bowed, London's grip still like a yoke around his neck, but to their surprise, London dropped his hand, and Simon was able to duck away, too. They stood there like that, the twins with their backs to the door, London's arms at his sides, the three of them simply watching one another.

"So," London said, "my time will be up soon. No Chairman has ever held the position for more than four years."

"But you're not ready to step down," Ruby guessed, and when he nodded, she shook her head. "I don't get it. You've broken every other rule. Why not this one?"

"This one," he said, "has been a little bit trickier to get around."

"But you've found a way."

"I have indeed," he said. "Which is where Simon comes in."

Ruby watched as Simon walked right up to London, his mouth set in a thin line of determination. "You want to use me," he said. "You want to rig the compass, make me the next Chairman, so that you can control me and keep doing all these awful things."

"Everyone thinks you're the next great Storm Maker. And they believe what they want to believe," London said airily, stepping around Simon as if he were nothing more than an inconvenient obstacle in the road.

"I'm not helping you," Simon said. "I'm not."

Even though she'd known this, even though she'd been so certain, it still shocked Ruby to hear it said aloud, to see her brother—with his knobby knees and too-big T-shirt, his spiky hair out of place—standing there announcing to this man that he would not be pushed into being some kind of puppet, that he would not be used in this way, that he would not become the Chairman of the Society of Storm Makers for the wrong reasons.

She looked from London to Simon, who were locked in an even stare, and thought desperately of Otis and Daisy, the question pulsing through her head over and over again, like a ticker, like a heartbeat: *Where are they? Where are they? Where are they?*

"I'm sorry to disagree," London said, still focused on Simon. "But you're just wasting my time now, and we have things to do."

He raised his hand and then, with a flick of his wrist, brought it down again. Ruby's mouth fell open as she watched her brother drop to the floor with a cry of pain. He rolled onto his side and grabbed hold of first one foot, then the other, howling as he did, and Ruby slid onto the carpet beside him, unsure what to do.

"What's wrong?" she asked. "What happened?"

Simon's face was red and twisted. "I don't know," he said, holding one of his feet and staring at the place where he'd been standing. "He burned me."

London stood watching them impassively. "Are we ready?"

It wasn't a question; Ruby knew at least that much. It was a demand, and there was nothing to do but help Simon up, draping his arm over her shoulders to help him walk on his scorched feet. He stepped gingerly across the carpet, and with each step, Ruby's mind worked frantically to figure out a plan.

She couldn't let them make it to the compass, couldn't watch it turn for Simon—whether because he was truly meant to be the next Chairman or because London had somehow rigged it. He was too young, too new, too powerless not to fall under London's control. And the only thing worse than watching London destroy all these cities and towns would be to watch him force Simon to do so along with him.

As they followed London out the door, Simon leaning on Ruby's arm and limping, they were greeted by rows of anxious faces, each of them a blur as they walked past one cubicle after another. There were probably close to a hundred in all, and from her conversations with Daisy and Otis, she knew they were a collection of the most esteemed Storm Makers in the country. Directors of Land Movement and Water-Related Disasters, Secretaries of Floods and Volcanic Eruptions.

The look of anger on London's face seemed to be lifting, replaced by a kind of showman's smile as they made their way through the crowd. They passed a big-shouldered man who tipped his cap at them, his face bowed reverentially. "Good man, Smalls," London said, patting him on the shoulder as they passed, then nodding at a woman in a black dress who was beaming up at him. With each step, he seemed to soak up the attention of his audience, waving at his followers like a politician.

"Cheers, sir," said a skinny man in a bow tie, the words shaped by an accent, and when they passed him, a little rain cloud sprouted over his head, dousing him in a brief drizzle before disappearing entirely. The man simply took off his glasses, wiped them on his shirt, and resumed studying his shoes.

London glanced down at Ruby and Simon. "Ward's with us on an exchange program," he told them, suddenly as friendly as a tour guide. "He has a propensity for rain, which is typical of the BPA, I'm afraid."

"The BPA?" Simon asked warily.

"The British Precipitation Association," London explained. "One of our many overseas organizations."

It was obvious that London was enjoying this, and Ruby could see the way certain Storm Makers gravitated toward him. But there were others who hung back, shuffling their feet nervously and exchanging subtle glances.

Ruby had been so busy wondering if they could tell how scared she and Simon were that it only now occurred to her that they looked just as frightened. Otis and Daisy had been right after all: Not everyone here was as convinced of London's philosophy as it would seem.

When they'd reached an open area of the office, London paused, giving everyone a chance to gather around.

"We're a few days ahead of schedule," he said, his voice booming, "but since we've been graced with a visit from our newest and youngest Storm Maker, I thought it might be an opportune time to visit the compass."

A hum seemed to vibrate through the crowd, everyone murmuring to one another. The whole place was tinged with nervousness and confusion, but there was something else, too, an undercurrent that Ruby could just barely detect: hope.

"As dictated by tradition, everyone is welcome to observe," he said. "And you all may take the opportunity to circulate the compass yourselves." He paused here, and looked around with a smile. "Sometimes leaders appear in unexpected places." He placed one hand on Simon's shoulder and the other on Ruby's, his fingers digging into her skin, which burned beneath his touch. "But in this case, I think we all suspect the outcome, which would be a truly auspicious beginning for our young prodigy."

A few people clapped, a small smattering of applause led by three men and a sharp-faced woman who had moved up front, all of them still beaming at London. Their pins glinted in the fluorescent lights of the office, and their smiles looked plastic, stretched wide over too-white teeth. Others began to step out of their offices, too, more tenatively, all of them falling into step behind the little trio as they began to walk again.

Ruby looked around wildly, trying to get her bearings in the maze of box-shaped cubicles, searching desperately for the entrance, or for an escape route of some sort. When at last they reached the hallway that led back out to the receptionist's desk, Ruby glanced over at Simon. Their eyes met, and in that moment, she knew that they understood each other perfectly.

"This way, this way," London said, about to steer them in the opposite direction, toward the heavy gray door with the little symbol. It was then that Simon gritted his teeth, planted one of his sore feet, and with the other one kicked the back of London's heel so that his foot knocked into his other leg, sending him reeling. At the same time,

Ruby gave him an extra shove to propel him forward, and then she grabbed Simon's arm, and the two of them wheeled around, ready to run.

A gasp went up from the assembled crowd, and in the confusion the twins were able to dart around the three burly men who had been trailing London like oversized rats. The rest of the crowd seemed to part at once, leaving a narrow path to the exit, and to Ruby's surprise, she found that not only were they allowing them to escape, they were actually urging them on.

"Hurry," yelled the woman who had been smiling so adoringly at London earlier, and two men in skinny ties shouted "Go!" as they ran. Ruby glanced back only once, and it was to see London struggling to his feet, screaming at his followers, his society, his people, most of whom had closed in again, making it difficult for him to get past.

"Stop them!" he yelled, his voice carrying over the noise. But they were already gone, moving fast down the hallway, with nothing ahead of them. Ruby's heart was bobbling around in her chest as she strained to keep up with Simon, who was quick in spite of his burned feet, and when they were nearly to the exit, both of them glancing desperately at the woman behind the reception desk, she punched a button and the glass doors at the end of the office slid open.

Breathing hard, they charged back through the narrow entrance and over to the elevator. Ruby hadn't had a chance to think this entirely through, and she realized now that she didn't know where the stairs were, so if the elevator wasn't there, they'd be trapped.

But in this, too, they were lucky; just as they rounded the corner, the man with the bright red hair threw open the heavy grate, motioning them on. Without a word, he let go of the handle, turning to punch a button on the panel. Simon leaned against the side of the car and let out a breath, and Ruby put her hands on her knees, the knot of terror loosening inside her.

But then a hand caught the grate in the split second before it slammed shut, heaving it back open again, and suddenly London was inside with them, his hair now disheveled, his face scarlet with anger. He stood facing the front without looking at them. "Rooftop, please," he said in a low, gravelly voice.

As Ruby felt the elevator come to life with a jolt, she closed her eyes, the world once again wildly unsteady beneath her.

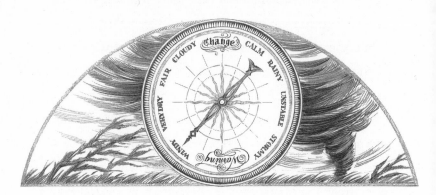

twenty-eight

WHEN HE WAS LITTLE, Simon was afraid of escalators. There was something about the appearance of the steps, each one with its own little set of metal teeth, the whole thing moving around and around like a song on endless loop. Mom and Dad had tried everything—carrying him on their hip, lifting him onto the first step, holding his hand while they counted to three before encouraging him to kick out one tentative foot, like testing the water before jumping into the pool—but none of it worked.

Simon would just hang back nervously, refusing to have anything to do with it, his eyes large in his pale face.

But one day, near Christmastime, as Mom and Dad tried to coax him onto the escalator at a department store, Ruby simply took his hand in hers and began to lead him away. They marched past the makeup counters with their clouds of perfume, past the stiff-looking Christmas tree with its painstakingly placed ornaments, past the menswear section, where the neckties hung like streamers from the walls. Ruby didn't have to look back to know that Mom and Dad were behind her, following closely, and she led them all around the corner to where she'd glimpsed an elevator earlier.

Simon looked so plainly relieved at the sight of the shiny metal doors that Dad could only laugh, but Mom bent down so that her face was close to Ruby's.

"It's nice of you to take care of your brother," she said softly, so that no one else could hear; Simon was busy jabbing at the up button. "But he's going to have to do it eventually. If you don't face your fears, how can you ever get over them?"

The doors to the elevator dinged open, and Ruby pointed. "You just find another way up," she said as

Simon bounded inside, punching the button for the second floor.

From inside the elevator, Dad had his foot wedged against the door to hold it open. But Mom was still watching Ruby with an odd expression, a look of amusement in her eyes.

"Find another way up," Mom murmured after a moment, placing a hand on Ruby's back to guide her onto the elevator. "I guess I hadn't thought of it that way."

But that had always been how Ruby's mind seemed to work; if there were two possible answers to a problem, either A or B, then Ruby was always on the lookout for C. If the escalator wasn't going to work, there must always be an elevator somewhere.

There was always another way up.

And now, standing grimly beside her brother in a different elevator—this one far less festive, far less inviting— Ruby found herself thinking again of that moment.

Nobody had said a word since the elevator had begun its slow climb, and this was more unnerving than anything else. London remained at the very front, standing absolutely still, his hands clasped behind his back as he watched each floor slip by through the slats in the grate.

The red-haired man leaned into the corner, his considerable weight cushioning him, and he had one hand resting on the emergency lever. Ruby kept cutting her eyes in his direction, willing him to pull it, but his gaze was fixed on the floor, his eyebrows lifting anxiously now and then.

Beside her, Simon had gone as jittery as a mouse. Whatever defiance he'd shown to London's face seemed to disappear as soon as the man turned his back, and now one of his eyelids was twitching. Ruby let out a deep breath as they passed the twelfth floor. It felt a bit like they were on a roller coaster, those moments of churning anticipation, her insides like something coiled and ready to spring, though she was pretty sure there was nothing good at the end of this ride, no free-falling, cartwheeling glee.

Even so, with each passing minute, she felt a great calm begin to overtake her. Somewhere around the eighteenth floor, Simon's breathing started to become raspy, a choked wheeze that nobody else seemed to notice. But at the same time, Ruby could sense a kind of steadiness of her own, and the clanging of the elevator as it rose seemed to tap into something deep inside her, a calming rhythm as clear as Morse code, constant as a drum and true as a heartbeat. Up they climbed, the numbers painted on each floor moving into the twenties, and then the thirties, and finally the forties.

Beyond this, at the very top, the elevator slowed and then jerked to a stop. It was enough to unbalance Simon, who half fell into Ruby. The elevator operator clearly wasn't sure what to do now that they'd arrived, and so he continued to hover near the emergency brake, despite the fact that they were already stopped. When the metal had quit shuddering and the elevator car had gone still, London spun around.

"Come with me," he said, as if they had another choice, and then he flung open the grate, turning around only once to give the red-haired man a hard look, in case he had any notion of following them, too. He didn't; the moment Ruby and Simon had stepped out of the elevator to where London was waiting in an area the size of a closet, the gate banged shut behind them and the man wrenched at the down lever.

The three of them stood and watched as he was lowered back into the building, disappearing from view a slice at a time, first his feet, then his knees, and so on until all they could see were his eyes, watery and nervous. And then they were gone, too.

Simon seemed to have regained some of his courage, and he was now glowering at London, his face dark. Ruby had only a moment to glance around at the concrete walls of the vestibule before London yanked open a heavy gray door marked NO ADMITTANCE and a blast of wind rushed in, forcing them to shield their eyes.

London waited, holding it open, and after exchanging a glance with Ruby, Simon went first, moving tentatively out onto the blackened surface of the roof, hundreds of feet in the air, where only the very tops of the other skyscrapers interrupted the cloudless sky.

The wind continued to whip at them, stinging Ruby's eyes, and she squinted at London as he began to walk over to the ledge, his dark jacket flapping wildly behind him. When he was near the wall, he turned around and crooked a finger at them, and Ruby and Simon—still rooted in place near the door—reluctantly picked their way across the uneven surface of the roof, hovering a few feet back from the edge.

"Do you know why I brought you up here?" he asked, his voice raised against the wind.

"To toss us over the side of the building?" Simon suggested.

London smiled. "So that you could see all this."

"We've already seen it," Ruby said. "Nobody's in the mood for sightseeing."

"Come," London said, laying a spindly hand on the wall, and it seemed they had no other choice but to inch over to the edge, where a concrete barrier that came up to their necks surrounded the periphery of the roof.

Taking a deep breath, Ruby looked out across the city, the dazzling height of the buildings, the shining surfaces turning the sunlight to splinters. When she glanced over at Simon, she could see that his eyes were busy at the horizon, and Ruby followed his gaze to the great expanse of Lake Michigan, vast as an ocean and silvery as a coin.

The wind whistled and the building moaned, but otherwise there was nothing; Ruby couldn't even hear herself breathe, and so she was surprised when a sound drifted up from below, faint and thin. She rose onto her tiptoes to see what it was.

At first there was only the dizzying drop and the steep angle of the building, forty-seven floors of sheer distance. But when she looked again, craning her neck to the left, she saw two men balanced on a narrow platform with railings on all sides, washing the windows just a few floors down. The whole thing was rigged up to a series of cables with a pulley to send them up and down the building, and they were laughing as they scrubbed at the windows, as if they were hundreds of feet below, their feet firmly on the ground. Ruby stepped away from the ledge, feeling light-headed, and she saw that Simon had done the same.

"You see that?" London said, pointing at a few thin columns of smoke in the distance, off to the south of the city. "That's why I brought you up here."

"What is it?" Simon asked.

"It's just one example," he explained, pacing near the edge of the building. "Just one of the many examples of how people are destroying this planet. They cut down the forests, and then act surprised when there's erosion. They pump smoke and chemicals into the atmosphere, and then can't believe that the climate is changing." He paused to look at them, his eyes glinting. "When Sophie died, it was Otis's fault for taking her there, and then for not getting her out. But it was also the idiot who threw a cigarette into the woods," he said. "And this is why they need to be taught a lesson."

Simon looked impatient. "If you care so much about

the Earth, why not show people how to take care of it, instead of making it worse?"

"Why should I help them?" London said, spinning around to face the city, so that his words were whipped behind them. "Nobody has helped me." He stood there for a moment, his hands on the ledge, his shoulders rounded. And when he turned around again, he was smiling. "Except you."

Ruby took a small step backward. "We're not helping you."

"No," he agreed. "*You're* not. But Simon will. As soon as that compass spins, we'll begin our work together."

"No," Simon said, the word landing heavily between them. He stepped forward until he was only a few feet from London, and he stood there glaring at him, his feet braced and his T-shirt blowing around his skinny frame. His eyes blazed, and he looked so angry that for a moment, Ruby could almost see what everyone was talking about, the potential in Simon, the possibility of greatness, the magic of it all. But then the wind fell abruptly all around them, the world going still, and he was just a boy again, his hands clenched into fists, his chin jutted angrily.

"I'm sorry," London said, waving a hand around him, and Ruby realized that he was the one who'd stopped the wind, and the magnitude of that—of that one impossible act—settled heavily over her. He tilted his head at Simon. "I couldn't quite hear you with all that noise."

But Simon didn't answer. Instead, he raised his hands the way he had that night on the road, and with his eyes squeezed shut, he snapped them in London's direction, a movement so purposeful, so powerful and full of intent, that Ruby was almost more stunned that nothing happened than she might have been if something had.

But it was indeed nothing, and Simon dropped his hands again in defeat.

London began to laugh. "And what was that supposed to be?" he asked. "Rain? Snow? Lightning? Wind?" At this last word, right on cue, the wind picked up again, so suddenly that Ruby stumbled forward as the pressure built at her back. London's smile remained frozen as he watched. "You should be thanking me," he said to Simon. "You've got hardly an ounce of natural skill, and here I'm trying to make you the youngest ever Chairman of the Makers of Storms Society. Who wouldn't want that?"

"You mean who wouldn't want to be your little puppet?" Simon shot back.

London simply shook his head, still chuckling. "You're no better than your sister," he said, and this time, when Simon lifted his hands again, a fleeting thought crossed Ruby's mind, a possibility that was horrible and thrilling at once, but tempting enough to make her linger on it for the briefest of moments. She looked at London, leaning there against the ledge with a manic grin, and she wondered what it would take to tip him right over the edge.

The wind was coming in from the west, rushing out toward the lake, and the numbers came to her almost automatically as her eyes bored a hole through him: speed of the wind, and weight of the object, and amount of leverage, plus a jumble of other calculations and factors, variables and measurements.

All this, in the seconds that passed while her brother—gathering himself, angling his hands, muttering something under his breath—aimed all of his concentration at that very same man. And with the quickest flash of movement, to Ruby's great surprise, it worked this time, and he seemed to channel the wind, directing it sideways at London, who—with a look of shock—was knocked backward, falling against the wall with his hands up, as if trying to block some invisible opponent.

And then, just like that, the wind died again.

Everything happened fast after that. Simon was still staring at his hands in amazement when London staggered to his feet and lunged at him. Ruby let out a yell that sounded as if it should have come from someone else, then threw herself at London's back, where he had Simon pinned to the ground, a big hand around his neck.

Simon's face was turning a deep red, and the only thing Ruby could think to do was grab London's tie and pull hard. A fog seemed to roll in all around them then, though where it came from Ruby couldn't be sure, and she heard voices behind them, halfway across the roof. Before she even had a chance to register who it was, whether they were friends or enemies, Storm Makers or just regular old people, she felt herself being hauled away from London, still clinging to his tie so that his face went purple, and he let out a gargling sound as he tried to claw at her.

"Let go," someone said, but Ruby held on, her teeth clenched. Through blurry eyes, she could see that someone else had Simon by the foot and was trying to wrestle him away from London, whose hand was still at his throat, and it wasn't until she saw his fingers go slack that Ruby dropped the tie. London slumped to the ground, breathing hard, and then it was Otis—Otis!—who pulled Simon a safe distance away, putting himself between them before turning to face London again.

Ruby whirled around to find Daisy, and she felt weak with relief, her legs wobbly and a lump forming in her throat. But Daisy said nothing, only moved out in front of her so that she was a few feet from Otis, the two of them facing down London, who was now backed into a corner of the roof.

He flashed Otis a smile. "It's been a long time."

"Not long enough," Otis said.

"You've heard about all my efforts, then?" London asked, looking pleased with himself. He flicked his eyes over to Daisy, whose hands were balled into fists. "Your father would have been impressed, no? Not just with my events on the solstices, but also my restoration of the Vacuum..." He turned back to Otis with a wolfish grin. "Perhaps that's something *you'd* like to try?"

Otis didn't even flinch. Instead, he raised one eyebrow in a look of amusement. "I'm not worried about your little machine, Rupert."

London paused for a moment, and a strange smile spread across his face. "I've missed this," he said. "You were always the only one who could best me."

"It was never about beating you," Otis said. "It was about getting good enough to protect people. Or have you forgotten?"

"Have *I* forgotten?"

There were a few beats of calm, the eye of the storm, and then London lunged forward again, a crazy glint in his eye, his arms outstretched. A wall of flame erupted between the two men as London moved forward, and the fire seemed to move with him, almost like it was something alive. The rest of them stumbled backward, but Otis—Otis didn't move a muscle. He should have been backing away; he should have been putting up a wall of wind, a blast of cold air, anything. But he just stood there, his face glowing in the heat as the flames moved closer.

"You were the one who forgot," London said as he stepped closer. "You were the one who stopped protecting someone."

Otis said nothing. He only stared down the wall of fire, his mouth set and his eyes curiously far away.

"And now look at you," London said, drawing near

him. "No fight left in you, old friend? Still haven't learned how to put out a fire?"

Beside Ruby, Daisy was poised to move, her whole body vibrating. Ruby, too, was torn; why wasn't Otis doing anything? He just stood and stood and stood as the flames drew closer. It was maddening and mystifying and brave all at once.

London was laughing now, his voice muffled by the rush of flame. Ruby watched, horrified, as it came within inches of Otis's nose, but the stony look on his face didn't change. She wasn't sure if he was trying to prove a point or just waiting for the right moment to strike. But as the first flames reached him, singeing his eyebrows, Ruby let out an involuntary cry, and it was this that finally shook Daisy into action.

She seemed to coil herself and then unwind again, jerking her head at London, and out of nowhere, out of the clear sky and the thin air, a rush of water met the fire, and Ruby watched in wonder as the whole thing died with a loud hiss.

For a moment, nobody moved. A thin trail of smoke rose between London and Otis, who reached up to remove his hat, examining the brim where it was charred black.

Beside him, Daisy stood breathing hard, her eyes darting from London to Otis and then back again. Time seemed suspended as they waited to see what would happen next.

"This is what you want?" London said finally, cutting his eyes over to Simon and practically spitting the words as he backed up to the ledge. It began to hail then, but irregularly, like something in London had been short-circuited. The pebbles of ice came down in patches from the otherwise clear sky, pinging off the rooftop like crickets. Ruby raised her hands above her head to shield her face, but she could see that London's eyes were focused on Simon with a bright fury as he backed right up to the ledge. "You'd prefer to throw your lot in with a nobody?" he said. "With a coward? With a *murderer*?"

Ruby's eyes traveled to Otis, who still hadn't moved, his whole body rigid, even as the stinging ice fell all around him.

"Fine," London said, hoisting himself up onto the ledge so that he was balancing above the whole of the city. The hailstorm tapered off, the last few pieces rolling to a stop on the speckled roof, and there was now nothing but the wind to surround him. "Best of luck to you."

He swung his legs around so that he was facing away

from them now, poised on the edge, and Daisy took a few frantic steps forward. London half turned, and from over his shoulder, the words sounded thin and distant: "You'll need it," he said, and then like some kind of horrible magic trick—here one moment, gone the next—he disappeared.

The rest of them stood in stunned silence, staring at the empty space where he'd been. Ruby's heart was thrumming like a drill in her chest, and a strange kind of electricity seemed to course through her.

She rushed to the ledge, standing on her tiptoes to peer over. Otis and Daisy were right behind her, and then Simon was there, too, and they all four stared down at London—not forty stories below on the sidewalk, but only a dozen feet down, on the window washers' platform, one of them helping him to his feet while the other gaped at them, his mouth open.

When he was up again, London threw his head back and gave them a jaunty little wave, and then to the utter astonishment of the two men, he lifted a hand and shot a bolt of lightning through one of the windows, the shattering of glass loud even from above.

Then, for the second time in as many minutes, London disappeared.

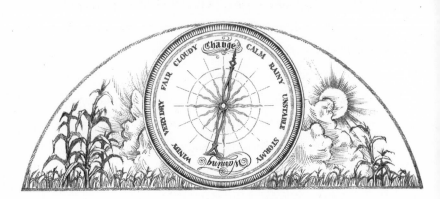

twenty-nine

IT MUST HAVE BEEN SOME TRICK OF TIME that made it seem to Ruby that one moment she'd been standing near the edge of the roof, and the very next she was in the elevator again. It was as if she was simply there, and then not.

Just like London.

The man with the red hair was no longer in the elevator, and so Otis was the one to pull the lever down, setting the car in motion with a heavy sway. Daisy and Simon stood off to the side, both of them looking pale and shaken by what had happened up above. Simon was still rubbing at his neck, as if surprised to find that London's hand was no longer attached to it.

Ruby kept blinking at Otis, trying to figure out which of her many questions to ask first. Now that the elevator was moving, he'd taken the opportunity to reach into his back pocket and pull out the floppy gray hat, but instead of putting it on, he simply clutched it in one large hand, rubbing a thumb over the fabric.

"Thanks for the note," Daisy said from the back corner, and Simon turned sharply to Ruby.

"You left them a note?"

Before she could respond, Otis spun around, his face serious. "And it's a good thing she did," he said. "I don't know what you were thinking, coming down here on your own."

"We were trying to help," Simon said miserably.

"Nobody asked you to do that," Otis said, his voice a low growl. They were passing the twenty-fourth floor, and then the twenty-third, and Ruby wondered what would happen when they got to the bottom.

"You have a plan, though," Simon asked, "right?"

Nobody answered.

They continued to descend, lower and lower, the

silence lengthening. Daisy tugged at one of her braids, and Otis shoved his hat back into his pocket. Ruby pulled out the barometer, looking at it hopefully, but the needle was still aimed at *warning*.

"No change," she said to Otis, who nodded wearily, as if he'd expected as much. Simon glanced over at the little device, then resumed staring at the floor. Two weeks earlier, he would have demanded to see it. Now there were too many other things he'd seen.

As they passed the lobby, Ruby's head began to throb at the thought of returning to headquarters, to whatever might await them there. She'd hoped Otis had planned to take them out a different way, to get out of there as fast as they possibly could, but they continued to drop, past the basement and the sub-basement, the elevator starting to seem too warm, so that despite their destination Ruby couldn't help feeling somewhat relieved when they finally came to a rough stop.

Otis put a hand on the grate, which rattled beneath his touch. "You stay with me, and you do what I tell you, okay?"

He was looking at Simon, but Ruby nodded, too. Neither of them asked what it was they were doing. There was something in Otis's face that told them not to bother.

As they stepped off the elevator one at a time—Otis, followed by Simon, then Ruby, and, finally, Daisy—they were met with a high buzz of voices coming from around the corner. The reception area was empty, the phone ringing without pause, and it looked like a different place altogether than the one they'd seen a short while before.

Beyond the entrance was a crowd of people, the same ones who had watched them earlier, who had trailed them through the office and then let them pass as they ran for the door. Ruby scanned the crowd for London, though she knew he'd be long gone by now; his loyal followers seemed to have disappeared as well. But the rest of them were huddled in small groups, their faces lined with worry. Around them, dozens of weather instruments warbled along unattended, and the binging and beeping of the various radar screens made it sound like they were in an arcade.

But nobody seemed to care. And when they saw Otis marching down the hallway, Simon just a half step behind him, they seemed to take a collective breath, and a hush fell over the office before giving way to a flurry of voices and speculation.

"*Otis Gray?*" asked a man with glasses, his eyes widening behind the lenses. "What are you…?"

A woman in a red suit pushed forward. "Where's the Chairman?"

"And why do you have the boy?" asked someone else, who Ruby couldn't see.

"He's back," others cried, their voices heavy with shock. "He's back!"

The questions came swiftly, but Otis made no attempt to answer any of them. He just stood there with a hand on Simon's shoulder, his eyes flicking back and forth through the crowd of his former colleagues, who were wedged into office doorways and around cubicles, all of them looking at him eagerly.

One man raised a weather vane in the air to call attention to himself, waving the rusted rooster until Otis cleared his throat and the others fell silent. When he stepped forward, Ruby saw that it was the elevator operator.

"Hello, Ned," Otis said, and for the first time, there was a hint of a smile on his face.

"Otis," he said with a nod. "The room's ready for you."

And with that, they were moving again, edging their way through the knot of people. Some of them stepped aside politely, while others looked troubled. "What about the Chairman?" they muttered. "Where's London?"

Daisy's hand was on Ruby's back to guide her, but they paused when a tiny woman, her face heavily mapped with wrinkles, stepped out in front of them. Daisy glanced up at Otis, unsure whether this signaled trouble, but the woman only reached out and touched a hand to Daisy's cheek.

"Your father..." she whispered, her eyes watery. "He was the greatest."

A few people standing nearby exchanged worried glances, and Ruby guessed that you weren't allowed to praise the former Chairman when you had a current one like Rupert London. But the woman was fumbling with the storm-cloud pin on her sweater, and when she had unclasped it she reached for Daisy's hand, pressing it into her palm.

"He hasn't been forgotten," she said, and around her, others began to do the same, slowly at first, and then all at once, unfastening their own pins from jackets and shirts, sweaters and ties, and lining up to hand them over to Daisy.

"In honor of your dad," one of them said in a voice of great reverence.

"Welcome back," said another, and still others simply murmured, "Thank you."

Ruby looked over at Otis, waiting to see if he'd follow suit, but then she remembered: That day on the farm, when Ruby had found the two pins attached to the collars of the dogs, Daisy had taken hers back wordlessly. But Otis had said the other was Ruby's to keep.

Her hand went to her pocket now. She'd been too embarassed to wear it all this time, knowing that Simon would point out the obvious fact that she wasn't a Storm Maker, but she'd been carrying it around ever since, and she realized now that this tiny piece of metal in her pocket must have been Otis's.

When she looked up, he was smiling at her. He gave a little nod, and Ruby placed it in Daisy's cupped hands, where it belonged.

"Thank you," Daisy whispered. She looked around the room, her eyes glassy. "Thank you all."

Someone handed her a jar that held a small patch of fog, and she dumped the pins inside, the cloud loosening as the metal clinked against the sides. She hugged it close to her as they all began to walk again, falling in behind Otis as he wound his way down the corridor. But as they arrived at a familiar juncture, the whole group at their backs, Simon came to an abrupt halt just ahead of Ruby.

"No," he said quietly, and Otis turned.

"No, what?"

"I don't want to do the compass thing," he said, his voice pleading. "It's not going to be me."

Daisy glanced back at the rest of the office, where everyone had gone quiet again, waiting to see what would happen. But Otis remained still, his eyes focused on Simon's.

"London was going to make me," he said. "Before."

"I know," said Otis.

"Then you know he was going to rig it."

Otis nodded. "Do you know why I came up to find you in the first place?" he asked, and Simon shook his head. "Once you're a Tracker, you've always got that sixth sense. For years, I've been ignoring it. Until you."

Simon swallowed hard, but said nothing.

"I had a feeling you weren't just any rookie. I had a feeling there was a change coming." Otis smiled. "And that change is you."

"But—"

"If it chooses you," Otis said, looking at him levelly, "then it's meant to be. You'd be the rightful Chairman of this Society. No tricks, no schemes. Just you and the compass."

"But there's no way it'll be me," Simon said. "Not without whatever London was planning to do." He dropped his voice so low that Ruby had to strain to hear. "I can't make any weather."

Otis smiled at this. "You just did," he said. "Up on the roof."

Simon still looked unconvinced, but he seemed to be steeling himself to walk into the room anyway. He glanced back at Ruby, who gave him a shaky smile, and then around at the rest of the room, the dozens of faces watching him with a kind of quiet faith.

"Okay," he said finally, and Otis straightened. When he cleared his throat, even Simon tipped his head back to look up at him, this scarecrow of a man, this quiet presence in a room roiling with nerves.

"This is long overdue," he began, and although there were murmurs, even a few muffled grunts, most everyone kept quiet. For the past four years, these had been London's people. But they were first and foremost Storm Makers, sworn to a set of rules that hadn't been followed, forced to carry out damage they might not have otherwise wished to do, and though more than a few seemed unfailingly loyal to London, there was also a feeling of great optimism in the room. Ruby knew that some of the people Otis had been talking about were here, too, the Storm Makers who disagreed with London's philosophies, who'd spent the past four years horrified over all that he'd done.

"I think many of us would agree that we could use a change," Otis continued, his voice echoing across the office floor. "And that the time is now."

"If it spins for Simon now," Ruby whispered to Daisy, "won't London just try it anyway when he comes back?"

"It only spins once every four years, and only for the person who's meant to have the title," she said, her eyes on Otis, who was still speaking to the group. "Always has. Always will. And the compass always has the final word."

"You're all great Storm Makers," Otis was saying. "And this is one of our oldest and proudest traditions. We may have abandoned some of the rest in recent years, but this one remains."

With that, he pulled open the door, which led down a narrow corridor, dark but for a few lamps scattered on either side. Simon was about to step through, but Otis held him back, guiding him so that they were both standing beside the doorway. Ruby looked to Daisy to see whether they were supposed to wait, too, but she was already moving through the entrance, and so with one last encouraging glance at Simon, she followed Daisy into the passageway.

Everyone was silent as they made their way down the long corridor. There was only the whistle of fabric, the pulsing breath of the crowd at their backs, the electric fizz of the dimly lit lamps. At some point, after they'd been walking for what felt like a long time, Daisy dodged sharply to the left. Ruby almost missed the turnoff, but the rest of the group moved seamlessly through the archway, as if they'd done it a thousand times before. By the time Ruby caught up, Daisy was turning the oversized handle on a heavy metal door, sending ripples of excitement through the crowd, everyone murmuring as they filed inside.

Ruby wasn't sure what she'd been expecting, but it wasn't this. In the center of a perfectly rounded room, almost like an arena, stood the most enormous compass she'd ever seen. It was the size of a grand piano, but entirely circular and trimmed in gold, the needle pointing in the direction of the door, due north. There was nothing around it, nothing to distract from its simple beauty, and as the others edged toward the back, making room for more, Ruby stepped forward to take a closer look.

She breathed in as she approached. For the briefest moment, she allowed herself to imagine it spinning for her, the long red needle under the heavy pane of glass following as she made her circle. She felt almost dizzy at the idea of it, the notion that she might be the one with the power, the one to be chosen, the one who would change everything. But even as she stood there, a hand on the cool rim, she knew it was silly to even pretend. It wasn't her. Of course it wasn't her. As she walked back over to stand beside Daisy, the needle remained absolutely still.

Soon, the last of the members of the Society had found their places around the edges of the room, and the brown-black walls seemed to fold everyone in.

"Why is it so...?" Ruby whispered to Daisy, who smiled.

"Simple?" she asked. "Because it's a weatherproof room."

Ruby's eyes traveled from the floor to the ceiling. There was nothing but dark walls and a darker dome above, and the great disc of a compass in the center. "Then how was London going to trick it into picking Simon?"

Daisy gave her head a little shake. "He's probably the only one powerful enough to overcome the room," she said. "Which, in my opinion, is how he got this the first time. But Otis thinks..."

"What?"

Daisy looked down at her. "He thinks London was bluffing. That he wanted Simon to believe he wasn't rightfully chosen, so he'd be indebted to him and remain under his control."

"So that means..."

"That Otis thinks Simon is really the one," she said. "Yeah."

Ruby turned to the door as Otis and Simon appeared, the last two to enter the room. When the black door closed behind them, there was a hiss of air as it sealed itself shut. They stood there for a moment without moving, all eyes upon them.

In the pause that followed, everyone seemed to lean forward. Ruby could tell that Simon was nervous, but he carried himself tall and straight, clearly attempting to play the part of the future leader of the Society of Storm Makers.

There were no more speeches. As everyone watched, Otis nodded, and then placed a hand on Simon's back,

and together, they began to walk. Ruby shut her eyes for a moment, afraid to look—afraid the needle might move, and afraid it might not—but then she forced herself to open them again. And just as she did, she saw it happen: The needle began to wobble, the smallest of vibrations, like a tuning fork, like a breeze.

She held her breath, her eyes wide. As the two of them reached the northwest side, the needle gave a little twitch, as if waking itself up after four long years of sleep, and then it began to move.

Simon was grinning and Otis was nodding, as if he'd known all along. Beside her, Daisy let out a whoop, and the crowd—which had been frozen in stunned silence—did the same, so that the little room was filled with the sound of cheering, all of it for Simon, who was passing just in front of them. Ruby reached out a hand, and he grabbed it as he walked by, his cheeks flushed, then let go again as he moved past.

Otis had stopped to let him finish on his own and was waiting beside Daisy, who couldn't help reaching over and giving him a sideways hug. He ducked his head and looked embarassed, but Daisy only laughed, her eyes still charting Simon's progress.

But as he continued his slow rotation, Ruby noticed what everyone else had missed in their celebrations, and her heart took a sudden dip.

The needle had stopped.

She looked around wildly, her gaze landing on Otis, and it was then that he saw it, too. His eyes widened, and he took an uncertain step forward. And then sideways. And then two steps to the other side. He stared at the compass in astonishment.

Others were beginning to catch on, and the noise in the room seemed to wilt. Simon passed the northeast marking now, headed toward where they'd started, but he hesitated as the crowd went silent, his eyes passing over the compass with a look of understanding.

For a long time, nobody spoke, though the room still seemed to echo with the earlier cheers. Once more, Otis took a huge step sideways. But it didn't change anything.

The needle was still pointing at him.

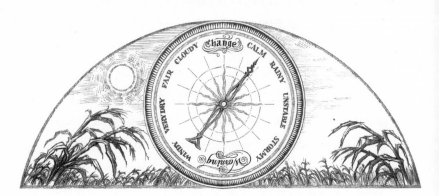

thirty

It was probably dark out by now, but from where Ruby and Simon were sitting—in one of the windowless conference rooms in the underground headquarters—it was impossible to tell. They'd been there for nearly an hour at this point. The receptionist, Summer, who—coincidentally—was hoping to one day become an expert on the vernal equinox, had shown them how to work the remote for the television.

But they were having much more fun poking around

the walls, where instead of photos, there were clear boxes that looked somewhat like fish tanks, only each had a miniature version of a kind of weather inside it. Simon was particularly intrigued by the lightning box, and he kept pressing his nose to the glass to make his hair stand on end from the static electricity. Ruby sat underneath the one that was snowing, watching the flakes building up into drifts halfway up the frame before they all melted and the whole thing started over again.

The door to the conference room was closed, but they could hear footsteps and voices outside, a flurry of activity that had begun moments after the needle spun for Otis. When the commotion in the compass room had died down, there was an unmistakable wave of relief that seemed to pass over everyone, even those who had appeared to be most loyal to London. Ruby could almost see them relaxing again, a weight falling off them after four long years.

Otis had looked more surprised than anyone, and even as the crowd started to drift over to congratulate him, to ask him questions, to beg for favors and make requests, he simply stood there rubbing at his jaw, a look of utter bewilderment on his face.

"He's probably just worried he'll have to start working in an office again," Simon told Ruby now, drawing back from the lightning box, his hair still frizzy.

"What makes you say that?"

"He told me he liked being on the road." He flopped down onto one of the rolling chairs, then pushed off the table, making it spin in circles. "That he liked riding trains and seeing the country and not being tied down. That's what he's been doing for the last four years. Going from place to place, helping out at disaster sites."

"Really?"

Simon nodded. "Cleaning up storms, rebuilding houses after hurricanes, things like that. Oh, and replanting that forest in California."

"What forest?" she asked, though she already knew the answer.

"The one that burned in the fire," he said. "The one where Sophie died."

Ruby watched her brother lean back in the chair. Just an hour before, Simon had been the key to everything, and now he'd been shuttled in here so they'd be out of the way while everyone else got things done. Ruby couldn't believe how fast it had all changed. She waited until

Simon had finished rotating and the chair was still. "Are you sad that it wasn't you?"

He gave her a long look, then shook his head. "I mean, it was fun to think I might be that important," he said. "But I'm actually sort of relieved."

"It would have been a lot to deal with."

"A *lot*," he agreed. "Besides, I'd rather be up in Wisconsin with Mom and Dad than have to worry about all this. Wouldn't you?"

Ruby didn't have a chance to answer because the door to the conference room swung open and Daisy poked her head in. "You two doing okay in here?"

They both nodded, and she slipped inside, collapsing into one of the other chairs at the conference table with a little sigh.

"It's been a *long* day," she said. "I feel like I got your note at the garage about a month ago."

"Is it weird being back here?" Ruby asked.

"It is," she said. "But I'm glad I came."

Ruby smiled. "Me, too."

"Where's Otis?" Simon asked. He'd grabbed a pencil from a canister in the middle of the table and was now absently doodling on a piece of blue paper. Ruby could see that he was sketching out the little emblem on the pins, the storm cloud and lightning bolt. When she looked over at Daisy, Ruby could tell she'd seen it, too.

"He's dealing with some things," she said. "There's a lot to do."

"Is he happy?" Ruby asked. She knew it was an odd question — there was a weather disaster to stop, and an office full of people to direct; London was still out there somewhere, and who knew how many other Storm Makers were still loyal to him. Yet the compass had spun for Otis, and in all the chaos of the day, all the madness, it seemed a kind of miracle.

"I think he's mostly surprised," Daisy said, swiveling in her chair. "Everyone is. I mean, this was what we all expected to happen four years ago, but now ..."

"Four years ago, like when London got picked?"

Daisy nodded. "The two of them were so talented," she said, gazing at the snow frame on the wall. "They were so far above anyone else, and with both of them flaring up around the same time, best friends and everything? It was like they were celebrities. The rest of us were always completely fascinated by them."

Simon was listening raptly, the pencil still in his hand,

and Ruby tried to imagine them together: Otis, with his weather-beaten face and wrinkled hat, and London, with those dark eyes and even darker suits. Something about the image just refused to match up.

"But even before Otis married Sophie," Daisy continued, "they started to grow apart. London began hanging around with some other guys, the kind who got a real kick out of their powers and didn't exactly use them responsibly. They started helping London with his first disasters, back when not everyone would bow to his pressure yet."

Ruby frowned, and in the brief silence, they could hear a tiny rumble of thunder from one of the frames, no louder than the purr of a cat. Daisy shook her head, as if to loosen her thoughts.

"Then Sophie died, and London blamed Otis, and it got worse between them. But when my father had his heart attack, and it was time to choose a new Chairman, everyone sort of expected it to be Otis. Of the two, he'd always had a slight advantage in power, and he was the one everyone really wanted. He just seemed more like a leader, you know?"

They both nodded; they did know.

"But he disappeared after the fire, and it was London who was chosen. Some people think it was rightfully so; others think maybe he somehow rigged it. And some believe he was just so charged with grief from Sophie's death that it was enough to move the needle on its own. But either way, the compass chose him, and the rest, as they say, is history."

"It should have been Otis," Ruby said, a spark of anger rising inside her.

"A lot of people thought that," Daisy agreed. "From the moment London started, the whole Society was divided. And even though most of them — the ones who believed in Otis, and who believed in my father before that — ended up eventually being forced to go along with London's plans, they were always hoping for change to come. So you can see what it meant for Otis to walk back in here today. What it meant that he was finally the one chosen. They've been waiting all this time. Since the day London became Chairman."

"Which is when you left," Simon said, and Daisy nodded.

"Which is when I left. I never trusted him. Neither did my dad. And I had a way out. I had the garage, and a whole other life. So I left."

"And Otis?" Ruby asked, though she already knew the answer.

"There were rumors about him from time to time, that he was traveling the country, helping people in the wake of natural disasters, cleaning up after London's messes. But he didn't come back until now, until he found Simon. It's like he couldn't. Like he wasn't ready yet." She paused and shook her head. "It's like all that time, he was trying to make up for the one person he couldn't save."

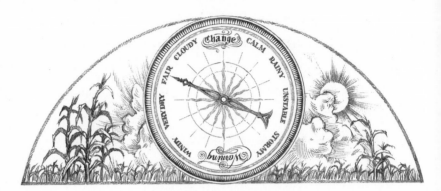

thirty-one

Later, after Daisy had left to check on things in the rest of the office and then returned again—looking shiny-eyed and frazzled but also energized by the buzz of activity, this newfound sense of purpose—she stood in the doorway to announce that it was time to get them home.

"I can take you myself, since Otis is going to be pretty busy with things here," she told them, but even as she did, the door was pushed open the rest of the way and Otis appeared behind her, his face lit with a grin.

"Actually, Otis is *not* that busy taking care of things," he said. "So we can head back together."

"But that makes no sense," Daisy said. "You've got all this stuff to do here...."

"There, too," he said firmly. "I've got a drought to fix. And a couple of young Storm Makers to take home."

Ruby frowned at the table, lost in thought, but Daisy's next words made her look up again.

"You've also got a solstice disaster to avert."

Otis nodded, pulling his hat from his pocket. "That, too," he said. "We're taking care of it."

Simon stood up from his chair. "How are we getting home?"

"Well, we drove," Daisy said, looking sheepish. "But my car broke down on the way."

"That's the thing about lost causes...." Ruby said, and Daisy smiled.

"I still haven't given up on it yet."

"Can't we catch another ride?" Simon asked hopefully. "I mean, you're the Chairman now. Maybe a limo or something?"

"We'll take the train," Otis said, smiling. "I'm still a train guy."

It took a while to say their good-byes. Everyone wanted to shake Simon's hand, to hear about what happened on the roof, to congratulate the youngest Storm Maker ever. Summer gave them both a hug, and Ned, the elevator guy, clapped them each on the back with a gruff nod.

"Mind yourselves," he said. "And come back soon."

"They'll be back, they'll be back," Otis kept insisting. They were nearly to the door by then, and he paused to look out over the room. "And I will, too. We've got a lot more work to do in the morning."

Another cheer rose up, and a few people whistled. As they walked out of the office, Simon looked up at Otis. "What sort of things do you have to do tomorrow?"

"Finish calling off the fires, for one," Otis said. "Restore all the dry land. Call in the old scouts. Weed out the bad eggs here at headquarters. Trash Rupert's office." He grinned at this last one.

"That's a lot," Simon said, looking awed.

"Tomorrow will just be the start of it," Otis said, putting a hand on Simon's head and mussing up his hair. "You would've been up for it, too," he said. "I would've helped you."

Outside, as they walked to the train station with the

lights of the city coming on all around them, Ruby cleared her throat. "You didn't say London before."

Everyone turned to her.

"When you were talking about all there was to do, you didn't say 'Find London.'"

Daisy and Otis exchanged a look, and in spite of the lingering heat, Ruby felt a shiver go through her.

"Is it because someone else is finding him?" she asked, her voice very small.

Otis bent his head as they approached the station. "No," he said. "It's because I have a feeling he'll be the one to find us."

Ruby could think of nothing to say to this. She followed the others into the train station, which was lined with little stores and newstands. Daisy and Simon wandered over to buy the tickets, while Otis hung back near one of the shop windows. When Ruby walked over to join him, she noticed there was a display of caps not unlike the one he always wore.

"Thinking of getting a new one?" she asked, and he looked over at her, stricken.

"No," he said, the word coming out with a force that neither of them had expected.

"Sorry," Ruby said. "Yours is great. I didn't mean..."

"No, no," he said, pulling his eyes away from the hats. "It's just that this one was a gift from my wife."

"Ah," she said.

"Just before she died, actually."

"In the fire," Ruby said quietly, and there was a flicker of surprise on Otis's face.

"So Rupert told you, did he?"

Ruby nodded.

"I suppose he must have given you quite an earful," Otis said with a sigh. He pulled the cap from his pocket and ran a finger along the brim. "We used to be best friends, you know."

"He said that, too."

"Did he?" Otis looked thoughtful. "We were college roommates. Completely inseparable. And Sophie was always tagging along." A shadow passed over his face at this. "Till the very end, I guess."

"You didn't bring her that day?"

He shook his head. "To a wildfire? Never. Those things are impossible to control, even for a Storm Maker with the ability to blow it back," he said. "Rupert was working at headquarters at the time. I'd been offered a directorship there myself, but I was never much for offices, so I took an outpost in California instead. I'd always been good with wind—perfect for blowing back all the fires out there—and Sophie had always had her heart set on living out west. Rupert took it personally, though."

"How come?" Ruby asked, glancing over at the line for tickets, relieved to see that Daisy and Simon were only about halfway through—she suddenly had about a thousand questions.

"When Rupert and I first met, neither of us had flared up. Do you know what the odds are that two people who know each other will both become Storm Makers?"

Ruby shook her head.

"Very small," he told her. "It was such a strange coincidence. I started about a month after him. We were both really young." One side of his mouth crept up in a half smile. "Not as young as Simon, of course, but young enough. Sophie wasn't supposed to know, but she figured it out. She was way too smart to hide anything from." Otis's eyes were glistening. "You remind me a little bit of her, actually."

Ruby smiled.

"She hated being left out."

"So she went to the fire herself that day."

Otis nodded. "She was always doing things like that, trying to be a part of it. I don't think she thought it'd be that bad," he said, his voice breaking. "She figured she'd see me in action, maybe help out if she could." His eyes were rimmed with red now, and he was blinking fast. "But it just got out of control so fast."

Ruby imagined the leaping flames, the popping of the brush going up in smoke. She closed her eyes for a moment, then opened them again when Otis went on.

"I did everything I could to save her," he said, looking at Ruby hard, as if there were words beneath his words, as if there was more he wanted her to hear. "*Everything*. But it wasn't enough."

They were both silent for a moment, and then Otis shoved the hat back in his pocket and put a hand on the store window.

"Is that why you didn't fight back?" Ruby asked, her voice very small. "Up there on the roof? Is that why you didn't put out the fire?"

There was something mournful in Otis's expression when he turned back to her. "It's a bit more complicated than that," he said. "But yes, I suppose there's a part of me that thinks maybe I deserved it."

Ruby began to protest, but Otis shook his head.

"Rupert still blames me," he said. "He always has. And he's not entirely wrong."

"Well, maybe he could find some less destructive ways of expressing his feelings," Ruby said, and was rewarded with a small smile from Otis.

"It used to be that if he was behaving badly, Sophie would just threaten to stop speaking to him, and he'd shape right up," Otis said. "She was the one person he truly cared about, and he'd do anything for her."

"And now?"

His face turned grim again. "Now I'm not sure there's anything left that he cares about. I don't know if he even remembers how."

The other two were approaching now, hurrying across the cavernous train station with the tickets in hand. Ruby looked back at Otis, who was once again gazing at the hats in the window.

"Your old one is better, anyway," she said, and he smiled.

"I wouldn't trade it for anything in the world."

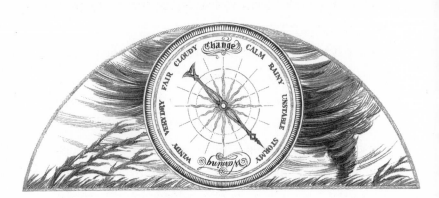

thirty-two

RUBY YAWNED as she looked out the window of the train. As soon as she'd found her seat a wave of exhaustion had come over her, and now she was struggling to keep her eyes from closing as they crawled out of the city.

They'd managed to get two seats facing each other, and on the opposite bench Daisy was also slumped against the window. Otis sat beside her, leaning forward to watch the darkening sky through the webs of phone lines and the shadows of buildings. Next to Ruby, Simon was playing with a loose thread on his T-shirt, his head drooping.

The day behind them felt like it should have been more than that—a week, at the very least—and Ruby realized she was happy to be going home. Even as the train moved into the suburbs, she was thinking of the farm in Wisconsin, the way it smelled in the morning—the crops wet with dew—and the now-familiar creaking of the house at night, as it seemed to settle itself all around them. She thought of Mom, paintbrush in hand, and Dad, out in the barn, and how they'd spent this day—this astonishing, terrifying day—assuming that Ruby and Simon were tossing a baseball around at Ben's house. They hadn't even known to be worried about them.

Out the window, the sun was slipping lower in the sky, and the clouds were nothing more than wisps. Ruby thought of the drought back home and wondered how quickly Otis would be able to fix it. She thought maybe Simon could help—after all, even though he wasn't Chairman, he was still a Storm Maker—and then she remembered something Otis had said earlier, the words scissoring through her with a suddenness that made her sit up in her seat.

"Why'd you say 'two Storm Makers' before?" she asked, and all three of them looked over at her. "Back at headquarters..."

"What're you talking about?" Simon asked.

"He said he had to take two Storm Makers home."

Simon frowned. "He was talking about Daisy."

But Ruby wasn't looking at him; she was looking at Otis, who shook his head and smiled at her.

"I was talking about you."

Daisy turned to him in surprise, and Simon's mouth fell open. Nobody seemed quite sure what to say, least of all Ruby. Her first thought, surprisingly, was of Simon, and how he must have felt that first day when he realized everything was different. She understood now that it wasn't just nerves, and it wasn't just excitement; it was like the world itself had gone wobbly beneath her feet.

How could that be true? Ruby wanted to ask, but the words seemed to melt before she could give voice to them. Across the aisle, a man's phone began to ring, and the conductor was approaching to take their tickets. He stood above them for several seconds before Daisy emerged from her thoughts long enough to pull them from her pocket and hand them over.

"Both of them?" she asked, once the conductor had moved on. She was talking to Otis, but her eyes were on Ruby, staring at her in wonder. It was the same look she'd had when she first met Simon. "How?"

"Did you notice what happened on the roof?" Otis asked Simon, leaning forward. "When you used the wind to knock over Rupert?"

"He couldn't do it," Ruby said, giving her brother a sideways glance. "And then, all of sudden, he could."

Otis nodded. "Has it ever happened like that before?"

"That night we saw London on the road," Simon said. "But it's not because I was scared...."

"No, that's true," Otis said. "Although fear can help, same as any other emotion. But in this case, I think it was something else that put you over the edge." He paused, then shook his head with a little grin. "So to speak."

They were starting to emerge from the suburbs now, the houses and buildings falling away so all that was left was the land itself, acres and acres of it, blue-gray beneath the deepening sky. The trees were all leaning in the wind, and Ruby saw a plastic bag blown up and away from them, set aloft by the wind or the train or both. Otis's eyes traveled over to the window, to the scudding clouds and unsettled sky.

"What were *you* thinking about up there?" he asked, turning abruptly to Ruby.

"I don't know," she said. "I don't remember."

"Yes, you do," said Otis. "When Simon was trying to make the wind blow, and Rupert was laughing at him, what went through your mind?"

A gust of wind buffeted the train car, making it rock just slightly on the rails, and Ruby inched closer to Simon. "I don't know," she said again. "I was scared, too. I guess I was just thinking about how much I hated him."

"And?"

Ruby tried to remember. She closed her eyes and was back there again, on the rooftop, surrounded by London's wild laughter and Simon's anger, the dizzying height of the building and the wind that swept across all of it, loud as waves in her ears.

Her eyes flew open.

"I was thinking about the mechanics of it," she said, sitting forward. "How even if Simon could make something happen, it would need to be a certain speed of wind to knock over someone London's size, and—"

"Exactly," Otis said, his eyes shining. "You were thinking about the science behind it."

"She's *always* thinking about science," Simon chipped in. Outside it started to rain, the drops slapping at the glass before streaming away, and it had become too dark for them to see anything but their own reflections in the window.

"I've had this theory for a little while now," Otis went on, "but I wasn't completely sure until today. Being a Storm Maker isn't just magic, and it's not just science. It's both."

Ruby nodded, but her eyes strayed to where a flash of lightning lit the sky.

"Maybe," Otis continued, "the key to this whole thing is that you're twins."

Daisy's face shifted as she began to understand. "You're thinking their abilities were split between them. So they're more powerful when they're together."

"They're two parts of a whole," Otis said with a nod. "The perfect blend of science and magic."

Neither of them was really talking to Ruby or Simon

anymore. They were facing each other, their eyes bright as they exchanged theories, the answer to the mystery of Simon unfolding between them.

"But what about...?" Daisy asked.

"The storm?" Otis asked. "I think that was purely a reaction. But if he wants to actually channel any weather, it's got to be the two of them together."

"Which is probably why they're so young," Daisy suggested. "Between them, they're more like twenty-four, which makes a lot more sense. Have there never been twins before?"

Otis shrugged. "Not that I've heard about. This has to be a first."

The rain was coming down harder now, drumming the sides of the train. The winds howled as they rolled past the many farmhouses with their windows burning orange through the dark.

"So what does this mean?" Ruby asked, and Otis and Daisy both looked over as if they'd forgotten anyone else was there. "I mean, how does it work, exactly?"

Daisy sat forward. "It's kind of amazing, actually," she said. "I'm guessing that if Simon focuses his thoughts on the physical result of the weather he wants—wind or rain, for example—and you think about the mechanics behind that particular phenomenon, and you both have the same goal in mind at the same time, then...voilà! Weather!"

Otis smiled. "Exactly," he said. "You could think of it like a bicycle. Simon's powers are like a bike without a rider. It can still roll if it's propelled by something like gravity—so, it can go flying down a hill, for example—but there's nobody to direct it, nobody to keep it focused and controlled. Nobody to make it go."

Simon made a face, but Ruby sat forward. "So what am I, then?"

"You," Otis said, "are the one pedaling."

There was a long rumble of thunder outside, followed by another spark of lightning. Around them, the other passengers had their noses to the windows to watch the worsening storm, their hands cupped around their faces to see. The train continued to sway from side to side in the wind, and Daisy's eyes sought Otis's.

"You don't think...?"

Otis shook his head, but he didn't look certain.

"What?" Simon asked. "London?"

The train's PA system crackled to life with a few coughs

of static as the lightning continued outside. "Well, folks," came the voice of the conductor, "we've been trying to outrun this storm, but it seems to be coming right along with us."

Simon and Ruby exchanged a look. If the storm was following them, that could mean only one thing: London was on the train, too. When Ruby turned to Otis, she could tell by his face that this must be true. Her heart thumped in time with the rain on the windows, and the sky was ripped open by another jag of lightning.

"He's here, isn't he?" Simon asked, but nobody answered. He rubbed his hands together and stared out the window, his leg bobbing nervously. When a few seconds more had passed and still nobody said anything, he looked over at Otis. "So why don't you go stop him?"

"Even if I were powerful enough," he said, his face grim, "the only chance would be to try to deflect it with some other kind of weather, and that's way too dangerous with so many people around."

Beneath her feet, Ruby could feel the train's gears shifting and slowing. But there was no train station here, no platform, and no town. In fact, there was nothing around them at all. She pulled the barometer from her pocket and saw that it was still pointing to *warning*. When she looked up again and her eyes met Otis's, she understood that this was something she didn't have to tell him. He already knew.

"The National Weather Service has issued a tornado warning," the conductor continued, "so we're going to make a brief stop here and give this thing a chance to move on. We're between stations, but there's a lot of debris on the tracks, so we think it's probably the best course of action. If everyone could just stay put for now, we'll try to keep you updated as best we can."

Otis was out of his seat even before the train had finished grinding to a halt, and now Ruby shot up, too.

"What're you doing?" she demanded.

"I don't know yet," he said, scanning the length of the train car.

"Otis," Daisy said, her voice low. "Don't."

But he ignored her. "Stay here," he said, moving out into the aisle. Ruby watched the back of his gray jacket as he walked away. She was vaguely aware that Daisy was speaking to her, but she was no longer listening. Her only focus was Otis, who was almost to the end of the car, about to disappear into the next one.

Before she could think better of it, Ruby ran after him, bumping into the edges of seats as she hurried down the narrow aisle. She nearly tripped over a stray newspaper, and an old woman gasped as she righted herself. Behind her she heard Simon shout, but she didn't stop until she'd reached Otis, whose hand was hovering over the emergency exit button on the door that led to the gap between cars.

"You said 'even if I were powerful enough' before. What did you mean by that?"

Otis's face sagged, and he cast a desperate glance out the window, where the storm was intensifying. Quickly, almost angrily, he lowered his face so that it was close to Ruby's. "Ever since..." he began, then stopped and shook his head, as if trying to rid his ear of water. "Ever since the day Sophie died, I can't make weather anymore."

Ruby stared at him, her throat tight. "Why not?"

"I did everything I could to try to save her," he said. "I used everything. Do you understand? *Everything.*"

"But when we first met..." she said, her mind thick with confusion. "You made it rain."

He shook his head again. "It was Simon's fever."

"But it can't be," Ruby insisted, though even as she did,

she was remembering London's threat up on the roof, the way Otis had only smiled at the idea of the Vacuum, a device that would have made any other Storm Maker tremble. She squeezed her eyes shut. "You couldn't have..."

"Lost it all?" he asked, a bit more gently.

"What about the compass?"

"I don't know why it chose me," Otis said. "I never could've imagined it would."

There was more thunder outside, and the wind sounded like someone banging on the door to the train. People were starting to panic now, pulling out their phones to reach loved ones or to call for help. Some were still glued to the windows, unable to look away, but others hunched low in their seats, as if that might somehow protect them.

"It'll pass, it'll pass," a man just beside her was murmuring.

But Ruby knew it wouldn't pass. Somewhere on this train, somewhere in the night, Rupert London was designing this storm just for them, all of it: the rocking of the wheels on the tracks and the pummeling winds, the rain and the thunder and the lightning. And for the grand finale, a tornado powerful enough to toss the train cars around like they were nothing more than toys.

Standing there beside Otis, the one person who'd always made her feel safest, who'd always seemed so powerful and sure of himself, Ruby felt hopeless. Because now she understood that he couldn't stop this, either, that there was nothing that could. She turned to look down the length of the train at Simon, who was twisted in his seat. He must have seen something in her face, because suddenly he was up, too, and Daisy followed, the two of them hurrying down the aisle.

"Where was he going?" Daisy called when she was halfway there, and Ruby shook her head, confused. But when she whirled around again, she saw that Otis was gone, that he'd slipped through the metal door leading outside. Without thinking, without waiting, she jammed her fist against the red button, and the doors opened with a hiss.

Outside there was nothing but a narrow metal platform that linked the cars together, unprotected and completely exposed to the storm. As Ruby stepped out onto it, the rain stung her eyes, and she had to hang on to one of the heavy handles to keep from being pushed off by the wind. There was a tang in the air, coppery and metallic, and Ruby pressed her lips together as she braced herself against the railing, leaning off the side of the train to get a better look. As she did, Daisy and Simon came crashing through the door, and Daisy grabbed her around the waist, anchoring her there.

Where the train had stopped, the track was slightly curved, so when she swept her gaze left and then right, she could make out both ends of it. Her eyes strained in the darkness to search for Otis; she knew somehow that he would be outside rather than in.

But he was nowhere in sight. The sky flared with lightning again, reflecting brightly off the metal cars of the train, and in that brief moment of illumination, Ruby saw something. All the way down, hanging off the last car of the train, was a silhouette that she would have known anywhere.

She stepped back, half falling into Daisy, gasping and sputtering.

"What?" Simon asked, his eyes filled with worry. "Did you see him?"

Ruby managed to nod, and Daisy looked relieved. "Where is he?"

"Not Otis," she said. "London."

They were all soaking wet now, and Simon's hair was in his eyes, beads of rain running down his face. But he was squinting out into the darkness, his eyes narrow. After a moment, he froze, his whole body going still.

"There," he said, raising a hand to point. "There he is."

Ruby saw him then, a tiny figure against the yawning landscape, bent against the wind and rain, swallowed up by the blackness as he made a slow trek away from the train. It was Otis.

Simon's eyes were wide. "Is he leaving us?"

"No," Ruby whispered, the word nearly swallowed up by the wind. Because in all the confusion, she was certain of only one thing: that Otis would never leave them. Not now. Not like this. There had to be another reason he was out there, alone and unprotected, forging ahead through the gathering winds.

"Then what?" Simon yelled. "What do we do?"

"We have to stop him," she said, casting about for something to help, some kind of answer. But her mind felt as blurry as the rain-soaked windows, slow and fumbling and scared.

"He'll be fine," Daisy was saying behind her. "We

should get you two back inside. Otis can protect himself."

Ruby whipped around. "No, he can't," she said, and Daisy stared back at her in confusion. "He can't make any weather. Not anymore."

A crash of thunder shook the ground, and lightning whitened the sky again. Daisy was shaking her head, unable to process this, or not wanting to. She opened her mouth as if to say something, then closed it again, and Ruby turned back to the thickness of the night before them.

"We have to do something," she said again. "We have to stop him."

"I don't think we can," Daisy said, her voice panicky. "I don't think he'd stop for anything. Not unless something he cared about got in the way."

Ruby spun around again, stricken by the words, and Daisy's face went white as she realized what she said. Because they knew; they both knew.

There were only two things Rupert London had ever cared about.

And one of them was out there in the storm.

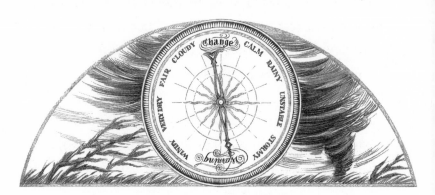

thirty-three

RUBY HAD NO IDEA how long she'd been standing there—struck motionless at the sight of Otis—when the door behind them was heaved open, a sound as deep as the thunder, but startlingly close. A man in a leather jacket poked his head out, the wind turning his long hair wild.

"Conductor's saying the tornado is almost here," he yelled over the noise of the storm. "Some people in the last car spotted the funnel. Everyone's supposed to get inside and stay down."

His eyes raked the horizon, but there was nothing out there, no safe place, no hiding spots. There was only the train, and the storm, and the land all around it.

And Otis, a lone figure hidden in the dark.

"Come on," the man said, jerking his head toward the inside of the train. But not one of them moved, not Daisy or Simon or Ruby, and after a moment the man shook his head at them, as if to say there wasn't much more he could do, and then withdrew back into the light of the car.

Out in the blackness, Otis was still pushing forward. Ruby watched numbly, helpless to do anything. She was almost afraid to pull her eyes away, not wanting to lose sight of him, as if it were that simple to keep him safe. He had one hand on his head, and she realized it was to pin down his hat. Something about this smallest of gestures cracked at her heart, and she swallowed the sob that rose in her throat. Leaning out again, she faced toward the end of the train where London was perched, and it was then that she saw the man had been right.

There, not a hundred yards away, was a tornado. Even in the dark, its shape was clear, a roiling funnel of wind and air and debris, narrow as a column of smoke moving fast across the land. Ruby felt as if she were watching it from very far away, and there was something almost beautiful about it, the way it danced across the fields like a puppet on a string.

They watched, spellbound, as it began to swallow everything in its path, snapping a tree in half like a twig, pulling up road signs and spitting out crops. And all this time, Otis continued to move toward it with a sort of gritty determination, bowed against the powerful winds, blown back again and again.

The door to the train flew open just for a moment before slamming shut again, and in that split second, they could hear screams from inside. Beside her, Simon cupped his hands around his mouth in a wordless shout, but this had no bearing on Otis, who continued to press on toward the heart of the storm.

It was like something out of *The Wizard of Oz*, Ruby thought as she watched. She'd always skipped the parts in black-and-white, moving straight on to the scenes in color, but here it was now before them: a twister in shades of gray. Only here, there was no Oz. Here, if a tornado took you, there was no second act to the story.

When Ruby turned around again, Daisy was no longer there, and she started to cry out, but Simon jerked his head toward the end of the train. Daisy had gone to find London.

The sky had turned a greenish black, and the air was full of wreckage. As Ruby looked on, her hands braced on the railing, she saw a bicycle go pinwheeling through the air. End over end it spun, carried on the edges of the funnel, and a tiny kernel of thought worked its way through her as it flew toward Otis.

You, he'd said, *are the one pedaling.*

There was no time to do anything but stir her muddled mind into action, and in the moment that the bike was aloft, she stared it down. She thought about velocity and she thought about torque. She thought about distance and weight and time. She could only hope Simon was thinking, too, his mind turned to whatever thoughts had propelled London back on the roof, or whatever had made it rain that night in the field.

In the space of an instant, she channeled all her energy in the direction of the bike, and just as she was convinced it was going to hit Otis, a force of metal and wind that she didn't want to imagine, it was blown off course, cast sharply to the left, missing him by mere feet.

Ruby turned to Simon, and his expression echoed hers:

It was somewhere between surprise and relief. Their thoughts had matched exactly, and together they'd managed to steer a bicycle as deadly as a weapon.

It had worked.

Out in the field, Ruby saw Otis hesitate—just briefly—and pivot in their direction. Even with everything spiraling around him, even in spite of the danger, Ruby had a feeling he knew what had happened. She jumped up and down, waving her arms frantically, trying to tell him to come back. But he was already in motion again, taking one heavy step at a time, looking frail against the might of the twister.

Ruby knew what he was trying to do. If Otis were to sacrifice himself, London might stop. It might prove to him that even if he no longer cared about people in general, there was still a part of him that cared for his old friend. Especially if his old friend was trying to make up for something that happened years ago, losing himself in the way that London's sister had been lost.

But it wasn't working—clearly it wasn't working—so why didn't he come back? Was he really planning to walk straight into the tornado for nothing? Ruby fought back tears, and before she had a chance to think it through, she was ducking beneath the railing on the platform.

Her feet hit the ground hard, sending a jolt up her spine, but she began to run anyway. On the train they'd been standing between two cars, which had given them more protection than she'd realized, because here in the open she felt powerless against the pull of the wind, which tugged at her like taffy, boxed at her as she stumbled, sent her skidding to her knees.

Her ears were filled with a rush of noise and something hit her arm, leaving a gash the length of a pencil. She staggered to her feet, only to get knocked back down again, and she realized — too late — that this had been a mistake. With great effort, she pulled herself forward, shouting for Otis, though she knew he couldn't hear. It was hard to see with all the debris in the air, but through slitted eyes she watched as his hat was carried away, disappearing into the storm.

Ruby tried to stand, wanted to go after it, but the thrashing wind hammered her down into the ground again, harder this time, and she felt the air go rushing out of her lungs. She squeezed her eyes shut, struggling for breath, wishing she'd stayed on the train, wishing *Otis* had stayed on the train, wishing they were anywhere but here, wishing and wishing and wishing until it all fell away, and the world faded from gray to black.

When she opened her eyes again, she wasn't sure how much time had passed, but Simon was beside her. He put a hand on her arm, his face etched with worry, and she let out a ragged breath, trying to focus her eyes, to slow the dizzying spin of her head.

Her first thought, strangely, was of the barometer. She propped herself up on her elbows, ignoring the pain in her arm as she fished through her pocket for the little instrument. Simon peered down as well, the two of them squinting through the stinging wind to read what it said. And as they looked on together, the arrow whirled beneath the glass, breaking its hold on the word *warning* and making three frantic circles before stopping solidly on *change*.

Ruby sucked in a breath, her heart thumping, and Simon shielded his eyes to look back toward the train, scanning the swirling darkness for answers.

They were still frozen there like that when, all at once, everything went still.

There was confusion on Simon's face as the winds died around them with unnatural speed. The twister slowed, like the deflating of a balloon, before falling entirely flat, the world abruptly going silent again.

The absence of the wind was loud in their ears as Simon helped Ruby sit up. Her head was still spinning and the cut on her arm had a heartbeat of its own, but she was too preoccupied to notice, her eyes searching the place where the tornado had come and gone with dizzying speed.

"What do you think happened?" Simon asked, glancing back at the train.

But she didn't answer.

Because there, limping toward them, was Otis. His head was now bare, and his jacket hung from his thin frame in tatters. There was a cut above his left eye and no sign of his glasses, and there was a bloodstain just below the torn knee of his pants. But he was smiling at them, his face marked by that familiar grin of his, and once Simon helped her to her feet, Ruby stumbled over and threw her arms around him.

"That was a really stupid thing you did," Otis said, but she could hear the smile in his voice. "You could have been killed. You shouldn't have done that."

"You shouldn't have, either," Daisy said as she came up

behind them, and Ruby stepped aside, relieved to see her, too. "You, of all people, should know what it's like to watch someone you..."

Otis tilted his head to one side. "Someone you...?"

"Care about," Daisy said angrily. "You should know how scary it is to watch someone you care about walk into a storm."

"I'm sorry," he said, his face softening. He walked over and put an arm around her thin shoulders, and to Ruby's surprise, Daisy—the woman who refused to cry—buried her face in his shirt. Otis simply stood there like that, his long arm encircling her tiny frame, and for a moment, it was as if the twins weren't there at all.

But then Daisy coughed and backed away, rubbing at her eyes with the back of her hand. "Just promise me one thing."

"That I won't do it again?" he said, and she scowled at him.

"No, that you'll let me come along next time," she said, then turned to Simon and Ruby. "And you guys, too. I hate that everyone's running into tornadoes without me."

Otis dabbed at the cut above his eye. "Where were you?"

"On my way to stop London," she said, gesturing at the train behind her. "But Ruby beat me to it."

Ruby stared at her. "No, I didn't."

"You did," Daisy said. "Both of you did."

"How?" Simon asked.

"By the time I got down there, he'd stopped it," she said. "He was just standing there, staring out at where Ruby had been knocked down, watching you trying to wake her up."

Nobody said anything for a moment, and then Otis bowed his head. "It was still Sophie, in the end," he said quietly. "The thing he cared about most."

"I think it was more than that," Daisy said, reaching out to take Otis's hand, holding it between her two smaller ones. "I think it was you, too."

Otis said nothing in return, though his eyes were damp. He only lifted his chin to look out beyond the train, where the tracks unfurled behind it like a ribbon. When the rest of them turned to follow his gaze, they saw a figure picking his way along the edge. As they watched, it grew smaller and smaller, until it was nothing but a dark speck on the horizon.

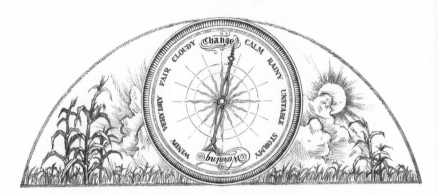

thirty-four

THE STARS WERE OUT by the time they neared the farm. Other than the sweep of their headlights, the world was wrapped in navy darkness, the acres of farmland quiet in the night. They were all silent as Daisy turned into the long gravel drive leading up to the house.

Earlier, after the storm had passed and the paramedics had arrived to attend to the passengers—bandaging Ruby's arm and patching the cut above Otis's eye—Simon had been the one to refuse to get back on the train.

"There's no way," he'd said, his arms folded. The train itself had actually weathered the storm fairly well, though Ruby knew that wouldn't have been the case if they'd stayed on board. Still, other than a few broken windows and dents in the metal siding, it was upright and intact, and what more could you ask for after such a close brush with a tornado?

But a policeman had offered to give them a lift into the nearest town, where they'd rented an old car. Daisy insisted on driving, muttering about the mileage and horsepower the whole way. She couldn't resist testing the limits of the little sedan, gunning the engine and then slamming on the brakes, jerking them around so much that Ruby started to think the train might have been the better option after all. But once they'd hit the miles of pin-straight roads near the farm, she'd eased up, coasting on the long stretches of asphalt between fields.

Now they could see that the lights were on in the kitchen, which seemed to Ruby like the beacon of a lighthouse, calling them home after a day spent lost at sea. Daisy slowed the car near the barn, far enough away from the house that if Mom or Dad looked out the window, they would think it was Ben's mom dropping the twins off early.

"Well," Daisy said, leaning back against her seat. When she turned off the car, the ticking of the engine was loud in the silence. Neither Simon nor Ruby moved to unfasten their seat belts. They all just sat there, watching the minutes pass on the dashboard clock.

Eventually, Otis reached over and opened his door. Ruby blinked as the interior lights went on. Daisy stepped outside, too, and after a moment so did the twins, pressing their doors shut quietly behind them. They all moved around to the hood of the car.

"Cheer up," Otis said, smiling at their long faces. "This isn't good-bye. Daisy will be coming down to headquarters a lot—"

"A *lot*," she agreed with a grin.

"And she'll bring you along as often as you'd like," Otis continued. "And we'll figure out some new things to show you, since you seem to have that wind gust down pretty well at this point."

Ruby nodded, though somehow, this didn't seem like enough. As if she'd read her mind, Daisy cleared her throat. "And in between visits, we'll keep working over at the garage," she offered. "You never know when you might need to whip up a decent snowstorm."

Ruby glanced over at Simon, expecting him to be thrilled at this, but his face was solemn as he ducked his head, toeing at the gravel on the ground. "I don't know," he said after a moment. "I mean, this was all kind of a lot."

"What was?" Daisy asked.

"Being a Storm Maker."

Otis smiled. "You're always going to be a Storm Maker," he said. "Both of you. Storm Makers with a gift for wind-making, from the looks of it. And I'm afraid there's not much we can do to change that. But hopefully it won't always be like today."

"Hopefully?" Ruby asked, looking up.

"Rupert's gone for the moment," Otis said. "And we'll get the Society back in order, fix what we can, reverse some of the damage that he's done. But that doesn't necessarily mean it's over. Or that he won't come back."

Ruby swallowed hard. "What happens if he does?"

"Then we'll just have to be ready again, won't we?" Otis said, putting a hand on her shoulder. "All of us."

Daisy looked from one to the other. "But he's gone for now," she said, her voice light. "Which means we can get back to normal."

Simon seemed relieved at this. "Like baseball."

"And school," Ruby chimed in, causing Simon to make a face.

"And the garage," Daisy said, then lifted her chin. "By the way, tell your dad he's just missing one of the currents."

Ruby frowned. "What?"

"On his invention," she said. "If he adds an electrical charge to the input, it should work like a charm."

"That's it?" she asked, and Daisy nodded.

"That's it."

Simon's mouth was open, and he turned to Ruby. "Does that mean we'll get to stay?"

She looked back at the farmhouse, huddled beneath the starry sky. An owl cried out from somewhere near the barn, and the crickets were loud all around them. It felt like they'd been away for so much longer than just a day, and Ruby realized how good it was to be home.

"Yeah," she murmured. "I guess it probably does."

"Good," Daisy said, beaming. "Because I'm counting on having you guys around from now on. It's actually sort of nice to have some company." She stepped over to give them each a hug. "See you at work tomorrow?"

Ruby grinned. "We'll be there."

Simon walked over to Otis and extended his hand. "Thank you," he said with a little nod. He looked so much older than he had just days ago, standing there shaking Otis's hand, his back straight and his shoulders squared. He seemed taller, more grown up, and Ruby wondered if she looked different, too. She certainly felt that way.

"Couldn't have done it without you," Otis said, and when Simon started to protest, he shook his head. "You're the one who made the difference. Really. It's like a stove that we couldn't get to light. I might be the flame, but you're the one who sparked the fire. You're the match."

Ruby could see the pride in her brother's eyes as he nodded. "Thank you," he said again.

"And I promise to teach Otis some sports metaphors before you see him next," Daisy teased. Otis laughed as he moved on to Ruby.

"Here," she said, holding the barometer in her flattened palm.

He smiled when he saw where the needle was pointing, but he shook his head. "You keep it," he said. "In case the winds ever shift again."

Ruby's gaze was unwavering. "I know why," she said,

and Otis tilted his head to the side in question. "I know why it says *change*. I know why the compass picked you. It's not about the most powerful Storm Maker, or even the one with the most potential. At least not anymore."

"Oh yeah?" he asked, the wrinkles showing at the corners of his eyes.

"Yeah," she said. "This time it went to the one with the best intentions. The one who'll replant the forests and soften the big storms. The one who'll help the most and hurt the least." She paused, smiling. *"You."*

Otis shoved his hands into his pockets and nodded thoughtfully. "Well, don't think it means I'll be cooped up in an office all day," he said with a grin. "If I get too stir-crazy down there, I might just have to hop a train and come up for a visit."

"Just don't pick the wrong train," Ruby said, and he laughed.

"Don't be surprised if I show up in the barn again."

"It's all yours," she told him, then glanced down as he pulled his hands from his pockets, both of them empty. "I'm sorry about your hat."

"It's okay," he said. "Maybe it was time."

"But you said you wouldn't trade it for the world."

"Well, maybe it wasn't quite the world," he said with a small smile. "But I think it was a pretty good trade all the same, don't you?"

An image of the tornado flashed through Ruby's mind, the spiraling air like a guided missile, and Otis, uncowed and unafraid, ready to sacrifice everything to save them all.

He leaned down as she reached up to give him a hug.

"Yeah," she whispered into his shirt. "It was a very good trade."

When they'd all said their good-byes—"Just for now," Daisy kept repeating, "just for now"—Ruby and Simon backed up to let them turn the car around. They lifted their hands to wave, then stood there as the red taillights grew distant.

After a moment, Simon turned to her. "I feel sort of like Dorothy, you know?" he said. "Right after she woke up."

"But it wasn't a dream," Ruby said, shaking her head in wonder.

"You might need to remind me of that in the morning," he said. "Otherwise, I'm gonna have a hard time believing that really happened."

She laughed. "Which part?"

"All of it," he said as they began walking toward the house, their backpacks slung over their shoulders. When they were close enough, they could see their parents in the kitchen, Mom making tea at the stove, Dad hunched over his diagrams at the table.

Ruby came to a stop, watching the scene before her. She thought again of what Otis had done today, and what she and Simon had done, too. How they'd all been willing to put themselves in danger for the sake of others, how there are things far more important than magic or even science, things that have the power to save you. And as if the two thoughts were one, Ruby was suddenly grateful for her family, for Mom and Dad and Simon and the life they'd managed to carve out for themselves here on this farm.

"What's wrong?" Simon asked, pausing to wait for her.

Ruby shook her head. "Nothing," she said with a smile. "I'm just happy to be home."

When Simon turned the knob on the front door, the dogs began to bark, rushing over to greet them both, all wriggling bodies and wagging tails.

"Toto, stop," Simon said, ducking one of their slobbering tongues.

Ruby laughed. "That's Oz," she said, rubbing Toto's ears. "Maybe that's why they've never liked you. Because you're always mixing them up."

"Nah," Simon said. "I'm pretty sure it's because I'm magic."

"Oh yeah," Ruby joked. "The Great and Powerful Simon."

They heard voices from around the corner, then footsteps, and Mom and Dad appeared near the stairs, both of them looking surprised to find their kids rolling around on the floor with the dogs.

"I thought you were sleeping over," Mom said, stooping to give them each a kiss on the forehead. "How come you're back so early?"

"I guess we just missed you," Ruby said, and Dad laughed.

"I'm going to choose to believe that," he said, putting Simon into a playful headlock, "even though it sounds like a load of malarkey to me."

"What happened to your arm?" Mom asked Ruby, and everyone looked at the white bandage.

"Let me guess," Dad said. "You hit the ball out of the park and went sliding into home to win the game?"

Ruby glanced over at Simon with a grin. "Something like that."

"Anyone hungry?" Mom asked. "I just finished making some cookies."

Simon nodded. "Always."

In the kitchen, they sat at the table while Mom poured them glasses of milk and set out a plate of cookies. Ruby eyed Dad's sketches over the rim of her cup, and when she'd finished drinking, she wiped her mouth and pointed. She was about to tell him what Daisy had said about the invention when she caught Simon's eye. He was looking at her with such undisguised hope that she dropped her hand and gave him a little nod. He should be the one to say it. He'd earned at least that much.

With a grateful smile, he turned to Dad. "You know," he said, gesturing at the crumpled pieces of paper, "all you're missing is one of the currents."

Dad stared at him openmouthed.

"Yeah," Simon continued. "You just need to add an electrical charge to the input, and then you'll be all set."

"How did you figure that out?" Dad asked, looking from Simon to Ruby in surprise.

"Science," Ruby announced at the same time that Simon said, "Magic."

Mom laughed, but Dad shook his head. "No, they're right," he was muttering, reaching for a pencil. "If I just connect this here," he said, making dark lines on the page, "then this will work better over here, and then it might just..." He looked up, his eyes shining. "We should go try it out tomorrow," he said. "All of us."

Simon beamed at him.

"I have a good feeling about this," Dad said. "It's all coming together." His hand was still busy on the page, sketching as he talked. "And did you feel how it's already cooling off out there?" He paused to glance up and wink at Mom. "I wouldn't start packing just yet."

He looked so pleased that Ruby almost wanted to tell him that he was right, that the drought would soon be gone, nothing more than a footnote in the record books. But he'd never understand how she could know something like that.

Still, by the next morning, the heat would have already lifted. Ruby would wake before anyone else, just as the orange ball of sun was rising—almost as early as it ever would, on the day before the summer solstice, the longest day of the year—coloring the fields a fiery shade of pink. For the first time in weeks, there would be a sharpness to the air, a coolness that would follow her into the barn, where she'd pause in the doorway, her heart lifting with possibility.

But for now, Dad was laughing at their good fortune, and Mom had walked up behind him, her arms circling his neck, her face pressed close to his. As Simon reached for another cookie, Ruby swiveled to look out the window at the farm that would be their home for some time now.

Tonight, though, there were no fields. There was no barn, and no scarecrow; no wheat or corn; no roads or trees. There was only their family, reflected back at her in the warm glow of the kitchen, the four of them gathered around the table, a small island of light in the darkness. She watched them there for a moment, their silhouettes dancing across the windowpanes, and then, once she was ready, she turned around to join them.

ACKNOWLEDGMENTS

There are so many people who helped make this book possible. I owe a great deal of thanks to MY AGENT, JENNIFER JOEL, AND MY EDITOR, JULIE SCHEINA, AS WELL AS MEGAN TINGLEY, ELIZABETH BEWLEY, JOANNA KREMER, LIZ CASAL, DAVID CAPLAN, AND EVERYONE ELSE AT LITTLE, BROWN BOOKS FOR YOUNG READERS. *I'm also very lucky to have had so much support and encouragement from* STEPHANIE THWAITES, BINKY URBAN, CHRISTINE BAUCH, NIKI CASTLE, JENNI HAMILL, AND EVERYONE AT ICM, CURTIS BROWN, AND RANDOM HOUSE. *This book has been made immeasurably better by* BRETT HELQUIST'S *gorgeous illustrations, for which I'm incredibly grateful. And finally, none of this would be possible without* MY FAMILY: MOM, DAD, KELLY, AND ERROL. *Thanks for always being there — rain or shine.*